I0634569

The Artist's Secret

Sonya Heaney

16pt

Read How You Want
LARGE PRINT BOOKS, BRAILLE & DAISY

Copyright Page from the Original Book

Title: The Artist's Secret

Copyright © 2020 by Sonya Heaney

Published by
Escape
An imprint of Harlequin Enterprises (Australia) Pty Limited (ABN 47 001 180 918), a subsidiary of HarperCollins Publishers Australia Pty Limited (ABN 36 009 913 517)
Level 13, 201 Elizabeth St
SYDNEY NSW 2000
AUSTRALIA

romance.com.au

TABLE OF CONTENTS

The Artist's Secret
Sonya Heaney

New South Wales, 1887

Peter Rowe's life is in the city, but his soul is in Australia's southern tablelands—a place he's never seen. Taking the new land manager's position on the thriving estate of Endmoor is the chance he needs to discover what happened to the family he has never met. What he doesn't expect to find in the bush is his employer's talented, beautiful sister.

Elizabeth Farrer's world is changing rapidly. An artist whose work has begun to gain acclaim, her brother's marriage has made her redundant in her own home and she intends to leave the country and make a life of her own. Her plans would take her far from her beloved New South Wales, but with the arrival of Endmoor's newest employee—a man unlike any other she has met—she discovers there might just be a reason to stay right where she is.

Just as they conquer their most difficult obstacles, old prejudices rise up and threaten to keep them apart...

About the author

SONYA HEANEY began her professional life aged eight, as the Changeling in Queensland Ballet's *A Midsummer Night's Dream*. After many more years of hard work, even more blisters, and plenty of pretty tutus, one too many injuries forced her out of her pointe shoes. Between then and now she has worked in a posh Dublin hotel (that didn't last long), pulled pints in London pubs (that lasted years), taught English in Korea (her apartment was broken into and her computer was stolen—along with many half-finished manuscripts), and worked on costumes backstage in various theatres (it was always chaos). Sonya holds a Bachelor of Arts in Professional Writing, and spent years putting it to use in nonfiction fields before turning her hand to romance. After working her way around the world, she once again calls Canberra, Australia's gorgeous capital city, home.

sonyaheaney.com
Facebook.com/SonyaHeaneyAuthor

Acknowledgements

Thank you to editors Nicola Robinson, for being sensible when I was ridiculous, and Chrysoula Aiello, who always knows how to make my books so much better. And a huge thank you to Christine Armstrong for another spectacular cover.

This book was written at a crazy time, and I need to thank my family—and Stinky the cat!—for providing me with sanity-saving distractions at the most important moments.

The Artist's Secret wouldn't exist without the inspiration provided by the stark beauty and unforgiving landscape of the Canberra and Queanbeyan regions. The town of Barracks Flat is based on Queanbeyan, a place many members of my family have lived over the years.

For Pauline Heaney

Chapter 1

**Southern Tablelands, New South Wales
September, 1887**

Elizabeth Farrer devoted two exasperating hours to her work before she put down her charcoal and admitted defeat.

'This is hopeless,' she muttered from her spot under the old eucalypt far out on her family's estate. Looking up from her sketchbook, she took in the expanse of dry, yellowed grass that stretched to the foothills of the Brindabellas. A pair of white butterflies fluttered by—such a bucolic vision that it hardly seemed real. A perfectly lovely afternoon, even if punctuated by the relentless bleating of a veritable army of sheep.

Light filtered through the leaves above, dappling the ground where her bare feet poked out from the sprawled skirts of her old burnt umber gown. So far out on the land it didn't matter if she gave up on a little propriety. She was hardly likely to outrage a kangaroo.

She had all the inspiration she could possibly want. And yet ... *and yet.* There wasn't a single spark of creativity in her that afternoon, just as there'd not been the day before, nor the day before that.

Cross, and grumbling not unlike her infant nephew, she gripped her charcoal determinedly to give it one last try and began shaping the curve of the creek on the page, drawing as much from memory as from sight.

A few minutes later she paused and gave her effort a frank inspection.

'*Utterly* hopeless.'

Setting her work—such as it was—aside, she groaned and brought the heels of her hands to her forehead, closing her eyes against the beautiful day. With the new accountant due to arrive from Sydney any moment, she really ought to get back in time to greet him. She might not be mistress of the house now her brother was married, but that didn't mean she could abandon all her manners.

'You're no decent company, I'll have you know,' she called to the largest kangaroo, a grey male with a suspicious look about him. He'd stirred the instant she did, ready to come at her with claws if she showed too much interest in his brood.

Reaching for her stockings and her boots, she put herself back to rights, preparing for the long walk home. Pushing to her feet, she strolled around the clearing to work out the discomforts of sitting still for far too long, kicking at a couple of little rocks that lay in amongst the grass. Not for the first time in the past few weeks she found herself thinking of a childhood in Cumberland, and the deep greens of the English countryside. Nostalgia was a dangerous thing.

Her wandering brought her to the fence that divided Farrer land from the countryside beyond. A couple of old huts nobody in particular laid claim to, the structures occasionally shelters for people passing through the valley, stood dilapidating on the other side. Leaning against a post, Elizabeth peered over at them, taking note of the dangerously overgrown surroundings and the weeds springing up out of the connecting path. There was an absolute stillness to the place.

Mr Towner had moved on again then. The old squatter rarely stayed for long, and because nobody could agree *whose* land the Irishman was actually squatting on, people tended to leave him be. He was far from the only man to pass through the valley and make use of the space, but he was certainly the most frequent visitor.

Or, Elizabeth thought, with a dawning and awful realisation, perhaps he'd died in there, and been forgotten all about...

'Oh, *Lord,*' she said, cursing the sudden return of her imagination. Now, she'd no choice but to check and see for certain.

Risking splinters in unfortunate places, she vaulted the fence at the post, catching the hem of her skirts more than once. Hovering there a moment, she uttered a few words she bet her family wasn't aware she knew.

Despite the few precarious seconds, she survived the trip over in one piece. After disentangling herself from the barrier and stomping her way up the path to scare off snakes, she hopped over a fallen branch blocking the way and reached the door of the more habitable of the buildings sooner than she would have liked.

Bracing for something awful, she lifted a charcoal-marked hand to knock on the weather-battered wood.

***

The railway station was so new it just about gleamed.

Peter propped his hands on his hips, tipped his face up to the near-blindingly blue sky, and drew in a long breath. Here he was, then, in Barracks Flat, the town he'd be calling home for the coming months; his first time so far south in the colony. After being in the city, it felt as if he'd entered a different world.

It may have been early in the season, but the spring air already held a great deal of warmth. It was a dry sort of heat, different from the humidity of the coast—harsher, somehow.

Around him new arrivals bustled with baggage and called greetings to various people, most of the travellers returning home rather than beginning a new adventure. As an outsider he was attracting a few curious looks, but nobody approached. The locomotive that had just deposited them in this dusty southern outpost of New South Wales steamed and hissed and spat like a restless animal eager to be on its way again.

An odd emotion stirred deep in his belly, but he was determined to ignore it for the time being and deal with practical matters first. These weren't the circumstances he'd ever imagined would bring him to the region, but he hoped to God it took to him the way he was determined to take to it.

'You're Mr Rowe? Peter Rowe?'

He turned to see a man of middle years standing beside him, battered hat on his head. He had a wizened country look to him that spoke of many hours spent in the sun.

'I am.'

Peter didn't miss the man's swift, assessing glance over his features, taking in the hints that his heritage wasn't entirely English. He was used to it, and the older fellow had the decency to not pry.

'William Adamson. I'm here from Endmoor to collect you.' He bent to pick up a bag, slung it over his shoulder, and then crouched to lift a larger one—all efficiency and genial gruffness even as he staggered back a step under the weight.

Peter stepped forwards 'Let me help you.'

The man was comically aghast at the suggestion. 'I won't be havin' that. Leave it to me, if you don't mind. You'll find Mr Farrer out with the coach.' He pointed in the obvious direction, where a pathway beyond the station led passengers to the road.

Peter began to put up another protest, but realised a moment later it was a matter of pride on the other fellow's part. Feeling decidedly uncomfortable about the whole thing, he headed in the direction he'd been sent.

Vehicles of various kinds awaited their passengers. Families gathered, eyes wide, some with rudimentary bouquets clutched in their hands, scanning the travellers for a familiar face. Servants hovered, ready to jump into action the instant they were required. Gigs and wagons lined the curved drive, and people from the surrounding farms perched around them, fresh produce on display. It was hardly the ordered chaos of an arrival at Sydney Terminal, but for a town so far from the city it spoke of a region on the rise.

It was not hard to find the carriage, seeing as it was the only one in sight. Nor was it hard to find the vehicle's owner. The man leaned against its door, arms folded, pose casual, watching Peter's approach steadily from the shadow of a grand, mature plane tree.

Robert Farrer was a young man of about thirty, tall, brown-haired, and—at present—giving him a curious, appraising look. Peter stopped a few feet from his new employer, stayed still for the scrutiny, and knew then all the obvious, usual questions would begin.

The assessment took only a matter of seconds, but it might as well have been an hour. Their gazes held while parrots chattered from the tree. Decision made, Farrer straightened and stepped towards him, emerging from the shade. He came to a stop in front of him, gaze assessing.

'Maurice Rowe is a man of about sixty-five,' he finally said, and—relieved—Peter grinned.

'My father had to stay in the city.' It was more or less the truth. 'He sent me instead. You should have received a telegram about the changed circumstances.'

The other man grunted.

'We didn't. But it doesn't matter either way.' He held out his hand and shook Peter's firmly.

Acceptance.

Pleasantries were exchanged, the luggage was loaded, and minutes later Peter found himself in the vehicle and off down the road.

They climbed the hill up from the station and then rolled through a town that was clearly in a time of transformation. Fashionable two-storey terraces rose up alongside smaller cottages and shops that looked like they'd been there a good few decades. A few people were milling around; others hurrying from one building to the next, focused on their errands.

Gum trees mingled with European imports along the roadsides, and the white seeds of the blossoming kapok trees floated around like fluffy snowflakes in the warm afternoon air.

'We're so grateful to have found someone so fast,' Farrer said as they passed one church, and then another. 'With John, my business partner, abroad trying to convince Europeans they really *do* want to buy Australian riesling, it's been a hard slog to take care of the property *and* the books. We'll be grateful for your help over the next few months.'

'Books are what I'm best at,' Peter replied absently, absorbing his surroundings.

It was far too early to rush to judgement. Everything had happened so fast, from his father calling him into his office to *inform* him there'd been a change of plans, to packing his belongings before he could even question why he—at thirty-two—was doing the man's bidding without putting forward an argument first, to the journey southwest into the country.

Talk moved on to the usual things strangers spoke of in order to sound polite. The cricket was the obvious first choice, with England's recently finished tour of the colonies.

'And to think of Moses with that left-handed batting. I'd love to have seen it,' Farrer said while they passed the last of the terraces and took the route westwards, past a park and then off the main road. The bush slowly enveloped them.

'It's not quite the city, but we're not complete bumpkins. Business picked up faster than we'd expected, and while I don't want to complain about it, it's been ... well.' Farrer chuckled. 'I *do* want to complain about it. A little break from the chaos would be welcome.'

The road got a little rougher and Peter braced his arm against the carriage's door. They passed an abandoned old wagon and then the trees took over completely as the sounds of wheels and hooves in the dust rose up around them. They passed a dirt track here and a scrubby clearing there. Small symbols of human occupation, small markings on the land.

Peter saw signs of the Endmoor estate long before they reached it. The bush had become tamer. The carpet of debris on the ground thinned. And then the trees cleared, giving him views here and there of a paddock off in the distance, merinos well camouflaged in their surroundings. And with each peek into the wide expanse of the valley, he was afforded glimpses of the green-blue foliage of the mountains far beyond.

They reached a set of gates and a large drive beyond it. Adamson paused to let them through, and then they were approaching a grand house that Peter estimated couldn't have stood on the land for much more than twenty years.

They rolled to a stop and then the door was opened for them. People began to emerge from various buildings, curiosity piqued.

'So, this is Endmoor.'

Farrer inclined his head and indicated for Peter to step down first.

'So it is.'

***

The door opened at the touch of Elizabeth's knuckles, swinging inwards and revealing a dark, one-room space with a table, a bed and a crooked old chair. An assortment of rubbish was scattered across the table—signs of past occupation, and of a resident who didn't much care about the mess he left behind—but when her eyes adjusted to the low light she saw the fireplace hadn't been used in some time.

The hut was empty.

Letting out a sigh of relief, she pulled the door closed and trudged across the clearing to peer into the second, even smaller building. She found it as dark and deserted as the first, and only then did she let out a full breath.

'Well. That's a relief.'

With that settled she headed back the way she came, pausing once at a scrabbling sound in the weeds until a startled, harmless skink darted away. Back up over the fence she went, catching her skirts all over again, but this time reining in the vulgar language.

Once she was safely on the other side she headed back over to her tree, brushing at something on her cheek as she walked, and then stopping still in surprise to stare at fingers that came away wet.

Why was she crying?

Oh, but she knew, because it had happened with more and more frequency in recent months, to her mortification. It was a private pain, one more than two years in the making, and—selfishly on her part—it had very little to do with concern for an old, crotchety nomad who was off somewhere roaming the hills.

Edward ... So much anger and frustration tied up in one name. And, to her constant consternation, heartache was bundled in along with the other emotions.

'You're absurd, Elizabeth Farrer,' she admonished, and began to pack her supplies away. She'd heard of people becoming maudlin around anniversaries, but it was no special time now. Just Wednesday.

Too much sitting around on her own, that was it. She couldn't change the past, but she could certainly change her future. Judging by the angle of the sun the train was due into town very soon, which meant she'd have to save the rest of her moping for another day.

The sketchbook went back in its bag, and the charcoal in its box. All the while the kangaroos watched her from some twenty yards away, pairs of pointy ears sticking out the top of the overgrowth. She offered them a frustrated look and a wave goodbye; they ought to know by now she hadn't any plans to shoot them. And then she gathered everything in her arms and set off east.

It didn't take long for the melancholy to pass. Once she got walking she spotted a giant wattle bush flowering, bright yellow and smelling divine, and soon after that stopped at the sight of a still-grey baby magpie chasing its parents and begging for food in high, ridiculous squeaks, his mottled feathers sticking haphazardly in every direction.

Almost home she paused one final time, removing her old hat before walking on to the house, smoothing her hair with her fingertips and trying to regain some semblance of tidiness. Holding the hat by its ribbons with one hand and her bag with the other, she climbed the last gentle slope of the land as the family homestead of Endmoor emerged from the landscape.

The sunshine reflected on the corrugated iron of the roof and veranda, and the garden, tamed and blooming with the first wave of spring, dazzled with its array of flowers. The main house was surrounded by a series of other buildings: stables and sheds in various states of newness and decay.

And, descending from a vehicle on the carriage drive were two gentlemen.

Robert turned her way first. The stranger, whose attention had been fixed somewhere off towards the mountains, removed his own hat and then turned too, revealing a wealth of jet-black hair and a set of strong, broad shoulders Elizabeth wished she'd not noticed.

It was brief before it was disguised, but she caught the change in his posture, the sudden alertness, and *oh* ... It had been a long time since someone had looked at her that way.

And it had been a long time since she'd looked at a *man* that way. This couldn't be the new employee. Her brother had told her to prepare for someone much older.

Elizabeth closed the distance between them and prayed nobody would notice she looked like she'd just emerged from a trek through the Amazon, or that her gown was so old the fabric was beginning to tear at the seams. *Burnt umber*—of all the colours in the world to choose. What had she been thinking?

Robert beamed broadly and stepped forward.

'Mr Peter Rowe, this is my sister, Elizabeth. Elizabeth, Mr Rowe is from—'

'*Rowe and Son Accountants,*' she finished for him, and then set her things at her feet and made herself look directly at the most interesting person to arrive at the estate in a long time.

'It seems there's been a change of plans, and we've been saddled with Mr Rowe, the younger.'

Robert, in the way of brothers, didn't seem to notice anything was amiss. He continued the introductions, all good breeding and fine manners. There hadn't been many times over the years

Elizabeth felt the need to strangle the man, but right then the urge was gargantuan.

All the usual pleasantries were exchanged, and Elizabeth supposed she said the right things at the right time, enquiring about the journey, remarking on the quality of the new railway that'd only reached town mere days before. She was fairly sure something was said about the weather. And she absolutely *refused* to break out in romantical shivers simply because a handsome man stood so close to her.

And then Alice, her sister-in-law, came out of the house, crossed the veranda, and proceeded to help lug a bag inside, and Robert was off to stop her, an admonishment on his lips and an indulgent smile on his face. Leaving Elizabeth and Mr Rowe alone and watching each other with caution and masked interest. It was dangerous, she knew, to put too much stock in first impressions, but as the world continued around them and she sought desperately for something halfway intelligent to say to fill the silence she struggled to take her own good advice.

While she dithered Alice won her debate with her husband, and Elizabeth latched onto the sight of the two of them walking off together wrestling a case.

'You might find us a little ... odd from time to time, this far out in the country,' she eventually said, and watched as a smile broke across the man's face, dazzling her into forgetting the rest of her words.

Well. If she'd been looking for a change in her world, she'd certainly just found it.

Chapter 2

The reality of Endmoor wasn't quite what Peter had expected. The thought came to him sometime between a close call with a roaming, clucking chicken upon his arrival, and an encounter with a hay-laden wagon that nearly ran him down as it passed by, headed for the paddocks beyond.

In truth, he'd expected something a little more ... idyllic.

With so many people around there was no way he could go poking about the property during the day without looking suspicious about it—and his intentions *were* suspicious, after all.

The cheerfully bickering Farrers disappeared somewhere with his luggage, and Peter assumed he'd eventually see it again. He knew he should step away and try to offer his assistance for a second time; surely that durable Mr Adamson could be worn down with persistence.

However, he stayed as he was, facing the most unexpected part of his journey so far.

'I do promise we're not mad all of the time,' his employer's younger sister told him, her brown eyes sparkling. He *really* ought not to notice that refined voice that carried more than a hint of England, or that her tone was refreshingly unguarded. She was of average height, and certainly not dressed to make an impression. And yet...

He was about to respond to the only Farrer left on the drive when a cacophony of deafening calls rang out above him. Black birds, tipped white on their tails, chased each other in a manic pattern above them and across to the rich green grapevines, continuing their call as they did.

As their hollering faded the bleats of the sheep filtered back across the landscape.

Miss Farrer grinned.

'You'll find the country as loud as the city, I think.'

'*Louder,*' he said with enough ferocity she laughed outright.

She glanced over at those vines and brushed back a curl of brown hair that had fallen across her ear, and Peter decided against mentioning the dark smudge on her cheek. Dirt? Soot? He hadn't any idea.

'Do you know much about wine?'

A pertinent question for a man who'd been employed to oversee the family's new business. Peter considered lying but knew she'd catch him out.

'I'm good at drinking it. Beyond that, I assume I'll receive a hasty education over the coming days.'

She wasn't, he decided, too appalled by the admission.

'In all honesty we're just happy to have someone take over those ledgers. Warring currawongs aside, I hope you like it here at Endmoor. The estate is named for our—mine and Robert's, that is—childhood home in Cumberland. I was so small when we left England, and not much bigger when my parents decided to move inland from Sydney and make a go of working the land.'

'You were probably horrified by what you found here. All those bushrangers and escaped convicts running wild.'

She tilted her head, thinking about it.

'Well, I didn't love knowing the Clarke Gang and The Duffer and all the others haunted the region, and I certainly wasn't thrilled about the size of the spiders.' She held up a hand. 'Some of them are this big.'

'Are you trying to scare me off on my first day? I promise I'm less cowardly than I look.'

'Oh, don't worry, if you're fine with the spiders, we'll find something else to frighten you,' she told him happily. 'When we first came out here it was just the four of us, a horse, and a couple of bollocks, and I—'

She broke off abruptly as she realised what she'd said, and a shocked look came over her face, her eyes going wide.

Peter tried; he really did. Even so, a huff of laughter escaped as Miss Elizabeth Farrer's porcelain skin flushed a distinct shade of pink.

'A couple of *bullocks,* perhaps?' he suggested.

She stared at him—or, rather, at a point somewhere on the wall behind him—and struggled to respond.

'Please tell me I didn't say that.'

There was no way—*none*—that he couldn't laugh again.

'I'm absolutely certain that you did.'

That got her eyes back on him. She gave her head a little shake.

'It's my accent. It just sounded like—'

'No,' he said. 'But nice try.'

The frustrated sound she made was dainty but audible enough.

'Could you perhaps forget you heard it?'

'Sorry, Miss Farrer, but there's no chance of that happening.'

She grappled in a few moments of outraged silence. The sheep continued to bleat.

'Aren't you supposed to be on your best behaviour on the very first day of your job?'

'Ah, but I'm not to begin until tomorrow, so I consider myself safe. Predictability is boring. Don't be afraid to be surprising.'

Somewhere outside a dog barked, and then Robert Farrer reappeared, handed Elizabeth a letter with a knowing look—'Post from town,' he told her unnecessarily—before switching his attention to Peter. He beckoned to a building to the side of the homestead, and whatever it was that'd passed between Peter and Farrer's sister was over. Miss Farrer turned her attention elsewhere with obvious relief, and Peter followed the brother to the cottage to the side of the homestead that would serve as his new home.

***

Elizabeth dreamt insignificant things that night.

After a friendly if stilted dinner, their new employee had made his excuses and returned to the cottage they'd spruced up for his stay, leaving her weak with relief. How fortunate that they'd never demolished the old house, as it was a convenient place to stash visitors who were either very unwelcome, too argumentative, or distractingly attractive.

Awkwardness was the way of things when people hardly knew each other, but she was certain the man thought she was an imbecile. Throughout the evening she'd spent an inordinate amount of time gripping her wineglass too hard, and swirling the straw-green liquid around inside it. Rather than try to participate, she'd let the conversation unfold around her.

'Are you all right?' her brother asked at one point, drawing unwanted attention her way.

'She's doin' research,' Alice had explained, nodding at the bottle on the table. It was Endmoor, after all, and they had a vineyard to develop.

If there was something strange about the evening, Elizabeth had been the only one to notice apparently. After the meal the men had discussed business. Mr Rowe spoke of revenue and expenditure the way Elizabeth might of the French Impressionists, while Robert became enthused about the topic of settling tanks and sediment. By the time their newest employee had made his excuses and returned to his accommodation Elizabeth found she'd spent a good deal of time staring a blank page of her sketchbook.

Alice put her little son to bed and then sat down with a book so sensational and scandalous it had Robert snorting and Elizabeth oddly curious. Even Gertrude, the aloof cat, had rolled around on the rug, purring her contentment.

Needing some time alone, Elizabeth took herself off to her room, only to discover there was no respite for her in her sleep. She dreamt of everyday things of no particular interest. Of helping Alice with the roses, and of numbing her mind with her brother's ledgers. She dreamt of wandering about the estate, but each time she tried to take herself beyond the property's borders some invisible power forced her back.

Supposedly it was the monotony that finally woke her. She'd quite literally bored herself awake. For someone whose heart lay in creativity, it was an utter disgrace.

Confused, uncertain how much of what was in her mind had really happened and how much had happened only in her head, she lay still for several moments, listening to the night as she came back to herself. Somewhere in the distance a bat let out a nightmarish screech that sent a shudder through her from top to toes.

Sitting up and kicking the blankets away, she lit the lamp and then untangled and braided her hair, going over the events of the previous day in her head.

In reality, Mr Rowe had displayed better manners that evening than he had in the afternoon, and not mentioned any aspect of the male anatomy once—not even the politer parts. He'd acted as though the whole event had never taken place.

Even so—even now—her face heated with the memory of it.

Still groggy, but certain she'd not get back to sleep any time soon, she slipped off the bed, reaching for a shawl. It didn't matter what he thought of her. She'd had enough of men in general. Robert, a brother, was all she needed.

Her mother's letter, the one that had arrived in the afternoon, sat beside her, stamped and marked with all the signs of a journey from Britain to Australia. Already she'd read it some half a dozen times.

Your brother was always more settled in New South Wales. If you were to return home, we wouldn't be surprised, and you'd be very welcome here.

It was the truth, was it not? Hadn't that been the reason she'd written in the first place? To return to England ... it was almost another dream. Squinting until her eyes became accustomed to the glow, she walked to the dresser and moved a couple of inlaid trinket boxes aside until she could reach the plainer one behind it.

Tracing the familiar dents and scratches in the old wood, she opened it and retrieved another, older, letter—one that had been read many more times.

Khartoum has fallen, and General Gordon is dead. We're to send a contingent to the Sudan.

Forgive me, but I'll be late to meet you this afternoon.

E.

It was such an inconsequential note, dashed off in an excited, barely legible hand, news delivered so casually a person would think he'd reported on nothing more important than what he'd eaten for breakfast.

It was so like Edward.

One day she'd find the strength of will to burn the silly thing, but not yet. Not this week, and probably not the one after.

She reread the note, smoothing out a creased corner as she did, and when she didn't burst into devastated sobs she put it carefully away again and wondered what else she might do for the remainder of the night. Precedent told her she'd not be sleeping anymore.

September nights were never easy. Not when every creature in existence thought spring existed solely for them to fight their rivals. And not when so many of them chose to wake well before dawn and announce their woes to the world, even earlier than the farmers did. Already, and despite it being hours from sunrise, she could hear various calls from the trees surrounding the house.

Moping about the bedroom was far too maudlin for an early Thursday morning. And so she would wander the house instead.

'Bollocks,' she whispered. For goodness' sake, she'd never said that word aloud in her life before.

Crossing the wooden floor on careful, bare feet, she eased her door open and stepped out into the hall, toes coming into contact with the plush rug that ran its length.

A few doors down she heard her infant nephew Duncan fussing, and the soft rustles of someone leaving their bed to care for him. Elizabeth plastered herself against a wall for a little while, feeling ridiculously guilty for a woman in her own house.

She stayed absolutely still until both the fussing and the murmurs died down, feeling like a fool for hiding from her family. She wasn't doing anything wrong, but she didn't continue on until the place fell silent again. Once she finally did, she winced with each new step as the parquet floor creaked beneath her feet.

It would never do if her cautious, protective brother came searching for an intruder. And it *certainly* wouldn't do if the night ended with him crowning her with their parents' antique vase that sat on the hall table, the one that had lost its brilliance since the elder Mr and Mrs Farrer had given up on the colonies and left their son and daughter behind.

There will always be a place for you in Cumberland, though you might prefer London, now that the Slade School welcomes women.

The suggestion in her mother's letter had made her heart leap with excitement. It was a heady thing to imagine, being welcomed into an academy in Bloomsbury. To be included along with men, and be taught by Heaven only knew who, but she was certain they'd be important.

It was a suggestion almost tempting enough to encourage her onto the next ship home. Life somehow seemed easier back there, and she wouldn't have to worry about all the dreadful things the Australian landscape inflicted upon them. There'd be no concerns about whether the elements would utterly ruin them from one year to the next.

A draught picked up from nowhere, and Elizabeth shivered violently and again curled her toes.

'Stupid, bloody weather,' she said as loudly as she dared, delighting in the freedom of saying appalling things when there was nobody around to scold her.

It was perfectly normal to startle at a shadow, she reasoned, as her heart began to beat too fast. It was also perfectly normal to stop still for a full minute to be certain the next shadow was normal and unthreatening and definitely *not* a poltergeist, and that it would not attack her if she continued on.

In the past, when she, Robert and their friends had been much younger, they'd scared themselves silly telling stories of ghosts drifting across the old, barren land. Nights had been worse for the Farrer children, living so far from town. A normal woman would have forgotten those stories a long time ago, but Elizabeth had a good memory—especially in the middle of the night, and *especially* when the air was alive with ... something...

She firmly ignored the sensation of fingertips crawling up and down her back.

The hall table, she finally realised. It was the hall table that had been there at least a decade whose shadow had appeared ominous a few steps back.

'Ghosts do not exist,' she breathed.

Once she was clear of the corridor she felt safe enough to move faster, but the word—that ridiculous word she'd said to Mr Rowe—chased along after her. To make matters worse, she'd not known until seeing her reflection half an hour after meeting him that she had charcoal smudged in various places on her face, and a scattering of burs attached to her gown in interesting locations.

Gliding through the dark house, she made her way to the drawing room, skirting around furniture and avoiding banged shins by memory. She used the shadows as an additional guide, and managed to not bump into anything important.

The curtains were drawn back from the large window, a nod to the sun that came through in the mornings and warmed the house naturally over the cooler months. And it was there that she dropped into a chair, curling her feet up under herself.

Bollocks, bollocks, bollocks.

Elizabeth buried her face in her hands. 'Argh.'

She stayed until the peace of the hour settled her, fixing her mind on her plans for the following day, and was about to return to her room when movement across the garden caught her eye.

Gasping, her instinct to flee hit her before common sense took over.

Ghosts were nonsense. Intruders, however...

Bushrangers were long gone from the tablelands, and there was more than one burly man on Endmoor grounds who'd willingly deal with an intruder. All she had to do was call for help—but she stopped herself before any words formed on her lips. Surely she was being overly dramatic.

Elizabeth hugged her knees as everything calmed again, and she was about to convince herself she'd imagined it but then the shadows shifted again.

'*Bollocks.*' The word formed on her lips, but no sound emerged. Her heart pounded so loudly she could hardly hear over it.

Rising slowly, she edged to the window, clasping at the gathered curtains and straining to see. If she could just convince herself it was a tree out there and not a man, or perhaps that it was an overly large possum, everything would be fine.

The clouds had come over since the sun set and now they moved on with the breeze. As the moon emerged, casting light across the estate, Elizabeth got her third glimpse of what had frightened her.

She saw him better this time, as growing confidence had him strolling right past the homestead and out of her view.

She rushed to the next room to keep sight of him: a tall figure whose striking features were almost entirely disguised in the night. Uncertainty had her clutching tightly at her shawl and walking on the tips of her toes.

From the dining room she spotted Mr Rowe again as he rounded the side of the cottage and continued on in the direction of the grapevines and the paddocks beyond.

Another instinct, one she didn't understand, told her to not announce herself, and she followed it as she followed him, creeping on bare feet out the kitchen door and making her way across the cool path that wound around the garden. Small pebbles and stray twigs pressed into her feet, and she cursed them silently but continued, her shawl pulled as tightly around herself as she could manage in an attempt to mask the white of her nightgown.

She stopped when the path ended, biting her lip and staring after him as he strode off into the darkness. The night swallowed him up almost entirely, but he didn't slow, even as the clouds came back across, masking her vision once more.

Frustrated, she shivered in the cool breeze. What did they really know about him, after all? Over the course of the evening meal they'd learnt that his education was impressive, that he'd never been to the area before, and that he had a deceased mother, a living father, and one sister named Edith. It wasn't exactly much to go by.

In that moment the town, along with its reassuringly large police barracks and magistrate's quarters, felt a thousand miles away.

Behind Elizabeth the house had fallen silent once more, but she took some comfort in the fact her brother kept a cricket bat in his office. What she lacked in size to the mysterious man out there stalking the countryside, she could certainly make up for with a lump of willow wood and a decent swing.

Chapter 3

It was madness to go wandering the property so late. Peter was well aware of it. He'd heard the country brought with it all kinds of dangers, and some of them had far better vision at night than he did. Thank goodness for the near-full moon, but it wouldn't do to succumb to a snakebite—or a hidden ditch—before he'd even taken his first look at Robert Farrer's ledgers.

And yet there he was sneaking about like a dashed criminal for no better reason than his infernal impatience. For a generally even-tempered man, it was a shocking thing to discover about himself.

He'd avoided a collision with Albert, the young butler, who'd come bustling along the path at an odd hour, smelling mildly like hops and mumbling something about a lost door key. Peter was fairly certain he'd come out the winner if the two of them got into a tussle, but he tended to avoid fisticuffs during the first week in a new position, and so stuck to the shadows until he had the night to himself again.

He wouldn't go far tonight. However, he felt the need to be out there, on the land, searching for ... well. It'd help a great deal if he knew precisely what he was up to.

Self-preservation had him startling like a jumpy kitten at the sight of movement up ahead, and then laughing quietly to himself at the sight of Mrs Farrer's enormous tabby ambling around the corner. He garnered one slow, bored perusal, the cat's eyes gleaming at him freakishly, and then she continued on her way at the same disinterested pace.

Dismissed, he walked on, attention fixed on the shadowy foothills. Dead leaves crunched under his feet the moment he left the path and he slowed his pace, half expecting to take a tumble down a wombat hole at any moment.

Wouldn't *that* be an interesting story to explain when he was found by an unsuspecting stockman at dawn?

He almost missed the movement off to the side of his vision. Had a bat not flown over at that exact moment, its eerie shriek coming from his right, he wouldn't have turned enough to see the woman.

Lit only by a dim light from one of the homestead's rooms, she was too slender to be the housekeeper, and it wasn't Mrs Farrer; Robert's fair-haired wife was so diminutive not even the force of her personality could disguise that fact.

Elizabeth Farrer, then. Peter froze.

'*Damn,*' he breathed.

***

'It's too big,' Daisy had no choice to concede two days earlier. She stood with Peter in the terrace on Glenmore Road, the light coming and going around them as the sea breeze blew the end of rain shower away west across Sydney's growing sprawl.

Brother and sister stood in silence for a little while, side by side as they gave the painting on the parlour wall a frank assessment. Peter really hadn't needed to pay a visit to the house to study the thing one last time before he left; he was fairly sure he could describe it in his sleep. He knew each rock and tree and shadow depicted in the valley, just as he knew each rise and fall of the mountains beyond it. A single building stood off to the left of the picture, a crooked and poorly formed blight on the wild landscape.

'It's *far* too big,' he agreed readily. 'And that's why I can't take it with me.'

In a house that had been furnished with all things masculine—the walls, it seemed, could always do with another image of a man on a horse—the sprawling depiction of a countryside so alien to Peter stood out each and every time. Long after his father's more obvious decorating choices had become stale and forgettable, his attention never failed to be captured by *this* one.

It was an unsophisticated work. In what Peter guessed had been a rare moment of sentimentality, his father had purchased the painting as he'd passed across the countryside back in the early 1850s, travelling the long, slow way from his own parents' modest home in Albury to begin his new life in the city.

'*I don't miss the bush*' Maurice Rowe had been known to say firmly—and often.

The man had arrived in the city with not only a somewhat battered painting but also a wife plucked from a small settlement in the middle of nowhere, a woman as eager to be gone from her own rural backwater as Maurice had been himself.

Daisy stepped closer, using the edge of her shawl to wipe at the dust on the brass plaque at the bottom. Peter watched her trace the title etched into the metal.

Namadgi Sunrise

Soon, *so* soon, Peter would see this view with his own eyes.

His mother's family had been there long before the bullock trains had arrived in the valley, and well before the bush had been tamed and the thick forest transformed into a maze of fields and roads. He knew it in a vague, distant way, but he could not yet feel it.

Another burst of spring rain misted the window, and a seagull sailed by, down the slope to the bay. It would be strange to leave the coast. His whole life had been spent within a few miles of the Pacific.

Rowe and Son was thriving, and even though the Farrer property was likely to do well in the future, neither Peter nor his father needed to take on the management of a brand-new vineyard in the middle of the country. The coincidence that the senior Rowe had somehow heard about Endmoor, of all the properties in New South Wales, wasn't just suspicious, it was telling.

Not for the first time since being asked—*ordered*—to pack his things and make a railway journey south, Peter found himself wondering...

'Do you think it's really like that there?' Daisy's focus was on the crooked little hut to one side of the picture. 'I can't even imagine ... The valley is so large you'd need some sort of map to navigate it.'

'I've made a sketch of the painting to take with me.' He hadn't intended to tell her; the words just came out. 'It'll have to do.'

She whipped around to face him. Her dark eyes danced. 'Am I allowed to see it?'

'*No!*'

She gasped with laughter at the power of his response. 'It can't be *that* bad.'

'Believe me, Daisy, it is.'

His sister had hugged him then. Tightly. 'What will I do without you here?'

'I doubt you'll even notice I'm gone,' he'd said, and received a little pinch on the arm and a kiss on the cheek for it.

***

Had Miss Farrer seen him? For long moments Peter stayed as he was, hoping that from so far away he looked like nothing more than a trick of the shadows or perhaps a small tree.

He watched until her attention moved elsewhere, and then carefully crept on, past his cottage, to where he couldn't easily be seen.

Imaginary tentacles stretched out in every direction, searching, seeking. Out in the paddock the merinos were a sea of hazy white figures dotting the plain, and beyond that rose the Brindabella Range. A painting could capture many things, but it also gave a man a chance to imagine the rest; the sounds and the scents of the country were opposite in every way to the bustle of a city and the breeze of the coast. The vastness was easy to picture, and yet it was different when it was actually *felt*.

Shaking his head at his own idiocy, Peter had to wonder what he'd expected to find at night that he'd not been able to see during day.

He took another step and grunted as something skittled under his foot, turning his ankle.

Crouching, he scooped his hand in the dirt and closed his fist around something small and hard. He ran a thumb over it.

A gumnut.

He tucked it into his pocket, and had just decided to return to the house when his head snapped up, all his senses alert. There'd been something out there a moment ago...

It was then he saw the bob of light some hundred yards away, maybe more.

Stilling, he strained to see, tracking the person's progress, occasionally losing sight of them as someone—*he*, he supposed—picked his way across the valley, the light disappearing here and there as the trees blocked the view, and then re-emerging further away. The light became less distinct as its owner carried it off to the west, and then faded away to nothing more than a whisper of a glow. It was as though a ghost had passed by.

Once he lost sight of it completely, Peter watched for another few minutes just in case, and then turned back.

'Tomorrow,' he murmured, his voice sounding too loud in the emptiness.

When he retraced his steps and rounded the corner the house was dark and Miss Farrer was gone.

***

'Are you finished with that?' Elizabeth asked Alice several days later as the other woman closed the cover of her novel with a satisfied sigh and set it aside, picking up her mending in its place.

Her sister-in-law focused on threading a needle, but the corners of her mouth still curved up as she nodded. 'Yes, I'm finished. Now, on to the next one.'

'There's another one?'

'There will be, just as soon as I can convince Robert to order it.'

That drew Elizabeth up short. 'What's so terrible that he wouldn't order it?'

Alice pressed her lips together, eyes laughing. 'I reckon I ought not to ruin your respectability by tellin' you.'

Elizabeth spluttered long enough for Alice to execute a couple of stitches. 'What on earth...?

Are you trying to preserve my modesty? What about yours?'

'I never had much of it to being with. And I'm a married lady now, so I can read whatever I want. I bet Robert wouldn't want your young mind corrupted.'

'Alice, I'm *five years* older than you!'

The younger woman grinned. 'Funny, isn't it?'

Elizabeth groaned. It *was* a little funny, how marriage changed things so much.

'You're impossible.'

The days were becoming noticeably longer, and even though they were now close to the evening meal, the drawing room was still bright. Elizabeth set the letter she had been reading aside—the art buyer in Goulburn wanted to discuss the pricing of her work—and eyed the book surreptitiously.

'I promise, one day I'll be so corrupted you'll all be astonished.'

Alice looked up and then looked appalled. 'If you do that nobody will come callin' on us.'

'I thought you didn't like callers.'

'Not most of 'em, but we've gotta give Mrs Adamson someone to impress.'

Sighing and admitting defeat for the time being—the housekeeper *did* deserve a guest or two now and then—Elizabeth returned to her letter.

It had been a complete accident that she had sold any of her work to Evanson and Associates to begin with. A delayed coach on a trip to Sydney at the beginning of the year, on a day everyone was so out of sorts thanks to the heat and the wait that they turned to the nearest person to moan about it, and the next thing she knew she was showing her work to a man she'd never seen before in her life.

Mr Montague Evanson, a married, ruddy-faced fellow somewhere in his forties, had been remarkably enthusiastic about the whole thing, and had waxed poetic about city buyers' enthusiasm for the romance of the bush.

In truth, at first she'd been sceptical. His offer had sounded too good to be true, and before their conversation had even ended she'd been sure it was an elaborate scam. It was only weeks later, with some investigative help from Robert and John Stanford, that they'd learnt the offer was genuine.

Soon after that she'd made her first sale, and then her second and her third.

'If you like,' Alice began generously once Elizabeth folded and set the letter aside, 'I'll lend the book to you. But maybe don't tell Robert, and don't mention it to me when he's around, because that's not a conversation any of us want to have.'

Elizabeth rewarded her with a happy sigh. 'I knew you'd come around.'

They shared a private, secret smile.

Alice added a few more stitches while Elizabeth rose from the chair, and then a couple more as she crossed the room and picked the book up, turning it over and examining the seemingly innocent maroon and black cover.

'Is it really such a scandalous story?'

'Uh huh, I reckon it is. Even by me own standards.'

Alice had grown up in different circumstances to her. It was something that made them seem closer in age than they were—at least Elizabeth thought so. And, as Alice had jokingly pointed out only moments earlier, she was also a married woman. A mother, too.

Some days recently Elizabeth had begun to feel like she was another child in the house.

'Speakin' of books, weren't you goin' to take some over for that Mr Rowe?'

'I was.'

It had been her plan back when she'd thought him less nefarious than he'd shown himself to be. She'd still not said anything to anyone about that night he'd gone wandering. When it came down to it, there wasn't anything illegal about taking a midnight stroll, and it wouldn't do to go about accusing innocent men of odd things.

'Last I heard, he's not there right now. Rode out with Robert somewhere or other. Probably lookin' at those fences to the east, though I don't know what a businessman like him wants with them. Maybe you want to wait a bit? Go over when he gets back?'

Elizabeth wasn't sure she trusted that look in the other woman's eyes. It was a look that said she'd noticed too much—*far* too much.

This wasn't good.

'No, I think I'll take them over now.' *And maybe snoop a bit.*

Chapter 4

Elizabeth felt incredibly guilty as she made her way down the path, past Alice's rose garden, and across the gravel to the cottage. The sun seemed angled to blind her. Cicadas sounded from every direction.

It was extremely hard to hurry with a stack of books in her arms and Hutton, her brother's dog, darting past, providing her with an excellent opportunity to take a tumble.

'Why aren't you off with Robert?' she asked the heeler after coming within an inch of stepping on a paw, and received a happy yip but no intelligible response.

Bessie the maid walked by, offering Elizabeth a smile, and a stockman stood on the drive, talking to Mr Adamson about something or other over the top of a wagon.

Elizabeth ducked around the dog, who'd become suddenly fascinated with the bottom of a wattle bush, and continued on her way. The books in her arms were rather heavy. With each step she imagined the men's eyes boring into the back of her, though the conversation that drifted across implied they'd not even noticed she was there.

Everything about what she was doing felt suspicious—probably because it was.

She sighed in frustration when she reached the door and realised she couldn't set the books down to knock, and then glanced in either direction before bracing for balance and giving the door a couple of decent whacks with her shoe.

How very, very ladylike.

The door opened of its own accord on the second kick; it struck her as naïvely trusting on the accountant's part.

'Excuse me?' she called when nobody came stampeding out to yell at her for intruding. 'Mr Rowe?'

The cicadas grew louder.

Wondering where on earth her well-installed manners had gone, and with arms starting to ache under the weight of an enormous pile of paper and binding, she stepped up into the building's cooler interior. She might have gone a little mad with her selection from the library. Mr Rowe would be reading his way into the next decade.

Nobody stopped her on the first step in, nor on the second, and before she knew it she stood in the middle of the cottage.

Looking around, chin resting on the cover of the top book, she found an empty space on the table. Setting everything down with a thud loud enough to have her looking over her shoulder in alarm, she took a slow turn about the place, flexing her fingers and shaking out the strain.

They'd not much bothered with changing the place's interior in the years since the main homestead had been completed and the Farrers had moved out. A fortnight earlier she, Mrs Adamson and Alice had done their best to make the space slightly less musty, and had moved a few items of furniture across from the main house to replace two battered old pieces that had been there since her childhood. The wallpaper was a deep but slowly fading red, a raised lozenge pattern print that she'd traced her fingers along a thousand times when she was a girl.

If they'd had more warning that Robert was bringing another man to work on the station, they might have done more. *'I wasn't sure anyone would want to move out here from the city'* had been his excuse when they'd devoted a whole afternoon to admonishing him about the surprise.

It was too small a place for a man to be hiding anywhere, unless he'd crawled under the bed. Elizabeth was definitely alone.

'What were you expecting to find?' she asked herself, and then cringed because her voice sounded far too loud, bouncing around the unoccupied space. Many a criminal wasn't very bright, but she doubted even the worst of them left giant, obvious clues out on the table, or pinned to the wall.

Maybe there was a much simpler answer to the man's odd behaviour that night. He might have had trouble sleeping in a new place, in such a new situation. Maybe the birds bothered him. Or the bats. Had she not also been wandering around in the middle of the night? Or maybe he was one of those men who walked in their sleep. She'd heard of such people, and also heard there was no rational explanation for it.

Mr Rowe wasn't a criminal. She realised she'd known that before she'd even invited herself into his house.

'You fool,' she muttered, and then looked this way and that in search of something she might scribble a note on to let him know why a library's worth of books had appeared on his table while he was out.

She came to a stop in front of the sole painting on the wall and made herself give it a frank assessment. Taken out of storage in the main house, it was one of hers, depicting two horsemen in the valley. She'd based it loosely on her brother and his business partner, with one rider's hair dark under his hat, and the other one a contrasting gold. With their faces concealed and their attention on the herd of sheep in the distance, it was certainly not a masterpiece.

Elizabeth shut her eyes for a moment and then forced herself to look at the picture closer still, assessing it as an expert might, wondering if anyone in Bloomsbury would see it and laugh her out of the academy.

Groaning quietly—and groaning far more loudly inside her head—she wondered if she could steal it from the wall and sneak it into the house without anyone seeing. Perhaps Mr Rowe hadn't even noticed it was there. He'd been very busy since beginning his new position. Perhaps he hated art, and perhaps he would rather it hadn't been there when he arrived.

Perhaps—

The crunch of a footstep behind her was such a surprise she spun too fast and stumbled over her own skirts, smacking a thigh into the table.

A touch, slight and fast, but firm on her waist saved her, and then she was righting herself and looking up into Mr Rowe's dark eyes as half of the books dropped to the floor, one heavy thud at a time.

'Oh my goodness.'

So much for a spot of stealthy snooping.

One of the books settled badly, wide open, spine bent horribly, but neither of them moved as Mr Rowe assessed the situation. Elizabeth's pulse raged at her, and she was sure she trembled in delayed surprise. It all made it hard to appear innocent.

'Good afternoon.' The man was more amused than offended, which was a blessed relief. When he ascertained she wasn't about to crash into anything else, he took a step back, placing a polite distance between them.

'Mr Rowe. I was...' There was probably a wonderful and convincing lie she could tell him then. What a pity she couldn't think of it.

Because there was nothing else to do but stand there and try her best to appear innocent, Elizabeth ignored the heat rising all over her, and also the excessive pounding of her heart, and tried to summon a smile that felt tight and comical as it stretched across her face.

'I've been looking at fences,' he told her, saving her from having to think any harder. 'I'm not entirely sure I've come away from the situation an expert, but it certainly explained some of the entries in the books. So much needs to be ordered. So much to be restored.'

Elizabeth grasped at the mundane offering with a pair of imaginary, desperate hands.

'Fences are the bane of a landowner's existence. They're always coming down, always needing to be maintained. And occasionally there's a thief with an eye to stealing an animal or two, and they cut their way in to do it.'

She should not, she remembered too late, mention thievery, considering her present situation.

'I'm not here to rob you.' It was a pertinent point to introduce to the conversation.

He tilted his head as he looked down at her, and even though his face gave nothing away, she knew with absolute certainty that he was laughing.

'That's very good to know. The idea never even struck me.'

She nodded, accepting it even if he didn't mean it. She pointed, first at the table and then the haphazard pile on the floor.

'I thought you might like some books. My plan, however, hadn't been to come over here and throw them at you.'

He seemed amenable to the idea but continued to study her silently.

'You should probably lock your door,' she added feebly, and then crouched to retrieve the book with the bent spine first.

He joined her down there and reached for the tome nearest to his feet, pausing briefly to examine it—should she have chosen something more original than Edwin Drood she wondered—and then reaching for another.

'Thank you. For thinking to do this, I mean.'

Their hands nearly touched as they reached for the same book at the same time. Mr Rowe's apology was a low murmur, and he reached for another and—too late—Elizabeth noticed the colour of the cover.

Oh Lord. How inattentive had she been when making that stack of books?

Task finished, they both climbed back up to their feet while she tried to decide if there was a way to snatch a book out of his hands without seeming impolite. There wasn't, of course. Which meant she could only hope he added it to the stack without paying the thing any attention. Surely he'd not pay much attention to one small, maroon...

Mr Rowe turned it over and read the title. His eyebrows rose, and Elizabeth wondered how she could have been so careless and *stupid*.

'I didn't mean to bring that one.'

His lips curved upwards a fraction.

'It's not mine. Really, it isn't.'

'*Lady Audley's Secret?* And here you were trying to entertain me with Dickens.'

It would be nice if Elizabeth had any idea what the book contained to put that knowing smile on the man's face, but Alice had been merrily tight-lipped about it. If she was going to earn a reputation as a connoisseur of scandalous stories she should be allowed to *read* them first.

He allowed himself another second to be entertained, reading the title another time for good measure, and then took pity on her, passing the offending item across.

'Thank you, again, for thinking of me. You may have this one back.'

**

'I've not read it,' Miss Farrer seemed compelled to tell him, which was a lie Peter was reluctant to let go. 'I haven't so much as opened the cover.'

Returning from the land to the surprise of her standing in the middle of his sitting room had quickly given way to amusement. She didn't like him feeling that way about her; he hadn't known her very long, but it was obvious in the almost-concealed frustration in her hazel eyes each time he saw them. He knew that and resolved to try harder to conceal his own thoughts in the future.

'Whose book *is* it if not yours?'

In such a small community he'd have expected the reading selection to be fairly limited. He expected a healthy collection of dull, dry guides on housekeeping, and wheat and sheep. There was likely an overabundance of Bibles.

'I don't know,' she replied, too fast to be believed.

Bigamy, abandonment, murder, arson—*Lady Audley* ran the gamut of outrageous topics. He wondered if Miss Farrer even knew what bigamy was. If she didn't yet, she'd know by the time she reached the book's end.

'There's nothing wrong with reading something other than Mrs Beeton's instructional guide every now and then,' she pointed out. 'I'm twenty-six years old. Well and truly of an age to read something a little controversial without fainting from it.'

'Controversial, is it? How do you know what sort of a book it is?'

'I *don't*. However, it's easy enough to figure it out when everyone reacts like you just did whenever it is mentioned. How about you? How do *you* know what type of book it is?'

'I just know. It's common knowledge.' It was the best answer he could come up with spontaneously, and he was well aware it was woeful. And the triumph on her face told him she knew it.

Needing a distraction, he scoured their surroundings. There was sturdy furniture, and a bowl of fruit on the table. They were hardly topics for riveting conversation.

Struggling, and aware she'd bested him, his eyes came to rest on the painting on the far wall.

'Is it an image of Endmoor?' He risked a glance back at those hazel eyes as he asked, and so did not miss the face she pulled. 'What did I say?'

'Oh, nothing. I was hoping you'd not notice the painting—or not comment, at least. It's not very good. I'm sorry we hadn't the time to furnish the place better before you arrived.'

Actually, he'd been thinking the piece was a sight better than anything he'd left behind on the walls of the Sydney terrace. It appeared there *was* a creative way to depict a man on a horse.

He examined the thing again, perplexed, and then met—and held—her eyes and again there was awareness between them.

The slow roll of a wagon's wheels passed by. Miss Farrer hugged the book to her chest with the title facing towards her, and began edging away.

'Um ... Do you need anything else? I mean ... you can always come by the house if you do.'

'I'm fine,' Peter murmured.

She stepped back further.

'All right then. I'll leave you to settle in. I ought to go and ... do something ... I'm sure I'm needed at the house by now. Mrs Adamson will be wanting to discuss tonight's menu.'

Peter smiled a little and let her flimsy excuse hold.

Don't follow her to the door.

She walked past him, primly and properly, cheeks a little flushed.

He followed her as she stepped out onto the path.

Don't watch her go.

Somewhere nearby a magpie warbled and then called across the clearing.

It took Miss Farrer until she was halfway down the path before her shoulders relaxed and her gait became more natural.

Somewhere, off in the distance, another magpie replied.

Step back inside the house, you fool.

Robert Farrer was waiting for her out on the veranda. The siblings spoke briefly, and then the sister headed into the homestead. Farrer saw Peter and raised a hand; Peter waved back and then finally stepped inside and firmly closed the door.

Chapter 5

Peter expected the stares as he walked along Monaro Street in town a few days later with Robert Farrer at his side. Several decades of practice meant he did a decent job of pretending ignorance.

The one saving grace of cities was that often enough there were too many people with too many things to do for anybody to stop and give a stranger a moment of their time. They were communities that bred a sense of self-preservation. Peter *almost* believed he could catch on fire in the middle of a pavement back home and people would politely ignore his predicament and continue on their way.

A small town was a disconcertingly different matter. It wasn't possible to go unnoticed.

'It's a struggle...' Farrer was saying as they passed a series of shops that ran the length of the road between the park and the river. Up above a few people wandered out onto the balcony of one of the terraces and rested their hands on the laced iron railing to watch the street in what, Peter thought, was a convenient display of timing. He pretended not to notice.

'Europe wants our wool and our opals, but they're not sure they want us providing them with wine. Why buy Australian wine when there's perfectly good booze coming out of France? The Germans are rather attached to their riesling and not all that thrilled to share their success, but we'll get there.'

He laughed quietly.

'John's a lot more charming than me. That's why he gallivants around Europe convincing everyone that New South Wales is the only place a man would want to buy from, while we stay languishing in the country, doing the dirty work.'

A young woman passing in the opposite direction shifted her attention their way, eyes holding Peter's for just long enough to convey a message. Unfortunately he didn't understand, nor did he want to interpret what it was.

He switched his attention to the man beside him. 'I wouldn't say bookkeeping is all that dirty.'

'Perhaps not, but there are a lot of people on Endmoor who would think so. My sister included.'

Peter took a sudden interest in a shopfront across the street. Conversations about Miss Farrer were best kept to an absolute minimum, especially when her brother was the other person involved.

It was easier, Robert had explained the day before, to come in and get all the business done in town rather than wait for mail and news to trickle out to them at Endmoor.

'And it's also good for your sanity,' he'd added with a flash of teeth. *'Things can get a little too lonely out in the bush.'*

Peter wasn't sure what was good for his sanity right then.

They reached the top of the street and came to a stop. Farrer called a few words in greeting to a Mr Addison who passed on a horse, and then adjusted his hat.

'All right. I'm headed to the church. Alice likes to maintain reasonable standing with the Salvation Army ladies, and I've been tasked with spending a few minutes of my day charming them on her behalf. Marriage,' he added with a sigh, and then waved to someone else near the churchyard's little gate.

Peter declined the offer of an ale at The Dog and Stile once the charming was completed and the ladies satisfied, and headed towards the post office on his own, trying out a few politely distant greetings for various locals. He was a stranger, and that was enough to earn anybody's curiosity so far out in the middle of nowhere. He supposed a newcomer was always worth a second look.

There was correspondence waiting for him, just as he'd hoped, as well as a parcel for Miss

Farrer that was reluctantly handed over into his keeping. Peter read and reread the return address on his own correspondence and realised he'd been away from home just long enough to begin missing it. He'd missed Daisy, and the pang at seeing his name written in her familiar, loopy hand was unexpectedly strong.

Not wanting an audience while he read his letters, he left the office and wandered through the gate and onwards, past the churchyard, concealing a grin at the sight of his employer surrounded by a gaggle of enthusiastic women. Popularity wasn't always a good thing.

The park was expansive and already well established—a surprise, considering the size of the town. Someone had put in a lot of effort and worked a few miracles to keep the place so green. It was, Peter couldn't help but notice, a very European sort of garden, with imported trees shedding the last of their spring blossoms and drooping lilac perfuming the air, alongside a whole lot of flowers he hadn't a clue of the name of. That dreaded fluff from the kapok trees still drifted around in the air. He sneezed.

Spring. It was a little different in Barracks Flat.

He wandered over to the artificial pond halfway into the grounds and sneezed again as he took a seat on a bench. Before he'd even unfolded the first letter he found he was smiling.

He read them both, and then read them again in case he'd missed something, and then stood and set off towards the mill-lined river to find The Dog and Stile. He could well do with that ale after all.

***

'What is he like?' Elizabeth's oldest and closest friend asked that afternoon.

It was a question she should have expected. Elizabeth blew a stream of seeds off a plucked dandelion and buried her first instinct, which was to tell the other woman about her distracting attraction to Endmoor's new accountant. Not only was that truth something she wasn't ready to admit to herself, but it was something she suspected might end up getting her hurt.

They sat by the river, not far from the Wright house, but hidden in an alcove of wattle bushes and weeping willows. It afforded them enough privacy that they could hear the occasional horse on the road, but the riders would never see them. The old rope bridge was up ahead, and beyond it the barracks, the town's namesake, stood abandoned and crumbling.

'He's tall,' Elizabeth said instead. 'And he has dark hair—darker even than yours. Dark eyes. He's obviously well-educated.'

Martha Wright's big blue eyes rolled. 'You sound like you're describing a horse.'

'An *educated* horse?'

Martha's little dog, the runt from Robert's own heeler's litter, moved from one end of the clearing to the next, as happy to be outside as his mistress was. It wasn't a breed designed to be a lap dog, and heelers were certainly thought to be too uncouth for a household as distinguished as the Wrights'.

Elizabeth threw the dandelion stem aside and wished there was more she could say without giving herself away. She'd done enough hurting over men to last a while yet. Spinsterhood and a career as an artist sounded like an excellent plan for her future, just as long as Robert was happy to put up with the sight of her on Endmoor for a few more years. She'd have herself sorted out soon.

She shifted her thoughts back towards the new, infuriating addition to Endmoor.

'He likes numbers. It's both baffling and wonderful. I was ready to burn all of Robert's ledgers.'

With John abroad she'd taken on a lot of the property's less than enjoyable tasks.

Unfortunately for her, she'd been good at them. Her brother, too amused about her predicament for his own good, had threatened to have her permanently assigned to the work.

Well aware of the expectant expression on her friend's face, Elizabeth considered what else to share. Even with Martha she wasn't quite ready to talk about bollocks or sleepwalking or broad, strong shoulders.

'His heritage isn't entirely British.'

'No? He's not German, I suppose.' They'd had Germans from the Rhineland out for a while, back when Robert and John were establishing the vineyards.

'No, his colouring is darker than that.'

The strong sun gleamed on Martha's pale skin as she absorbed that piece of information. She really ought not to be without her hat, but Elizabeth knew better than to point it out.

'Dark, you say? Perhaps he's all the way from Italy, or Greece? Maybe Spain. Or even India?'

'He's not Italian. I think he's Aboriginal, at least partly, but he hasn't said and nobody has asked. My brother—'

She paused, gauging Martha's reaction. Nothing had come of her friend and Robert's affection for each other during their youth, but she usually tried to avoid the topic of her brother altogether.

'Well, anyway, Mr Rowe seems to be very good at his work, which is all that matters at the moment.'

'If you say so,' Martha replied, and bent to pat the dog, who'd just arrived at her feet.

'It's really no different with him there than before, the ledgers excluded.' It was a fib, and the fact her friend didn't reply was telling.

The water bubbled and gurgled and sparkled, and the dog ambled off to investigate.

'I think you like him,' Martha finally said, sounding awfully smug about the situation. 'And by *like*, I mean—'

'I know exactly what you mean, and I won't admit to that.'

Her friend seemed far too pleased by that particular development. Not that there *was* a development, Elizabeth amended silently. Spinsters didn't worry about men. They were too busy doing other, far more interesting things.

One attempt at a grand romance was sufficient, and she'd already done that, with spectacular results—spectacularly*bad* results, that was. In fact, it had been a cautionary tale that men had wandering eyes, and it was one she was still ashamed to share, even now he was gone.

Victoria Abraham: the name bounced around in her head sometimes, on quiet days when she hadn't enough to occupy her mind. Victoria was an unfortunately common name—inescapable. Why hadn't Edward's other love been called something more obscure and forgettable?

'Not all men are wicked,' Martha began, voice careful and even.

Elizabeth made sure to keep her attention on the slow, steady course of the river.

'Oh, no, I know they're not. Robert's always been too good for—well—for his own good. I have my doubts about them as a group, though ... Marriage is inevitable for most people. I consider myself fortunate to have avoided it so far.'

Martha didn't agree, Elizabeth knew. This was not a new debate.

The dog completed his hundredth lap of the clearing and flopped down in the shade, and Martha stretched her hand out to run her fingers through his short fur.

'What about John Stanford? He's outrageous, but not wicked, I think. You've a lot in common, and you get on.'

'John!' Elizabeth tried to imagine it. A romance with the man who as a boy had convinced her to spend an entire afternoon upending buckets of water onto spitfire larvae in the garden? The man who had her believing the little insects would set Endmoor alight if she didn't? The man who teased her better than her brother ever could?

'It would be like marrying an especially maddening cousin.'

They both turned sharply as a familiar barouche passed by, the vehicle tall enough they could see the top of it from their hiding place. Martha sighed.

'My father will expect me back. It's time to go upstairs and play the invalid again.'

Two years earlier a robbery gone wrong had left Martha wounded, and her recovery had not been fast. It had given the older Wrights the excuse they needed to control their overly beautiful, extremely admired daughter more than ever before.

Removing the hat had been a small rebellion, really, but Elizabeth's friend truly wasn't well.

And suddenly Elizabeth was ashamed. Recently she'd devoted so much time to feeling sorry for herself. However she could go out and about as she pleased, and not only because she could manage it physically. Robert would find himself clobbered over the head if he refused her her freedom.

The sounds of the vehicle's wheels came to a stop and Martha sighed again and made her apologies to the dog. Neither one of them looked happy to be heading home.

'I've a book,' Elizabeth said as she stood and reached out a hand to yank her friend to her feet.

'A book?'

'You could *try* and sound a little bit excited. It's not instructional. I've been reading it, and it's definitely the type that would give your mother the vapours. Next time I'm in town I'll bring it with me for you to borrow.'

Interest flared in Martha's eyes, but she was already shaking her head. 'If it's that sort of book, my mother will *really* get the vapours, and that's never much fun. She'll probably burn it, and then I'll never be able to return it.'

'I think it's worth the risk. Why not hollow out a Bible and store it in there?'

'Like Valeria Brinton?' Martha now sounded interested. *The Law and the Lady* was the first sensational book either of them had ever read back when they were girls—and the first of many to be confiscated by Mrs Wright. They'd idolised the story's heroine.

'It could actually work. For all their preaching, nobody in my family actually cares much about church.'

***

With Martha and her dog returned home without too much fanfare, Elizabeth walked back alongside the Murrumbidgee River, turning onto Monaro Street at the same time Robert and Mr Rowe emerged from the pub.

'How is she?' her brother asked when the three of them met at the bottom of the street.

'All right. Better.' It wasn't entirely true, but she'd recently developed a habit of fibbing. Not all lies were bad. 'Shall we head home?'

'This was waiting for you in the post office,' Mr Rowe said, clearing his throat and drawing her attention his way.

Elizabeth thanked him and absently reached out for the small parcel he held out to her. She was constantly ordering some supply or another for her work, and received at least as much mail as Robert did.

'I suppose we should probably—' She broke off when she got a better look at what she held. It was not a delivery of art supplies.

Later she'd have no recollection of what she thought they *should probably* do. Later, she'd not even remember how she got from the centre of town to her home in the bush.

The parcel was battered and oddly yellowed, as though it had been sitting in some dusty, sunny corner of an office for longer than it ought to have, forgotten all about. The initial address had been crossed out, and a new direction—to

Barracks Flat—written in a messy and unfamiliar hand in its place.

'For me?' she asked stupidly, even as she saw her name scrawled across the paper.

Robert peered over her shoulder. 'Were you expecting anything?'

'No.' She turned it over. 'Maybe a friend in Sydney has—'

Cascade Street.

Edward!

The world whirled. Elizabeth reached out blindly as her head grew light, gripping her brother's forearm as she fought off a wave of emotion so strong it all but engulfed her. A hand was at her back, the touch feeling a long way away, but it anchored her enough to keep her on her feet.

Someone said her name once, and then again, but there was too much ringing in her ears for her to hear the rest.

Edward. Edward Sumner.

A man who was supposed to be dead.

Chapter 6

The journey back to Endmoor was a subdued one.

After having the carriage brought down, the three of them—Peter, Farrer and Elizabeth—had set a steady pace directly for home.

Peter tried to stay removed from the situation, whatever it was. It was clearly a private matter, and he was far from being family. There might have been more conversation between the siblings if he wasn't in the confined space with them, but he didn't think so. It was clear Robert Farrer didn't have any more idea what had happened back in town than Peter did.

He tried to give the two of them all the space he could, squashing himself into a corner and not shifting his position even when various parts of him began to cramp. It was not an especially successful way to hide.

It was hard—impossible—to not keep sneaking glances Miss Farrer's way, but each time he did, he was left more confounded than before. On other days he'd been entertained that he could dislodge her control with apparent ease, but it wouldn't happen here. She'd regained her composure almost as soon as she'd lost it, and now sat as straight and silent as she could manage on the rough road. The distance she'd placed between herself and the rest of them wrapped around her in layer after layer, daring anybody to even attempt to converse with her.

So far, neither man had been brave enough to try.

His attention was captured once more as she adjusted her grip on the parcel in her lap, but she kept her focus on the trees through the open window. Peter and Farrer might not even have been there.

The bush was never truly silent, he'd learnt over the past weeks, but there was usually a peace to it he'd come to appreciate. That afternoon was not one of those peaceful times. The rustling of leaves as the breeze picked up felt amplified to his ears. The pollen in the air made him want to sneeze again, and he fought it off with more determination than he'd ever applied to a task before. He concentrated hard on an insignificant eucalypt until it was out of sight, forcing his mind off his hay fever.

The various screeches and squawks of birds grated. He glared at a bright white cockatoo that watched them trundle past. It seemed like the bloody creature was smirking at them.

The bumps and ruts in the road worsened, but Miss Farrer sat as primly as she could, back defiantly straight. Every now and then there'd be a jolt too great and some of her poise was rocked, but her hands only tightened on the unopened parcel as she pressed her lips more tightly together.

He hadn't paid close attention to the thing when he'd collected it, nor at the park, and not in the pub afterwards. He'd not wanted to be intrusive, had been too absorbed in his own correspondence, and it really was such a small and insignificant-looking thing. Now he wished he had given it a closer inspection.

Peter looked across at her again, noticed her brother doing the same, and accidentally met the other man's eyes.

An uncomfortable moment passed, and then both of them again looked away.

They passed the couple of dirt tracks that led off to small huts and cottages, and then finally arrived at Endmoor's gate.

Robert himself hopped out to open it, and both Peter and Elizabeth watched the mundane activity with an intensity he was sure nobody had applied to the task before. They passed through, Farrer closed the gate behind them, the vehicle rocked as he climbed back in, and then they were off up the drive.

Peter didn't let out a full breath until they'd come to a stop in front of the homestead and signs of normalcy finally appeared around them.

In looks, nothing drastic had changed since they'd left a few hours ago. The spring flowers had finally given up for the season, and petals lay scattered across the path, some of them dancing in the breeze. Peter heard the sounds of a broom being put to work further into the garden. A stockman he'd been introduced to on his second day offered them a casual greeting as he passed by, headed for the stables. Farrer's heeler bounded their way, gleefully oblivious to the tension around him.

Elizabeth hopped down from the carriage unassisted, parcel still clasped tightly in one hand, and disappeared into the house as though there wasn't a single other person on the estate.

***

She couldn't open it.

Elizabeth wasn't one of those people who lived by superstitions. She never worried over supposed death omens as so many were inclined to do, and was quite sure a spirit could not get trapped in a mirror—no matter how many ghost stories she'd heard to the contrary. She liked to think she was a rational sort of person, which was why it shocked her so much she couldn't find that rationality then.

She had to open it. She had to know. The news it brought, whatever it was, wouldn't go away simply because she ignored it.

Oh, how she wished it would.

She felt suspended between the past and the present, and that the parcel was surely the key to her moving in a new direction. Only, right then she wasn't certain she *wanted* to move on. Some memories were too important to her to end.

And yet ... Edward had been far from perfect. Not all of her memories of him warranted dramatic displays of nostalgia.

The package still sat there on the dresser in front of her, haunting her and taunting her, begging to be opened. It was originally addressed to her in Edward's distinctively messy handwriting, but in the time since, someone had somehow found her out in the country and had it redirected.

She was well aware she was behaving strangely, and more than aware that she would have to give the others an explanation for her behaviour in town—*and* her behaviour now. What she ought to have done was keep her emotions private, and make some general, casual conversation on the way back home, because she was fairly sure she hadn't said a word the whole way. She should have hidden her shock until she could be on her own.

It wasn't as though she hadn't any experience hiding such things in the past.

Robert had noticed. Alice had been out working in the rose garden when they'd returned, but by now she too would know something was wrong, because Mrs Adamson had also noticed.

And Mr Rowe had seen.

Soon someone—probably Alice, but maybe the housekeeper—would come to check on her, and by then she had to have done two things: pulled herself together, and opened her accursed post.

'It means nothing,' she told the room at large. The still rational part of her mind was well aware of that fact.

Things became mislaid all the time, and she knew it could easily happen with mail. She couldn't and wouldn't allow herself to start hoping a miracle had happened.

The handwriting, though...

Feeling too hot and too cold, she cracked the window open and then went to her dresser and shifted several books aside. Once again she took the old, battered box from the back, near the wall, and removed the letter from within it.

As hiding places went, it was hardly well concealed, but there'd never been anyone in the household who might snoop through her personal things. Robert was nothing if not honourable, and they got on better than most siblings, she thought. They always had.

The box contained only a few things. There were a couple of diaries she'd kept as a girl. There were a few letters from her parents, chiefly from her mother. There was a note scribbled to her by a boy from some years earlier; it amused her now that she could hardly recall what he looked like, let alone why the handful of sentences he'd put on the paper had meant so much at the time. They had, though, and so she couldn't bring herself to throw them away.

But it was Edward's letter, until now the only one she thought he'd ever written to her, that mattered the most. And for so long it had lived in that box alongside the now-old betrothal announcement that had changed everything. She hadn't been able to throw that away, either.

Ensuring her bedroom door was locked, she took Edward's correspondence—old and new—across to the bed and laid them side by side on the mattress.

The parcel's wrapping seemed to yellow more with age with every minute that passed. It spoke of a moment frozen in time, never again to change. Gathering her courage, she began to unwrap it with careful, gentle fingers.

The cord knotted about it snagged, and she had to find a pair of scissors to cut it free, snipping out the remnants of the first address as she did. Because it was written in Edward's hand it felt like sacrilege to do so.

The paper crumbled a little more and then all but disintegrated in her hands.

'Old,' she reminded herself. 'It's *years* old.'

There was an envelope inside with her name scrawled across it in big, masculine lettering, and a small box bearing a jeweller's name beneath it. She set the box aside and picked up the envelope with unsteady fingers, carefully opening it and drawing out the little card within.

She couldn't read it; she *had* to read it.

Something clattered on the paving stones outside, and not too far away she heard the rise and fall of voices, the words indistinguishable to her from where she sat. A breeze drifted to her, playing with the tendrils of her hair. The real, living world surrounded her.

She lifted the card and forced her focus onto the words.

Dear Elizabeth,

There's no reason for this gift other than that I thought you would like it.

Love, E.

It was not the sort of letter a lady expected to receive from a man about to leave for the Sudan.

The disappointment was huge, sudden, and overwhelming.

'That's it?' she asked, her voice loud with an unexpected, enormous anger.

It was dated the second of March, 1885. The day before Edward had set sail from Sydney Harbour for war in Suakin.

Had the man no common sense? No ability to feel anxiety or fear? As much as he'd painted the campaign as an adventure, she had always known there'd be a great deal of danger involved. How had he not?

The little box contained a pendant, the gold manipulated into soft swirls and decorated with small pearls and Ceylon sapphires. A solitary sapphire a little larger than the others dangled from the golden drop at the end.

Elizabeth touched the stone gently and then lifted the pendant, turning it this way and that, and then held it up to the light to appreciate its gleam. It was no little bauble, not any old trinket. It was expensive, and much more than Edward could usually have afforded. It was so fine it brought a seizing to her chest and a sting to her eyes.

She fixed it around her neck with hands that shook and fumbled with the awkward clasp, tucking it, *concealing* it, behind the collar of her gown, and then returned to the letter—such as it was—reading each word over and over, tracing them with the very tip of one fingernail, absorbing each one for the treasure it was, and furious with the casual tone.

Less than twenty words. The last she would ever hear from the man on whom she'd pinned so many hopes and dreams for the future, and she had less than twenty words.

She touched the sapphire again through the fabric of her clothes, pressing it as firmly as she dared so that she could feel its imprint against her skin, and held it there until it warmed. It was not the sort of piece that could easily be explained away to the others.

How foolish of me, she thought, and then carefully returned the card to its envelope. How foolish to have hoped there might have been so much more.

***

Whatever had happened earlier that day was gone from Miss Farrer's expression when she emerged for the meal in the evening. She smiled her way through the soup and the roast and joked with her brother about a pair of escaped ewes he'd found halfway to town the previous day. And she laughed at Mrs Farrer, who could barely conceal her disgust when a plate piled high with green beans appeared on the table.

'Are you convinced we'll be able to raise the wages by a pound?' Farrer asked, turning his attention Peter's way and picking up a discussion from the day before.

'Very confident. Possibly two pounds, provided summer doesn't bring on too many challenges.'

The evening was warm, and once they'd eaten they lingered, first at the table, and then in the drawing room, enjoying the breeze from the open windows.

It was high time for him to make his excuses and be off, but first young Duncan insisted on a lengthy game of *watch Peter bounce a ball of yarn about,* and he couldn't quite make himself go. The infant tired of the game eventually, and Peter climbed to his feet with an exaggerated groan and a complaint about creaky knees—only to discover that the boy's father had produced a bottle of something from the mantle.

Both women saw it and groaned.

'As you can see from that enthusiastic response,' Farrer said as he went to the cabinet for a pair of crystal glasses, 'this is not the most popular bottle in the house.'

The drink in question was, Peter discovered *after* he'd been handed a glass, a sickly sweet homemade sherry. The strong scent of the drink, a combination of dark currant and far too much sugar, was almost overpowering.

'It's a present from a neighbour. A well-meaning if slightly misguided neighbour,' the other man said apologetically.

'It's what passes for a good tipple in the country—until we here at Endmoor change the state of things, that is. Manners oblige me to drink it rather than pour it into the garden.'

'Robert,' the man's wife said, 'if you pour that into *my* garden it'll kill something. And then I'd feel obliged to kill *you*.'

Farrer raised his glass in a toast.

'Here's to our neighbours. The tablelands' second-finest vintners.'

Miss Farrer scoffed without looking up from the papers she'd spread across her lap.

'I suppose you've placed yourself at the top of that list.'

'Naturally. It's early days, but I'm quietly confident.'

The siblings shared a grin and then the brother turned back Peter's way.

'You do, however, have permission to pour the drink into the nearest vase when my back is turned.'

The room fell into a comfortable silence, save for the occasional babble of the baby, who'd been hoisted onto his mother's lap. The sounds of the staff reached them from other parts of the house, and the calls of birds headed home for the night slowly faded away, leaving the endless chirping of insects in their wake.

Elizabeth continued to pore over her papers, a pinch of a frown beneath her brow, her finger tracing the lines as she read—and then read again. Peter gave the sherry a polite sip, eyed the nearest vase, and then sipped again.

'What's that you have there?' he asked her when she sighed and looked up.

'Notices and accounts from Goulburn and Sydney. Nobody warned me that when my painting sales increased I'd be expected to pay attention to the finances.'

She cast her gaze to the Heavens and sighed again.

'It's utterly boring.'

'But a necessary evil of success,' her brother chimed in and she rolled her eyes.

'I know I oughtn't complain ... At least I don't have to touch Robert's ledgers anymore. I can hardly moan about working on my own...'

Peter shifted in his seat, drawing her attention his way.

'Then you're very lucky I came to Endmoor to take on the task. What would you have done without me here?'

She shrugged and tapped the papers to her chin, pretending to think about it.

'I couldn't say for certain, but I think we'd have increased our expenditure rather a lot, and business would be going so well we could offer a one—or *possibly two*—pound raise in our workers' wages, and—and...'

She floundered.

'And I daresay we'd have also increased our revenue to a point we were forced to employ an accountant from Sydney to assist us. And then—'

'My sister,' Farrer said, interrupting her good-natured tirade, 'has plenty of talent for, but no love of numbers.'

Miss Farrer smiled at Peter, looking apologetic.

'I'd prefer to create something than analyse it.'

'I really don't mind looking at them, if you'd rather work on your art. It'd be a pleasure to help.'

She looked so hopeful about the prospect he almost laughed, but pride had her hesitating another moment before she arranged the papers and handed them over.

'A man must be utterly mad to consider tallies and sums *a pleasure*.'

'We all have our quirks.'

She seemed to like that observation.

'I could do it myself, you know. It's only that staring at a page of numbers for any length of time is hardly conducive to creativity. Or sanity.'

'Well, then. You're lucky I was willing to come out to the tablelands to help.'

She looked from the glass dangling from his hand to his relaxed position on the chair, assessing, judging—smiling.

'Oh, yes. I can see that living in the country has been a terrible hardship for you so far.'

He held her eyes a moment longer than was gentlemanly, thinking several things that would've been incredibly inappropriate to say, and then noticed the brother watching them and came to his senses. It seemed a good time to leave.

Downing his sherry and sparing a thought for his poor teeth, Peter collected the documents, rose, said all the right, polite things and nodded and bowed at all the right people—other than Duncan, who, in his growing fatigue, had become a bit grizzly—as he headed for the door. Elizabeth rose to see him out, and when he was at the bottom of the stairs he looked back once; she still stood on the veranda, watching him go.

Outside in the lingering warmth the countryside felt alive. The gravel crunched under his feet as something nocturnal ferreted about in a bush. The light from the house arched outwards across the darkening land, a light breeze rustling the homestead's curtains.

And, because of those open windows, as he rounded the corner Mrs Farrer's words reached him, as clear as crystal.

'Well. This has been an interestin' night.'

Peter's step faltered.

'I'll say,' Farrer replied. '*Very* interesting.'

Chapter 7

Peter hadn't expected work in the country to be the same as any experience he'd had yet in his life, and it was gratifying to discover he was right. What he'd not expected was how much he'd enjoy it.

In between writing invoices and corresponding with people everywhere from Bethanien to New Sheffield, and going over Miss Farrer's *utterly boring* notices and accounts, there was always a bucket to carry for Mrs Farrer or Mrs Adamson, or an opportunistic chicken to feed on the way to or from his cottage.

He spent his nights reading, beginning with the Dickens, and studiously avoiding too many glimpses in the direction of the homestead. However, as he read he could not stop himself wondering how Elizabeth was getting on with a certain bigamous Englishwoman.

And, he'd started to reason with himself, a man really ought to ride out and see for himself the property he worked for—and ride out quite often if it was sunny. It was an awfully convenient way to poke about the estate without looking guilty when he did it.

He was a decent horseman, despite living the largest portion of his life in the middle of suburban Paddington, and he took to his borrowed horse well enough. Not that it was exactly a challenge, when the fellow knew the land so thoroughly that he plodded on along of his own volition, following favourite routes, as determined to stick to the direction of his choice as a locomotive on railway tracks.

Peter didn't mind, and let the horse have its way. He hadn't a particular destination in mind that day anyway, supposed the horse wouldn't get them hopelessly lost, and was happy that it gave him an opportunity to get a better look at the land in daylight, and more or less on his own.

He was taken along an overgrown but previously worn track that encompassed a few small buildings in various states of repair and *disrepair*, coming across the river or one of the streams now and again, all sparkling ripples and the occasional gliding bird.

Peter saw a few animals: sheep—there were always sheep—silent to him now they were so far off in the distance, as well as the occasional kangaroo.

What he didn't see was any other man.

As the horse wandered Peter made a point to turn his mind over to the coming week. The arrangement with the vineyard further north was coming together nicely. Though there'd been doubts of the region's viability for wine production, both Farrer and Stanford were determined, and there was a kind of brilliance in their bloody-mindedness.

Some dew had gathered overnight, and the last of it glittered like a thousand crystals on the leaves of the trees as the sun grew in strength.

The Murrumbidgee reappeared at a bend up ahead, and Peter considered how long he'd been out, and how much further he could expect the horse to amble along for and still be happy to make the return journey. They were almost at the foothills of the Brindabellas, and he suspected they'd long ago crossed over from Farrer land to the wilder countryside beyond.

He drew them to a stop and dismounted. The animal took an immediate interest in a nondescript patch of grass.

Whomever was responsible for *Namadgi Sunrise* hadn't sketched from where Peter was then, so far from where Endmoor now stood. The angle was wrong, but he'd wager the image *had* been captured from somewhere in the valley. It was a start, even if the valley in question was absurdly large.

He thought back to that painting, to that parlour in Sydney. His appalling sketch was as good as useless, and it was a pity he hadn't had Elizabeth with her charcoal about at the time to do it for him. The mountains were a lot vaster than he'd imagined, their scope so much greater than the artist had given the impression they'd be. A person might be out there for months—or even longer—and still not find any clues, nor any answers.

He pulled the utterly unhelpful and crumpled sketch in question from his pocket anyway. Holding it up to the horizon, he strained to make a comparison.

'Disastrous,' he concluded.

Giving up for another day, he removed his hat to wipe at the perspiration on his forehead and then decided it was time to interrupt the horse from his snack. He was almost there when the animal's ears pricked.

Peter froze, listening. Careful now, he moved in a slow circle, searching.

He saw the swag first, leaning against a rock, its colour blending in with the plants around it. Tempering his steps, he moved slowly around a tree, and then around a scrubby bush.

It was then that he saw the lantern.

***

John Stanford's return was a complete surprise.

One moment there were three adults in the house taking their midday meal, and the next there was a tall, fair-haired man standing there, grinning at them, two generously sized, open and overflowing bags at his feet.

'What are you doin' here?' Alice was the first to react.

Robert pushed back from the table at the same time Elizabeth came to her senses. 'Why didn't you say you were home?'

'Welcome home, John. How was your journey?' Robert offered in a chiding tone, sending amused looks at both women.

The man accepted his best friend's handshake and then granted them all with another grin. 'Who'd want to write ahead when a fellow could receive a welcome as wild as this?'

It was designed to snap them out of their surprise and trigger a flurry of affection, and he could not have been disappointed. Alice got there first and was hefted all the way off the tips of her toes in a hug Robert would surely have taken issue with had it been another man.

When she was free, Elizabeth's embrace was a little more dignified but no less warm.

Predictably, the barrage of questions began the moment the greetings were complete. John staggered back under their enthusiasm, hand at his chest.

'Good Lord, a man forgets the force of a full set of Farrers. Give a man a chance to recover from the long, dusty journey home before you bombard him.'

Elizabeth crossed the room and poured him a drink from the pitcher on the table, watching as he took a swill, every movement measured and coloured with false exhaustion.

'John ... didn't you come home on the train, not in a coach? Is it not comfortable? Mr Rowe seemed to think so.'

'Shh.' He winked and leaned across to refill his glass himself.

'How was your trip? Were the exhibitions everything you hoped for?'

'I'll save stories of the snobbery at the Paris and Vienna shows for another day. Nobody's particularly fond of Australians, but they'll learn. Give them a few more years and we'll have Europe convinced ours wines are equal to those from Bordeaux or the Rhineland.'

'John,' Alice began as Elizabeth smoothed a leaf off his sleeve and then stepped back, 'what's in those bags?'

They all knew. There was only one reason the parcels sticking out of them came wrapped so finely, and tied so neatly with bows.

'Why don't you come and see.'

They didn't need any more encouragement.

'I should have started with the presents,' John grumbled minutes later as the women exclaimed over delicate lace and little carved wooden figures from Germany. They found a paint box with a London name on it that made Elizabeth gasp, as well as a book on English gardens.

'I'll leave the two of you to decide who wants what,' he joked. Alice already had the book open on her lap.

There was even a hobby horse for Duncan, who was brought to the room to be introduced to the toy, chubby hand extended to pat the pony's mane. As they should all have predicted, he gripped the hair in his fist instead, and then yelped when Robert removed the hair from his hold.

'Perhaps not until he's a little older,' John cautioned. 'Heaven forbid I'm blamed for maiming the Endmoor heir.'

Elizabeth half listened to the men talk as she looked at her new art supplies. Something was said about the uncomfortably long journey from Europe to Australia, and she half heard a comment about the inherent snobbery in the winemaking industry.

The paints in the box were so fine she hardly dared use them. It would be a shame to waste them on any old thing; she'd have to save them for something special.

She was aware of Robert watching her carefully. He'd done that quite a bit since she'd gone strange in town days earlier. Even though he'd sworn more than once that he believed her flimsy excuse about being overwhelmed by the demand for her work, she knew he only said so to appease her.

For her part, Alice had been uncharacteristically quiet about it, watching her as carefully as Robert did but not pressing. Elizabeth knew it was a reprieve, not an opportunity to escape the conversation entirely. The younger woman had ascertained time was what she needed, and time was exactly what she'd been given.

And Mr Rowe? Elizabeth wasn't familiar enough with him to know what he thought of the whole silly thing, but she *did* know he was too polite to pry. It had been a little tricky looking directly at him ever since, and if he had a notebook somewhere with a list of all the odd things she'd done in his presence since he'd arrived at Endmoor, she wouldn't blame him.

She was dragged from her wool-gathering as Alice looked up from a page of petunia illustrations and let out a small sound of exasperation.

'Duncan, no. The horse's upside down. It's—*Lord*, here, I'll turn him up the right way.'

A lot of banging and chattering ensued; the hobby horse was at risk of losing his elaborately painted exterior before he'd been in the house half an hour. For his part, the infant did not end the exchange convinced he wasn't right.

The men and Elizabeth watched the exchange end when Duncan gave up on being cross and took a firm interest in the pattern of the parquetry floor, and again she felt her brother's eyes rest on her a fraction too long.

She pulled a face at him and it did the trick. Seemingly convinced there really wasn't a thing to worry about, Robert bent to scoop an increasingly cross and tired son from the floor for a walk about the room.

The inevitable gossip began, and Elizabeth again set her present in front of her, contemplating the selection of colours. The paints were of the highest quality. It was a luxury beyond anything she'd ever find in such an isolated part of the world as New South Wales. Perhaps now she'd be able to mix the exact blue shade of the local parrots. She'd been attempting to create it for so long...

'And that's why I came via Victoria,' John said in response to something she missed.

'*Victoria!*' The name really *was* inescapable.

The room fell instantly silent at her vehemence; all of that effort Elizabeth had put into appearing composed and normal evaporated. Drat. Robert would again feel obliged to play the part of concerned older brother.

John spoke first. 'Not a fan of our Queen?'

Elizabeth didn't think much of the Queen either way—they were quite a long way from London. She wasn't, though, about to correct anyone's assumptions.

'She wears too much black.'

'I can't argue with you about that.' John glanced around. 'Now. Where's this Mr Rowe you keep speaking of? Have I been permanently replaced, or is there room for three of us in our business?'

***

Peter found the man by the water.

He was old and wiry but looked like he'd once been much more formidable.

The stirring inside him wasn't suspicion as much as anticipation. It took everything he had to not approach the fellow immediately, and to watch him instead, gauging his welcome.

With the river so loud and so close there was enough distance between them that neither could hear the other, and Peter trod carefully through the grass as the man disappeared behind a rock, and then a tree, and then re-emerged slightly south.

He watched as he paused to take a drink from a flask and then set off again, clearly familiar with the land, a weather-beaten white man treating it as his own.

Peter moved faster.

A group of currawongs, mad with the need to protect their territory, chased each other around the sky, their deafening calls further disguising the sounds of Peter's approach. He was within yards of the man when the birds moved their dispute on to another part of the valley, and finally the swishing sounds of his boots in the grass alerted the stranger he was no longer alone.

He stopped still in an instant and turned slowly, cautiously, holding his ground.

After so long, after decades of imagining and wondering, of inventing elaborate histories for himself when he thought real answers would never come, at the sight of the man's face Peter found he could hardly take another step.

A wattlebird made its odd unmusical call, and then launched off from a gum tree in a rustle of feathers and leaves. Cicadas sent up near-deafening chants in every direction around them.

'Excuse me,' he began when he was in easy earshot, 'I was wondering if you...'

He lost track of his words then, as the other man shifted slightly, just enough for the light to reveal the details the shadow of his hat had not.

A gasp of air passed between them; it might have been Peter who made the sound of surprise, but he suspected it was not. It was only a hint here and there, but what he saw in the stranger's features ... there was something very familiar there. Not unlike what he saw in the mirror every day, but at the same time so different, so confusing.

'I was wondering,' he tried again, but again the words in his mind evaporated.

In the shabby, grubby, wizened fellow he saw in front of him, exactly the sort of person he'd expect to find wandering the bush, Peter saw someone who might have answers about the past. And, for a fraction of a second, it seemed the man might bolt.

Peter didn't move. He didn't dare.

The old man's jaw firmed and the ragged beard covering it shifted as his expression did. And still he stayed mute.

'I'm Peter Rowe,' he began again, the simple introduction sounding inane to his own ears.

Disinterest warred with something older and more powerful in the man's face. Skin that would once have been pale had tanned to the colour of leather, and deep crevices marked his features. He was a man used to solitude; that much was plain to see. Conversation wasn't designed for someone who'd long ago given up company for isolation.

'Vernon Towner,' the man replied in an indistinguishable accent, as though they were meeting at a garden party. And then, with certainty, he continued.

'You're Charity's boy.'

'Yes, I am.'

There was a good six feet between them, but it might as well have been a mile. A fly buzzed around Peter's face. The horse, almost forgotten now, snorted once from where it waited behind him.

'Huh,' Towner said. 'I'd say you've a few questions for me.'

Chapter 8

For a man who took pride in order, Peter found himself standing in the centre of his Endmoor cottage one stifling December afternoon, wondering how he'd accumulated so much *mess*.

A generally neat person, both by nature and schooling, it was quite the surprise to see just how corrupted he'd become in two and a half months. Cups and a decent collection of Minton plates and bowls borrowed from Mrs Adamson were stacked on the table and yet to be returned. Books had continued to migrate from Endmoor's library, and covered many surfaces—they could be excused, he'd reasoned more than once. A man had to do something during the evenings he declined invitations to stay in the homestead after the evening meal. The Farrer family didn't need him intruding on every moment of their time.

He added some trousers to his pile of clothing and glanced at the mantle.

The growing assortment of oddities from the land was a little harder to justify, but also difficult to throw away. An old hinge, more rust than metal now. A feather, blue-tipped with indigo, from a bird he'd yet to learn the name of. A gold sovereign, dated thirty years earlier and with a significantly younger Queen Victoria in profile on its back, had been discovered in the dirt at the bottom of one of the new grapevine trellises. He paused in his packing to pick it up, using a fingernail to flick specks of dirt from the grooves of the monarch's hair.

'Absurd,' he told the room, and then forced his mind back to the task at hand. It was difficult to prepare for a journey when a man hadn't any idea how long it would be.

The jangle of reins near the cottage caught his attention. Even though Christmas was upon them, the estate continued to work as it always had. It was impossible to explain a holiday to a sheep.

He set the coin back alongside the rest of his odd little collection and reached for the next garment that would travel with him back to his family in Sydney.

A dull *thwack* came from somewhere outside and he paused in the middle of laying out an overly formal wing-tipped shirt. What was that?

When the echo died away he shrugged and turned back to the shirt. What had he been thinking bringing it in the first place? Barracks Flat was hardly a place of balls and soirées, though he supposed there might be a time or two the Ladies' Auxiliary threw something respectable together.

Trunk or valise? He was still undecided. The trunk seemed a little excessive if he was only to be away for a few days. Another *thwack*, and he paused again. When the tail end of a giggle reached his ears he decided he wasn't in imminent danger.

He might as well take the shirt back to Sydney. The mere sight of that starched collar made him want to expire. The relentless sunshine was oppressive. It made a man want to snooze over his ledgers.

He set a waistcoat on top of the shirt and swiped a hand across his sweaty forehead, contemplating the valise again. With the afternoon sun hitting the cottage from every direction, the place felt more than a little like a furnace. Or like the depths of that Hell his childhood tutors had constantly warned him about.

Another *thwack* came as he picked the gumnut up off the table and tried to remember what had been so important about the blasted thing that he'd kept it. Superstition, maybe.

Whack.

Something glanced off the side of the cottage, surprising him into a stumble. His thigh clipped the edge of the chair, sending it clattering, and sending the contents of his Gladstone bag scattering and coins bouncing and rolling across the floor.

Not an absolute disaster, he supposed, but not exactly what he needed right then. He'd a long letter in there, the pages not fastened or numbered.

'Only a *small* disaster,' he muttered.

Another laugh—louder and far more childish—sounded. Curious, he collected the papers and sorted them into a messy pile as he wandered over to the door, pulling it open to let a stream of sunlight through.

Miss Farrer stood half in the shadow of a tall rose bush, her little nephew perched on a blanket nearby, waving what looked to be a miniature, homemade cricket bat in a manner more suited to a man charging into battle than a connoisseur of the sport. Peter watched as she laughed at the child's antics, which in turn made the boy squeal with the smugness of one who knew he held someone in his thrall.

Peter set the papers aside and stepped out of the cottage, pausing on the step.

The baby was in the throes of an excitement only one so young could manage, delirious with the effect of bashing the miniature bat onto the pavement beyond the blanket, and then onto the nearby trellis—and on his own shin, squawking with outrage at the impact of the third hit, and then looking about as though there was another person to blame for the insult.

'Did that hurt?' Miss Farrer asked, kneeling and doing an excellent job of masking her amusement with concern.

The infant waved the bat again, and Peter stirred.

'You might want to help him with his backlift. The technique's a little off.'

She turned and beamed at him.

'Mr Rowe. What do you know about cricket?'

He started towards her.

'Nowhere near enough to justify that hopeful look on your face.'

He spotted the ball beneath a drooping plant. Bending to retrieve it, he gave it a squeeze, relieved to find it was far softer than those used in a normal cricket match. Rising, he approached her, taking in the pink of her cheeks and how she inclined her head in thanks.

The tip of one of his fingers brushed hers when he offered her the ball.

'Um,' she said drawing her hand back, 'I'm sorry. Were we distracting you from your work?'

'Not at all. You've given me a perfect excuse to procrastinate. There aren't many things I dislike more than packing.'

A shadow crossed her expression. The little bat whacked against the paving stones again and both of them, with obvious determination, fixed their attention on Duncan. They watched the child as he continued his enraptured inspection of the wrong end of the toy.

'He enjoys the game, or so Robert assures me. As long as I do all the throwing *and* the catching, that is.'

'To be fair, the general consensus seems to be that a fellow should be able to stand on his own before he's sent out onto the pitch.'

'I figured as much. Don't tell my brother, but if this is the future of colonial cricket, then England is in no danger. He certainly deserves an award for his enthusiasm, however.'

Peter took pity. 'He's no Billy Murdoch yet, but give him a chance. He's not a year old, is he? I daresay he still has the time to learn the handle end of a cricket bat from the toe.'

Miss Farrer shifted the ball from one hand to the other, squeezing gently.

'You *do* sound like you know what you're talking about. Perhaps you could help him learn. Are you a good player, Mr Rowe?'

Peter debated—and discarded—a fib.

'I'll say I am, just as long as you don't ask for a demonstration.'

'Perhaps you could at least teach him which end is to be held. I don't think he believes I'm right.'

He grappled. He'd not been a star batsman at Sydney Grammar.

'Uh, I might not be the best person to ask. I've ... I've an injury. A strained hamstring.'

He shouldn't be discussing his thighs with a respectable lady—his father would be appalled. However, instead of taking offence, Miss Farrer laughed; the baby laughed in turn.

'I suppose I could give it a try,' he conceded, and knelt.

'That,' the woman beside him said smugly, 'was very elegantly done for a man with such a grave injury.'

Child and man regarded each other. The boy was still young enough to be fair in that way of many small English youngsters. Soon enough he'd sprout, and the babyish fair fuzz would no doubt darken to something more worldly. Peter hadn't the largest family in the world, and—as yet—not a single nephew or niece to educate him in the ways of small children. It was a terrifying moment, but it wouldn't do to let the woman watching him know it.

The boy seemed amenable to the lesson, watching intently and silently as Peter, feeling the idiot, carefully extracted the little bat from a set of chubby hands and turned it around, demonstrating.

He was halfway back to his feet when Duncan, with impressive concentration, turned the bat back around and again slammed the blunt end of the handle onto the paving stones. He was clearly delighted with the racket it made as he did it again and again.

'Oh dear. Don't worry. You did better than I managed.'

The baby paused in his play to give the two adults a curious look, and then stuck the end of the bat in his mouth and gave it an experimental gnaw.

'Ah well, he'll make an excellent spectator one day.'

Miss Farrer glanced beyond him, giving the interior of the cottage a swift, discreet perusal.

'You're packing?'

'I am.'

It felt like there was something more to say. An explanation of—or an excuse for—why he had to go. He'd nothing to feel guilty about, he reminded himself. Nothing.

That huge family cat ambled past, not the slightest bit interested in the discomfort in the air, and they were saved by the infant, who managed in his garbled way to inform them he needed the ball placed back in front of him.

Immediately. Elizabeth lay it within his reach, and then they waited to see what would happen. The child appeared as curious about the outcome as the adults did.

'No, Duncan. It's not for—oh for goodness' sake, you'll injure yourself and then your parents will have to thrash me, and then Christmas will be ruined before we even decorate the tree. It's for—'

The three of them watched in abject fascination as the ball—bumped rather than hit—rolled off sideways into the dirt.

Peter chuckled.

'I think that was more luck than skill, but I don't want to crush the poor fellow's spirit. I'd better leave the two of you to your test match.'

Miss Farrer nodded, seemingly distracted, and he set off back the way he'd come. *The valise*, he decided while the thwacking and chortling began again.

***

'What are you doing here?' Martha Wright asked two days later, her voice hushed as she glanced over her shoulder to the presently empty entrance hall of the grand Wright house, and Elizabeth sighed with relief.

The stars had aligned. Bessie was watching the baby, Alice was tired of looking at her browned, sun-roasted garden, and Elizabeth had not only completed an oil painting of the ridgeway but was also hugely pleased with it. It was time for a break.

And now, continuing their good fortune, they'd arrived in Barracks Flat to discover that not only was Martha up and about and looking relatively well, but she answered the knock on the door herself. Things had gone perfectly so far.

Too perfectly?

Feeling eyes on her back and a silly guilt at sneaking about that should have been beneath either woman at their age, Elizabeth fought the urge to duck behind the rose bush beside the door and drag her friend along with her. Digging for dignity, she leaned closer and whispered.

'Where is everyone?'

Taken aback by the furtiveness, Martha glanced over her shoulder; there was nobody there. It was when she turned back that she spotted Alice slinking down the path, appearing as suspicious as she should, all things considered.

'Good afternoon, Miss Wright,' Robert's wife called.

'What's going on?'

'We're abductin' you,' Alice, who'd promised to stay in the carriage, announced cheerfully, 'if you're willin' to go along with it.'

'Like Romeo an' Juliet,' Alice had commented as they'd hatched their plan on the way in from Endmoor. 'But with too many Juliets.'

Martha looked from one woman to the other, face pale, a frown between her brows. A single ivy ribbon to mark the season hung above the door, the leaves stitched carefully enough they wouldn't dare rustle in the breeze.

'*Abducting* me?'

Alice was taken aback by Martha's tone. 'Don't look at us like it's a crime.'

Elizabeth stirred. 'Alice, I'm fairly sure it *is* a crime.'

'Yes, but only if the victim isn't willin'. You're willin', aren't you, Miss Wright?'

A simple outing was about to dissolve into chaos thanks to Alice's enthusiasm and Martha's obvious reticence. Elizabeth struggled for a way to save it.

'We've a chance to escape for the day, and thought you might come along with us.'

A shadow crossed by in the hall then, and the squeak of a floorboard decided it for the lot of them. Martha gasped and stepped out into the sunshine in a hurry, pulling the door firmly closed behind her.

'All right, then. Abduct me.'

She checked over her shoulder one last time, quickly, panicked, and then—hatless and gloveless—she hopped down the step and reached for Elizabeth's hand.

'We'd better hurry.'

None of them were giants but Elizabeth could have sworn otherwise then, their feet on the pavers were that loud as they rushed, and the gate to the road seemed just as far away when they were halfway down the path as it did when they'd begun their escape.

'Oh, bloody hell, there's someone comin' around the side of the house,' Alice said in a whisper loud enough to raise the dead, and the three of them moved faster, bumping into each other and stifling giggles.

Rushing and fretting and stumbling, with Alice playing scout, Elizabeth and Martha finally sneaked past the fence and onto the street and—with the help of Mr Adamson, who'd driven them in—everyone clambered up into the carriage. They were off before they'd even had a chance to settle into their seats.

***

Travelling up Monaro Street posed a definite risk of discovery, but Elizabeth and Alice had decided in advance that skulking around the web of smaller roads surrounding it would only raise more suspicion.

'People will wonder why our carriage is taking off down a side lane,' Elizabeth explained when Martha arranged her skirts and noticed—alarmed—that they'd passed the river walk and the town's busiest bridge.

'Best to commit our offences with everyone watchin',' Alice added. 'Makes us look less guilty.'

'I'll have to take your word for it. It's good to be away,' Martha admitted after a short pause.

Elizabeth arranged her gloves neatly in her lap and watched the town roll by. She saw a few familiar faces, and a healthy crowd at The Dog and Stile. A few currawongs—*still* at war—chased each other past the vehicle's windows. Spring might have melted into summer, but the birds still protected their territory.

And then, from the corner of her eye, she saw Martha suddenly drop forwards with a gasp.

'Oh my *Lord*, what's goin' on now?' Alice asked, following Elizabeth in a downwards dive, both of them reaching for the collapsed woman before they had a chance to see what'd happened.

Elizabeth's mind returned to a time two years earlier, when Martha had been injured, and when, had they dared admit it to each other, not a single person in Barracks Flat expected her to survive. Trembling badly, and with a pulsing in her ears, she gripped her friend by the arm and tried to tug her upright. The space was too small, and all three women were tangled in a swirl of cotton and plaid skirts.

She could not free herself enough to achieve a thing. She ought to call to Mr Adamson to take them back to the Wright house. This outing was the most horrid idea she had ever had...

'Goodness,' Martha said then, in a perfectly reasonable—if muffled—voice, 'that was close.'

She wriggled free of the other women's grips and had the decency to look abashed.

'It was that Mr Addison my father does business with,' she explained, hoisting herself back up onto the seat with all the grace and composure Elizabeth and Alice lacked right then. The women glanced at each other and then at Martha, uncomprehending.

'And he made you faint?' Alice sounded sceptical.

Martha seemed only mildly offended at the suggestion. 'Of course not.'

As they left Monaro Street and the quality of the roads worsened, it became an effort for the other two women to return to their perches. The vehicle rocked and swayed as they hauled themselves back onto their seats. Alice swore quietly as she was thrown one way and then banged another.

'Then why the dramatics?' Elizabeth asked once they were back to rights—more or less.

'He spends far too much time with my father these days. If he'd seen me, he would have run off to tattle, and then we'd be chased down by the magistrate and hauled back by force before we even reached the edge of town.'

Alice plucked a piece of fluff off her skirt.

'Far as I know it's not a crime for three ladies to leave the house durin' the day.'

Martha fixed her bright blue gaze on Robert's wife. 'You'd think not, wouldn't you?'

They were almost free, almost around the corner and headed past Church Lane, beyond the leafy and quiet side streets of town that felt a world away from the bustle of Monaro Street and the bridges crossing the river. Martha had just mustered the courage to peek out the window again, and Alice had barely finished muttering something about weeds taking over the park, when Elizabeth straightened, peered around the corner and tapped the carriage's roof.

'Oh, stop a moment! Mr Adamson! There's Mrs McCoy.'

And so they added two more passengers to an increasingly cramped carriage. Moira and David McCoy, wife and son of one of Endmoor's stockmen, had picked up what looked like a year's worth of parcels in town and were headed out the same way the rest of them were. On foot. It was going to be a long and uncomfortable walk back.

Naturally, it was only polite to offer them a ride. Of course it was too stifling for five people stuffed into the carriage, but with Elizabeth's persuasiveness, Martha's quiet charm, and Alice's bloody-minded determination, the pair were overwhelmed and overruled.

The first half of the journey was a study in awkwardness and uncomfortable sideways peeks and dull comments about the drought. Parcels were stashed in every corner and under their feet, alongside the picnic basket the women had prepared before setting out.

The McCoys, the young son as much as the grown woman, were both so intimidated by the presence of Miss Martha Wright in the same vehicle they were, neither one could stop themselves sneaking glance after glance at her perfectly formed features, and at her lovely posture, despite her overly pale face. Not that the boy tried especially hard *not* to stare, Elizabeth noticed.

Nobody relaxed until they'd passed the last of the houses, a half-constructed row of terraces, and the bush came into sight. Not a single other person dared to dive onto the carriage floor for any purpose now; it was far too cramped for that.

They spoke of the drought long enough to bore themselves thoroughly silly, and Alice rescued the lot of them from uncomfortable silence with a story she'd heard involving the priest and a cassock with a rip in a disastrous location.

'At least half of it's even true,' she assured them when she was finished.

It was when they passed the first farm gate that the discussion moved to the selling of property and land.

'Da'll need to give up on it sooner or later,' Mrs McCoy said of her own family plot.

It was the first Elizabeth had heard of anyone selling land on the outskirts of Endmoor. In recent years people were in the business of acquiring *more* land, not relieving themselves of it.

'He'll have to? Why?'

The boy, piped up. 'He falls all the time. He keeps lyin' about it, but when we see him he's always got a new cut or bruise, or he'll be wearing something hot and woolly in summer to hide a new bandage.'

'Davie...' his mother tried, but the boy had warmed to the topic.

'What d'you think he'll have done today?' he asked her. 'Gash on his head? Broken leg?'

'*Davie.*' She regarded the others with an apologetic smile. 'What *I* think is that I'll need to find someone to help with the selling of the land.'

Struck by inspiration, Elizabeth spoke before she thought.

'Mr Rowe might be able to assist with that. I don't know the particulars of his work, but he clearly does it well. I've heard no complaints from anyone. If you'd like, when he returns from the city, I'll ask him about it. I'm sure he'd be happy to assist.'

White fluff sailed by the window, a distant cow lowed—and nobody said a thing in response. Elizabeth didn't trust those carefully bland expressions looking back at her.

'What's the matter? What did I say?'

Mrs McCoy felt an immediate need to fuss with her son's collar; in turn the son tried to politely swat his mother's hand away.

Martha looked as pleased as punch. 'Mr Rowe sounds pretty special, doesn't he?'

'I reckon she fancies him,' Alice said to the carriage at large.

Martha sat taller and slanted her eyes Elizabeth's way. 'I reckon you're right.'

Chapter 9

Peter had been away from Sydney just long enough for it to feel foreign and familiar in equal parts. It was a thought that occupied his mind from the instant he stepped into the office in his father's house.

On his return home the blessed relief of anonymity had wrapped around him immediately. He'd not realised exactly how much he'd missed it, how on display he'd felt from the moment he arrived in the tablelands to the moment he left the day before. He'd allowed himself to be swept up in the bustle of the busy city streets, enjoying little things he hadn't even realised he'd missed.

That morning, feeling frivolous but knowing it was necessary, he'd taken himself down to the nearest cove. Alongside a motley crowd, he'd dipped his feet in the ocean. Yes, many of the people beside him had been several decades younger, the tops of their heads only reaching the vicinity of his hips; and—yes—he'd felt decidedly silly about the whole thing, but it had been a compulsion he'd been unable to bat away.

He'd even stopped on the way to the Paddington terrace to have his shoes thoroughly polished. There hadn't been much call for that where he'd just come from. Not much point in a man having his boots buffed when they'd only be covered in dust again—or worse—two steps down the unpaved street.

Father and son sat now, talking about everything and nothing in the distant way their conversations always unfolded. A festive angel, tinsel twined around her skirts, hung from the window, sparkling madly in a small concession to the season. Daisy must have sneaked the thing into the office when their father wasn't looking.

Beyond the window and past the ordered little garden between his father's terrace and Glenmore Road, a steady stream of traffic bustled one way and the other. From another part of the building strains of a piano reached his ears. One of Chopin's Nocturnes, Peter guessed. His sister had retreated to give father and son some space.

What was it Elizabeth had said to him that first day back in September? *'You'll find the country as loud as the city, I think.'*

One thing was certain: they were *different.*

'I'm hearing South Australia is thriving. Making a decent name for themselves in riesling and even sherry.'

While Peter had been wool-gathering, his father hadn't ceased speaking. He tried to force himself to concentrate, but the mention of sherry sent his mind back to a different house and the overpowering scents of currants and sugar.

One of the first things he'd discovered upon arriving on his father's doorstep that day was that Mr Rowe, senior, had inexplicably but not unexpectedly found the time to educate himself about Australia's burgeoning wine industry. And, as ever, he'd opinions to share.

'I'd say we're several years off that sort of success,' Peter replied ruefully, well aware his father's brows had raised at the mention of we.

He was a little curious about the slip himself.

'Farrer and Stanford are still only in the early stages of establishing the vineyards. Grapevines don't grow overnight, and convincing people of influence to give them a chance will probably take even longer.'

'Yes, well. They won't want to miss out and be robbed of success by the South Australians. I'd say they've got a lot of hard work coming their way.'

'They do. We do.' Peter braced himself.

'We?' his father repeated faintly.

'Robert Farrer asked if I'd be interested in a more permanent position at Endmoor,' he admitted, and tried to gauge what his father thought about that.

The older man grunted and pressed his fingertips together, forming a peak as he thought.

The mantle clock ticked more and more loudly, and Peter felt rather a lot like a boy who'd been dragged in front of his instructors for misbehaviour.

'We're inundated here,' his father said.

Peter's attention had again been snagged, this time by the sight of a seagull perched on the low brick wall that ran between one terrace and the next. The bird had found an enormous lump of bread somewhere and attained a determined mien, picking the whole thing up in its carmine-coloured beak.

He forced his attention back to his father. 'Who's inundated?'

Maurice Rowe was probably entitled to the chagrined sound he made.

'Us. The business. Rowe and *Son*,' he replied with exaggerated patience. 'I was thinking on taking on another man or two.'

His father went on about his plans in some detail. Clearly he'd been thinking about the situation for some time.

The gull would not be deterred by the colossal size of his prize. Head tipped back, small beak open as wide as he could manage, he attempted to choke the entire thing down in one go—and failed miserably. Peter tucked both his smile and the silly little story away to tell Elizabeth later.

'It's all dependent on how the Farrer situation works out,' his father said, and Peter abandoned the bird to its quandary.

'If you're asking me for a definitive answer on that, you might be disappointed. At this point I'm not even sure if the Farrers know how the business will go. There're plenty of people who'd be happy to see the enterprise fail. Wine, they're told at every turn, is something they ought to let the Europeans handle.'

Another noncommittal grunt came from across the desk.

'And you can stand it out there? Not bored yet?'

Before Peter gave the first answer that came to mind, he gave the question serious thought.

Several carriages clattered past on the road outside, and in the side of his vision Peter saw a streak of white as the gull was frightened off.

'It's ... not Sydney, that's for certain.'

His father chuckled and let out a breath. 'I'll believe you on that. Know a thing or two about the country myself. Bored senseless, are you? I know I was, in the past. Does that mean you're ready to give up on riesling and make a return to Cascade Street?'

Peter looked across sharply.

'Is that what you're expecting me to do?'

'Did I say that?'

Peter closed a fist around the arm of the chair.

'It was incredibly convenient that you, of all people, heard of a position available at the foothills of the Brindabellas.'

His father's smirk was swift and sneaky.

'Son, I've never not kept track of the goings-on in the tablelands. I thought ... one day after your mother was gone...'

Nothing more needed saying. The senior Mr Rowe suspected that one day one of his children would want some answers about the part of them that wasn't white.

'You're right,' Peter said after a pause, attention drifting to the portrait behind the desk. It was a decent likeness of his mother, he thought, even though the years had softened his memories. She'd been a difficult woman to know, and talk of her life before Sydney had been strictly, silently forbidden. She'd been beautiful.

Chopin drew to an end, amplifying the sounds of the shouts from the road outside as they drifted in the open window. They ricocheted around the room as the final notes faded away.

The boy, the one who'd shined Peter's shoes, passed by the gate, a large smudge of polish streaked black across a prematurely ruddy cheek.

'Barracks Flat, the whole region, it's growing fast. Too fast, some might say, but there's no stopping it now. If you're willing to rusticate there a little longer, maybe you'll take to it.'

'You can't stop change,' Peter murmured. People always tried all the same.

His father grunted. Another seagull cawed, and Peter's eyes instinctively moved in that direction, to the abandoned hunk of bread. A breath of breeze stirred the angel in the window. The tinsel glittered like a thousand crystals as she twirled.

***

Once they were free of town streets cluttered with gossips and busybodies, and after the McCoys had been safely deposited at a fork in the country road, the women continued on past Endmoor, where there were visitors at all times of the day, at every moment of the year. There was no point in an abduction without the adventure.

The carriage could only be taken so far as the road became a track and then became something else entirely. Farrer land became free land as they continued westwards, and then the women hopped down with Mr Adamson's assistance.

They left the carriage at the place where the road had long ago been abandoned to nature, and left Mr Adamson along with it. The servant produced a wrapped sandwich from somewhere, devoured it in the time it took everyone to organise the basket and the blanket, and had put his feet up and lowered the brim of his hat for a nap by the time the lot of them waded off into the bush.

'Is this too far to walk?' Elizabeth felt obliged to ask Martha when they were halfway to their chosen—secluded—spot. She knew how much it irritated her friend to be the constant invalid; she also knew that it would be a tall order for her and Alice to carry Martha all the way back if she fainted.

'I'm fine,' her friend said, shaking herself free and pointing at the basket. 'If you two deal with the burden of that, I'll follow behind you, offering suggestions and motivation.'

They sneaked in through a track they'd used a lot more often as girls than in recent years, breaking orders to take turns to furtively prop Martha up as they went, slowing their pace to match her steps. They were surprised to find the place missing a few of its old eucalypts. Someone had been at work clearing the land.

Martha's steps faltered when they broke free of the trees.

'We're going to picnic beside those old graves?'

Elizabeth tugged her along. 'It's a lovely spot, and there're no prying eyes. Are you afraid?'

'No! I'm ... sensibly cautious.'

Alice kept walking on. 'That sounds like a fancy term for *scared*.'

The clearing was one of the few markers on the land an inexperienced person could navigate by, thanks to its misshapen pond and small graveyard. The graves were near the water and from decades earlier, from when bushrangers ran wild and only the brave—or stupid—travelled the roads beyond the biggest towns. The inscriptions on the headstones were largely overgrown with moss, and the remaining few that hadn't yet slipped down the bank and into the water pointed crookedly in each and every direction.

They took themselves around the pond and to a spot in the shade. The sounds of the river surrounded them, soothing. Elizabeth dug around in the basket and handed across Martha's contraband: *Lady Audley's Secret*.

'It's your turn. We've both finished it.'

While the other two set out refreshments, Martha opened the cover carefully and skimmed through the first few pages. The angle of the sun changed, and Elizabeth tried to give the other woman her spot directly beneath the tree. The offer was politely refused.

'I'm quite happy to be sitting with my back to those graves. The view this way is much less morbid.'

Alice wasn't convinced. 'I think I'd rather see a poltergeist approach than have my back to it. Gives a person the chance to build up the energy for an appropriate scream.'

Martha looked up from the page.

'Poltergeists? I always imagined if I came out here often enough I'd find some handsome bushranger waiting to run off with me. Now the place seems more creepy than exciting.'

'A *handsome* bushranger?' Alice pulled a face. 'Needle in a haystack, that'd be—the bushrangers I know of looked more like bearded goblins. But if anyone was to find a handsome one, I bet it'd have been you.'

Elizabeth started at the statement and, for the briefest of moments, felt a stab of something dreadful: envy.

What would Mr Rowe think of her dearest friend? What would he think if they were side by side? Elizabeth would fade into the background like dated wallpaper, she suspected. They'd been a pair for almost their whole lives, she and Martha, but only occasionally had looks mattered to her.

Elizabeth was pretty, and Martha was the declared beauty. Elizabeth was the artist, and

Martha was ... Martha wasn't allowed to be anything other than a beauty. At least not publicly, and certainly not since her illness.

'I'm happy to not have to worry about an outlaw sweepin' me off my feet. What d'you say, Elizabeth?' Alice bit into a mince pie as she waited for a response, drawing back to give the thing an astonished look, and then nibbled more carefully.

'I'd say I agree with you.'

All the beauty in the world hadn't changed the fact Martha had nearly died two years ago. And Edward was long gone.

She pointed at *Lady Audley*. 'I think you'd better read that before doing anything too mad. There are consequences for falling madly in love with a stranger.'

Alice propped her chin on her knee and stared off into the distance.

'Hard to imagine such a proper lady not bein' scandalised by that book. I don't mean offence, Miss Wright. I'd love to be more like you. Decent, with good, proper manners.'

'That's it,' Martha said after a significant pause. She seemed outraged by the suggestion she was *proper*. 'I'm going to do something horrendous just so I can no longer be accused of being *good*.'

'Elizabeth?' she heard Alice say, and only then realised her friends had fallen quiet.

Reaching into the basket, she retrieved one of the mince pies, distractedly taking a big bite, and then gasping. *Goodness.* Mrs Adamson had not skimped on the brandy.

She bit the little pie again and thought about fickle, superficial gentlemen as her eyes watered.

'Strong, isn't it? That was a big bite, Elizabeth. I've gotta say I'm impressed you haven't spat it back out.'

Elizabeth finished the pie in increments and listened to the other two debate the merits of the city over the country, a discussion that swiftly moved to the merits of marrying an outlaw rather than a businessman. Martha was still intrigued; Alice was mildly appalled.

'There are a lot of women in the city,' Elizabeth said into a lull in the debate, and she all but wished she could take the words back the moment they were out. Envy was a pointless emotion. What was Mr Rowe up to, she wondered.

'There are a lot of gentlemen, too,' Martha pointed out gently.

A fly buzzed between them. Elizabeth watched until it moved away.

'Lots of ladies, lots of gents,' Alice told her then. 'It evens out.'

It was then that they heard the rustling in the bushes.

All three women froze, eyes darting from the movement to each other and back.

Martha lowered her voice.

'Elizabeth Farrer, if that's really a ghost coming, I'm never letting you abduct me again.'

Chapter 10

The ghost was Ada Hall. After a few frightful seconds, sense set in and Elizabeth realised the sound and shape of the person emerging from the shadows was too familiar to her to be an apparition.

The three of them, Elizabeth, Alice and Martha, sat there, half-eaten brandy pies in hands, as the woman gradually emerged from the scrub. At first the newest arrival was just a hint of rust-coloured skirts and the occasional unintelligible word making its way through the bushes.

'Utterly ridiculous,' Elizabeth heard her exclaim before the words trailed off again.

The branch of a banksia rustled. Elizabeth brushed at her skirts and wondered if offering the older woman assistance would cause great offence.

'Should've brought a machete,' the old lady said quite clearly.

She came into the clearing backwards, small and old enough to be grandmother to the rest of them, a nondescript woman who'd likely always been that way, and one who couldn't care less about silly superficialities.

Once she was free of the final pesky wattle bush blocking her way, she spotted them across the grass and came to a halt, final words about *that blasted miserly man* trailing off. Elizabeth thought that particular insult could reasonably be applied to one of many people in the district.

'It's Miss Hall,' Elizabeth told the others unnecessarily as Alice crumbled the rest of her pie and scattered it across the ground for the ants.

'I don't know whether to be relieved or disappointed.' Pink-cheeked, Martha dabbed at her forehead. She'd declined an offer to borrow either of the other women's hats. In hindsight they should have wrestled her down and forced one on her.

'Relieved,' Elizabeth said immediately.

'Disappointed,' Alice said at the same time.

The older woman's bonnet looked more fossilised than the Queen herself, and it slipped forwards to cover her eyes twice before she got it under control. She held a wild bouquet in one hand, and had a little pail over her wrist with a cloth sticking out of it. Petite and hardy, she was largely unremarkable—until she got talking.

Miss Hall came to a stop in front of the three of them, noting faces and not looking especially surprised to see them.

'Well. It's as crowded as Sunday morning at St John's here today. This is a surprise I won't whine about. Good afternoon, Misses and Mrs.'

As return greetings were offered the woman inspected the flowers in her hand.

'It's too late in the season for good bottlebrush.' She held the native flowers up to the light so their stems glowed a brighter red.

'I don't know why I bring them. They'll be rotten brown by tomorrow.' She shook the bouquet, revolted, and the flowers flopped more. A few skinny crimson stems fell to the ground.

Elizabeth got to her feet and went to the woman, gently removing the flowers from her grasp before they were ruined entirely.

'It's the thought that counts. I'm surprised they've survived this long into the season.'

'Ben's lucky I come out here to visit him at all. Those old flowers'll do.' She started off towards the headstones.

'Miss Farrer?' she called over her shoulder. 'Would you like to come and give me a hand? I've a headstone to polish. While we're at it you can tell me about this new Ngambri man I hear's working for you. Half the town is talking about him in the streets, and I'll bet the other half are doing the same behind closed doors.'

It was a summons, not a request, and Elizabeth, still holding the bottlebrush, had no option but to follow the older woman as she ambled off towards the cloudy beige pond and the little old cemetery past it. She was not finished speaking, however, and raised her voice—Elizabeth thought deliberately—as she said the rest.

'You can get me some water from that pond and arrange the flowers. And while you're doing it, you can tell me about this rumour that you're returning to England.'

Shoulders tense as she continued onwards, Elizabeth felt two pairs of accusatory eyes boring into her back the whole way.

***

Despite the scorching heat, the sort of weather that sapped a person's will to do anything, everyone at Endmoor prepared for Christmas. They decorated and decorated. And decorated. Most of the ornaments been made in spare minutes and moments in the past weeks, but there were some delicate baubles imported from England, most of them miraculously surviving the long sea journey unscathed.

The grapevines continued to thrive in absolute defiance of the weather, and the summer evening skies became increasingly spectacular, even as the ground underneath them dried and browned and threatened fire at the slightest provocation.

When the holiday arrived, Mrs Adamson organised the Farrers and their guests a meal designed to make them forget their hunger for at least a week, before she would head off with her husband for their own family's celebrations.

The Farrers went to church, and they performed all the correct duties expected of one of the most respected families for many miles. And then it was time for the better, less public part of the occasion.

Through it all, Endmoor continued to function.

Occasionally one person or another disappeared in order to take care of some task, or some other task. The sheep, the cows, the chickens and the pets demanded as much attention as ever.

Baby Duncan was spoilt and fussed over, though the child hadn't much an idea of what was going on, and was at least as interested in the paper the presents came in as he was in anything else.

Midway through the day Elizabeth devoted a good ten minutes to tossing and retrieving Duncan's ball while he laughed uproariously and made no effort whatsoever to participate. It was, she supposed, decent and necessary exercise after she'd consumed more rich food than anybody ever required.

In the afternoon, and in a complete departure from her usual work, Elizabeth chose new, human subjects and sketched a few festive family scenes. She might have been feeling a little giddy—from the heat, the occasion, or those mince pies—she couldn't identify the exact cause.

It was briefly entertaining, but after several hours of it she gave up on reality and drew her relations as caricatures. Robert laughed at his own exaggerated portrait, and even threatened to hang it in the sitting room. When John Stanford came by on Boxing Day and echoed the sentiment about his own portrait, Elizabeth confiscated the things when their backs were turned and tucked them safely away in the bottom of a drawer in her room.

'Imagine what the guests would say,' she told them when, a few hours later, they discovered the drawings gone and came at her with glasses of wine in their hands and forlorn expressions on their faces.

They'd heard nothing from Sydney the days Mr Rowe was away. It was perfectly normal, and perfectly reasonable for a gentleman they'd known only a few months to not be wiring them news on the minutiae of his family reunion. But it didn't make Elizabeth any less anxious for information.

Despite Elizabeth's enjoyment of the holiday, the restless part of her worried. She was not a girl anymore. As a woman in the middle of her twenties she ought to be beyond girlish foolishness and romantical worries. She was known as a rational sort of person—anybody would call her that, including those who knew her the best. People came to her for advice on all sorts of things, always expecting her to offer sense where others used emotion.

What she needed, if she ever gave up on spinsterhood, was a man like Mr Evanson from Goulburn. Stable and supportive and encouraging of her art. He should also be unattractive if he could possibly manage it. Handsomeness was too much of a distraction.

The biggest problem in Barracks Flat was finding such a fellow who was unmarried.

Outside to take advantage of the cooler evening breeze, Elizabeth watched Duncan set aside the bright violet ribbon he'd extracted from the pile of gift packaging. It had diverted him in a way little else had that week, but then he reached for that little bat that had somehow, inexplicably, made it out onto the veranda when Elizabeth had left it securely stashed away.

When it was in the child's hands, upside down it went again, the toe up and the handle pointing towards the wooden boards—and that was terminology she'd *not* known a week before.

Surely it was time for another of Mr Rowe's lessons in batsmanship.

'I'm not sure he has a future in the sport,' she felt obliged to tell her brother as he paused to watch, but the man didn't seem especially devastated by the news.

'It's all right, I suppose. As long as his talent for viticulture develops, I'll be content.'

Elizabeth decided, as she watched the baby watch them, huge eyes curious, a career in winemaking was an argument for a later date.

'Robert, please don't get carried away and start investing in trellises and wine presses for him yet.'

As the holiday drew to an end John obediently polished off a glass of riesling before turning to his favoured red Château Margaux. Robert again argued politely that they should probably be drinking riesling, *'For appearances.'* Alice spent more time running off to assist the housekeeper than any landowner's wife had ever done before. And, to maintain her sanity, Elizabeth fussed over them all. It was tolerated with more indulgence than she thought she deserved.

It was all so familiar it was wonderful. Elizabeth felt guilty for how little she'd appreciated such things in recent months, and guiltier still for not mentioning her thoughts of England until Miss Hall had blurted it out.

The sun reached the worst of its power not long before it would retire for the night and everyone rose from their places on the veranda, moving their chairs to a slightly cooler spot around the side, where the view of the Range was far better. An increasingly tired Duncan alternated between whacking everything in sight with the bat and drawing the ribbon around the wooden boards he perched on, fascinated by its snakelike twists and curves.

The brilliance of the sunset had almost faded away when they all heard the horse's hooves.

'Today? Guests today?' Alice asked, and it was a completely reasonable question.

Nothing more was said as everyone present—Farrers older and newer, along with one Stanford—rose to see who had the courage to disrupt a perfectly enjoyable evening.

The mysterious guest came around the corner on foot, a silhouette in the face of the colourful December sky.

Alice made a sound of utter relief when the man's identity became clear.

'Oh. All right, *he's* welcome. Happy Christmas, Mr Rowe.'

'Mrs Farrer,' Peter said with the barest hint of a bow, and then looked around at the rest of them. His eyes might have lingered on Elizabeth longer than the others, or perhaps she merely imagined it.

She moved forwards on reasonably steady legs and beamed.

'Good evening, Mr Rowe. Come and join us.' She glanced back at the bottles and glasses on the veranda. 'We've been doing some research.'

'A *lot* of research,' Alice amended as Elizabeth went into the house for another wineglass.

Chapter 11

Peter returned to the country feeling refreshed, despite the stuffy and long trip to the city and back. The railway passengers hadn't *quite* been packed like cattle in a wagon on the journey back down south, but there wasn't much to be said for being forced to spend several hours with *very important* people who fancied the sounds of their own voices far too much.

When they rolled into town he'd stepped out onto the platform at Barracks Flat for a second time not with trepidation but with relief. He knew what to expect now—sort of. At least he'd an idea of the welcome to expect when he again set foot on Farrer land.

On his third morning back in his cottage with its diamond-patterned wallpaper and decreasing stack of books, he finished a report from the Incorporated Institute of Accountants that was nearly too dull even for *his* analytical mind, and was about to take up a paper on the benefits of noble rot on riesling grapes when a woman's voice drew him to his front door instead.

With Christmas celebrations dealt with and festive cheer soon to be dispatched for another year, the property was a hive of activity. Several vehicles and even more horses crowded the drive, and when he spotted Elizabeth Farrer in amongst it all, dressed for an outing and presently laughing with that blasted John Stanford out by the family's coach, Peter found his feet carrying him her way before his mind could order them to stop being so stupid.

Elizabeth Farrer. Never Lizzie or Beth or any other name he'd known other Elizabeths to go by.

She paused at his approach, but hardly seemed delirious to see him. That alone should have stopped his progress.

It didn't.

'You're going out?' he asked her when one of the farmhands drew Stanford's attention elsewhere. It was possibly the silliest thing he could have said, considering all the evidence that made the answer obvious.

'We are. Off to deliver some things to the McCoys over to the west, and then to town.'

'Ah, well. It's a fine day for it. Not too hot compared to yesterday.'

Why, he truly wished to know, did uncomfortable people always start nattering on about the weather? He strove to do better, and shoved a second comment about the heat back where it had risen from before it could be voiced.

'I was about to read a paper.' *Oh yes, that was a vast improvement.*

'You were?' Her polite disinterest was expected, but he just kept on speaking.

'Yes. About *botrytis cinerea*. Grey mould, some people call it. Noble rot.'

He couldn't blame her for not swooning.

'Grey mould?' She smiled then. 'How lovely.'

It had been a few years since Peter had had his manners drilled into him, but a fellow didn't have to be a genius to know he shouldn't discuss fungus with a lady first thing on a Thursday morning.

'Yes, I'm told that if an infestation is introduced at the right time, it works for the production of botrytised wines, and—'

And that's where the conversation ended, because Stanford was back, his infernal Aurelian hair shiny in the sunlight, and Elizabeth was looking at the man with blatant relief. Peter knew with absolute certainty that the other man had not once, not *ever* felt the need to say a word like *infestation* to a beautiful woman.

'Well, enjoy your day,' he finished pathetically, and she had the decency to look at him one more time—with sympathy, he was sure—before taking Stanford's proffered arm and moving away towards the carriage.

Sense had him thinking of that letter to Moss Vale that needed composing, but pride won over, and he'd called Elizabeth's name before he could stop himself.

She came back to him, which meant she'd finally stopped clinging to her brother's business partner, but he'd not thought beyond regaining her attention and struggled again, thinking it would have been better to have stayed in the house.

The *house*. Aha.

'You've created a picture I've an interest in. The smaller one I saw two days ago, the one of the homestead. I was wondering if it was one you were willing to sell. To me, I mean, if you've not got a buyer already.'

'You want to buy my painting? Why?'

Because I made a fool of myself a moment ago and am trying to recover.

'I thought I might send it to Sydney. People there would be interested to see it. Also, it's a very good piece.'

He probably should have begun the conversation with the compliment.

'If you're serious about purchasing it, then—'

'I am.' Now that the idea had come to him he realised it was the truth. Daisy could find a home for it in amongst all of those manly horses.

'Then...' She thought briefly and then named a price that left Peter incredulous.

'Miss Farrer, that's little more than the cost of a loaf of bread!'

She named a higher price.

'And for that I could just about afford some jam to go with it.'

The Farrers' horses stamped, impatient now.

Peter leaned closer. 'Think of a price that's at least halfway reasonable, and we'll negotiate this evening.'

There were worse ways to end a morning than with a smile from Elizabeth Farrer and a new piece of art.

***

It was later that day, on his third journey out along the Yealambidgie trail, that Peter finally found the ramshackle cottage from the old painting in his father's house.

After taking a look at a few reports, and then discussing those reports with Endmoor's owner, and then rereading that infernal piece about mouldy infestations, Peter took himself off across the land, moving fast in an attempt to outrun his own discomfiture. It hardly worked, but as the bush enveloped him he allowed his mind to drift beyond the estate and the people living on it.

The day was ideal for investigating the land. Clouds had managed, for once, to blow across the valley and provide the hapless residents within it some shade, and the cooler air was a blessed relief. He'd never realised a man could become sick of the sun.

It would have been much easier to find the collapsing hut had the landscape not changed so drastically in the years since his parents left it behind. Search after search was wasted taking a wrong turn at the same clearing; time after time he veered back towards Endmoor by accident.

So many frustrating days of searching, and of thinking he'd finally taken himself off northwest, only for the homestead's straight, neat chimney stacks and pristine corrugated iron roof to reappear in his view, taunting him as they emerged on the horizon ... The land was constantly tricking him.

The whole search had been an exercise in frustration from the outset. While settlers slowly carved away at the bush everywhere else, the trail was one place they'd left for nature to reclaim. And it had done just that, in all its messy, scrubby, infuriating glory.

Yealambidgie ... it was a word that odd, aloof Vernon Towner had given him that day they'd first met, one Peter had repeated the whole way back to Endmoor, worried he'd forget it. In his experience luck always came in bursts, and it turned out it was both a name Robert Farrer recognised and a place he could direct him to.

'It's been unused for years, so I'd tread carefully. You'll find it a little wild,' he'd cautioned.

As understatements went, Farrer's had been enormous.

Just as he had the first two visits, Peter took pity on the horse and left him tethered in the shade a way back. It was only when he was stomping his way in, imagining killer snakes ready to pounce at every turn, that it occurred to him that not once had Farrer questioned *why* he needed to find the trail. The discretion was pretty nice.

Pausing once, and then again, he consulted his memory of that painting back on the wall in the Glenmore Road terrace, and could not match it to what he saw around him. There were too many changes to find his bearings.

Moving through the bush, and selecting a direction at random, he walked a good half-hour through trees and clearings so monotonous they could send a man out of his mind before he stumbled upon something interesting.

And when he did, it was *very* interesting.

Peter stopped suddenly, sending something scurrying away in the undergrowth.

Up ahead was a rundown hut emerging bit by bit from the trees and the weeds with each step he took. The rusting iron rooftop shone dully in the daylight, and off to one side was what might once have been a little vegetable patch.

He was almost within reach of the place when he caught sight of the oversized chimney, hanging a little sideways as though it had been built by a drunkard.

Aha.

'Found you,' he said, and walked towards the door.

***

'He cannot be serious.'

Elizabeth was going to faint. Right there, in the middle of the post office, on a busy day in a place that was filled with familiar faces, she was going to collapse in a heap there on the floorboards.

Hands shaking, head swirling and her vision dotted with a kaleidoscope of colours, she tried very hard to focus on maintaining her balance rather than on all the activity around her.

Once she'd regained a few of her senses, she dared to have a second look at the telegram in her hands. Mr Evanson's words had not changed, and nor had she misread the sum he'd offered for a commission. It was three times the price anybody had offered for her work in the past.

It was enough to make her dizzy yet again.

Stepping forwards, she gripped the bench firmly with her free hand and tried to force her way through the muddle in her mind to form a coherent thought.

'Miss Farrer?' the man behind the counter asked, a thousand questions rolled into two words.

She found a bland smile somewhere, and offered it to the fellow as she clasped the message tightly and looked over her shoulder. Several other people waited to be served; Barracks Flat was uncharacteristically busy at the exact moment she could have done with privacy.

'I'll need a few minutes. Perhaps you could help someone else first?'

Stepping aside, she drifted over to the building's large widows and gazed out at the street, searching for Alice who'd gone visiting Mrs Hobson at her shop.

Who knew buyers could make her offers so high? Somehow her name was becoming known, which meant Mr Evanson was working magic greater than she had ever expected.

What of England? What of London?

Her sister-in-law emerged on the opposite side of Monaro Street then, purchases stacked in her arms, marching across the road too fast for anybody who'd noticed to catch up and offer assistance.

Elizabeth tucked her message away and left the building, rushing across to relieve Alice of the top package so that she might actually see where she was going.

'I thought you were merely *visiting*.'

The smaller woman darted to the side before she could be divested of any more of her burden.

'Imagine how much I would've come out with if I'd gone in there to shop. Are you ready to head home? Duncan'll be wakin' up and makin' a fuss for Bessie, if he isn't already. She's got patience, that one, but I think I shouldn't test it too often.'

'I'm ready.'

Elizabeth tucked the package under her arm and reached out to grab at Alice's skirts with the other, using them like reins to guide the woman to the carriage, tugging her to the side before she managed to turn an ankle in a ditch.

'It's nice that you worry, but we must look like a pair of loonies,' Alice shot over her shoulder.

'Probably,' Elizabeth agreed, but she didn't let go.

A reply to the telegram would have to wait for another day, because right then she had no idea what that response might be.

***

Nobody came rushing to stop Peter from entering the house.

He'd felt a right idiot standing there knocking on a door in the middle of nowhere, especially as he'd had to wade his way through enough weeds—the gardeners in town would faint clean away—to reach the thing.

The door didn't creak so much as swing wildly on rotting, rusting hinges, and once it had slammed back against the wall with enough force to make him wince, Peter had all the proof he needed he had the place to himself.

He nudged aside a small collection of discarded shoes, some with holes and some clearly mended a time or two, and stepped inside, smelling the age and neglect seeping through every wall, and even up through the floor.

It hadn't always been that way, though. The disintegrating hearth was stacked with what he supposed was once intended as kindling, and spread across the little table was a cloth he was fairly sure—underneath several generations of dust—bore a floral pattern. A little wooden chest had been shoved to the back of the table, and dozens of spiders had spun their webs around it.

That, Peter thought, was a better form of security than any lock or key.

An assortment of old books and horrendously yellowed newspapers stood near the door. As far as hoarding went, it wasn't precisely what he expected of a rundown hut in the middle of a scrubby bit of nowhere.

He moved in further and made a thorough inspection of the ceiling. It wasn't new, but he didn't think it'd cave in on him. At least not that day.

Unlike his much larger and more comfortable cottage on Endmoor grounds, this one was devoid of any real decoration, except for...

He crossed the floor, attention captured by the framed sampler hanging crookedly on the wall and also yellowing with age. Peter touched it gingerly, moving it more or less into alignment. There was a name stitched in the bottom corner, finished a bit crookedly, like its creator had lost interest before she was done. He tried to imagine Daisy's meticulous governess excusing such careless work.

Shaking his head, he was about to move on to examine the rest of the tiny place when he froze. The initials in the stitching...

C.T.

It could mean nothing. It could mean a lot more than that. There were Catherines and Claras aplenty in the colonies, but the missionaries had named his mother *Charity*. And her maiden name had been *Towner*.

Releasing a breath, he removed his hand. His fingers came away covered in an impressive coat of cobweb and dust as the sampler immediately returned to its odd angle. The nail it hung on was as crooked as everything else surrounding him.

He took himself on a turn around the four walls, which was a task that lasted all of four or five seconds, and then dug a discarded knife out of a particularly thick patch of dust and used the thing to hack away at the worst of the spiders' webs surrounding the chest. He wasn't in the right mood to risk death by arachnid attack.

Task accomplished, he eased the latch open, not expecting treasure, and found only a single item inside it.

There wasn't much point being disappointed. Finding the hut was more than he'd expected out of his day. It suggested his father might just have sent him off into the right unobtrusive spot in a massive colony. Not that his evidence was infallible yet.

He repeated little appeasements in his mind while reaching into the chest to lift out a small case. Kept safe from the elements for an age, it was the best-preserved item in the whole place. He inspected the simple design stamped into the metal before opening the clasp with his thumb and forefinger.

It took several seconds to comprehend what he found inside.

'My God.' Apparently he'd found treasure after all.

Peter cupped the frame in his hand and took it over to the door to get a better look at the image within it by the sunlight. Encased in the metal was a miniature daguerreotype, an old sort of photograph favoured in his parents' generation, an image created on silver-plated copper. He'd not before seen one so small, but once his eyes focused it was more than enough.

It showed a small family lined up in front of an unfamiliar building, which itself stood in front of an unfamiliar landscape. And in the centre, dressed in the fashion of her girlhood—dressed as a white woman and with her hair harshly parted and looped around her ears—was his mother.

Hardly daring to touch it, worried that it was as fragile as everything else around him, he traced the line of her face, fingertip hovering just above the picture.

Charity Rowe had died when he was still emerging from boyhood, and before he'd developed the courage to ask who he was and where they'd come from. Her portrait sat in his father's office, there for Peter to study whenever he wished, but in the picture in his hands as he stood in a tiny house in the middle of the country, she seemed different to him. Alive, even.

The sketch in his pocket crinkled as he moved and he pulled the thing out.

Even though the light was dim, seemingly made worse by the ancient, earthy smell of the small space, he removed the disastrous map and placed it on the table. He doubted it could be any more help than it had been so far.

Feeling like a thief, which is what he supposed he was, he tucked the case away in his pocket, not trusting the ramshackle building with it a moment longer. He closed the chest and placed the knife back where he'd found it, and then again started for the door.

He paused on the threshold and turned back one more time. Nobody might live here anymore, but the well-trained, ordered accountant in him desperately needed to straighten the pile of old books and papers someone had left by the door, and the only decent—and matching—pair of shoes in the place begged to be set side by side at the entrance.

He'd be back another day. For now there was a woman two-hundred miles away who deserved to know his news.

Chapter 12

Once he'd successfully negotiated a rational price with Elizabeth, Peter sent his new painting off home, mildly confident that, thanks to its small size, it would arrive at the other end unscathed. He noted that the stares he'd garnered in town in the past had gradually transformed into an occasional nod and, once or twice, a brief conversation. *Progress,* he supposed. It was probably too exhausting for everyone involved to continue with suspicion.

The visit to the bank that followed took longer, thanks to a gentleman with a wealth of carrot-coloured hair who lingered at the counter.

'What in the blazes is taking so long?' the fellow asked several times while Peter shifted his weight from one foot to the other and stifled a yawn. Forbearance was an attribute he'd cultivated over the years, but when his toes numbed and the debate moved to interest rates—which neither of the men seemed to actually understand—he shifted forwards.

'I might be able to—' he began, only to have the man whip around and give him an impressive glare, dissolving any desire Peter might have had to help resolve the situation. Some days were better ruined by sore feet than rude strangers.

Business in town eventually concluded, and with reluctance to return to the estate coursing through him, Peter found himself wandering along the river walk.

He reached the bridge where Monaro Street crossed the Murrumbidgee, and then wandered onto it. It was the furthest south he'd been ever in his life, which was a startling thing to comprehend. It looked like Barracks Flat had begun its sprawl across the water some time ago, but now the sprawl had become a wave of development. The entire area rang with the sounds of hammering and sawing.

Advancement people called it. Peter didn't know if he'd describe it quite like that.

He watched a pair of black swans emerge from directly beneath him, gliding downstream with a pair of half-grown cygnets in tow. Raising his gaze to the riverbank beyond he took in the sea of European weeping willows that ran the length of the water, their branches sagging into the stream.

A few stone cottages formed a row on the river's southern side, their tin roofs glinting blindingly in the sun. Another, newer inn sat below the level of the bridge on the other side, and on the street leading uphill beyond it, he made out what might have been a small convent, the silver spire of a chapel nearby the structure pointing high into the sky.

'Good afternoon.'

Peter didn't need to look to know that the last person he wanted to see had decided to appear out of nowhere.

Because he was just annoyed enough to be a little rude, he waited for John Stanford to walk over to him before reluctantly accepting the proffered handshake.

'It's been a busy few days,' the man commented, and rested his forearms on the ledge. 'I'm of a mind to hide away for a bit so nobody else can chase me down in the street and ask for one favour or another.'

Business was briefly discussed then, but there was another purpose to the man's appearance. Peter knew that without a doubt when most of what was said between them then had already been talked about the day before, or the day before that.

Stanford was stalling for some reason.

'Did you hear what happened last Sunday?' He started off south across the bridge, which dictated Peter follow.

'A lot of things happened last Sunday.' All of them mundane as far as he could remember. 'You'll have to be more specific.'

And so the other man launched into an anecdote involving a respectable member of the Ladies' Auxiliary and a missing pair of drawers as he continued drawing Peter to the southern bank and then turning right along the river walk. The story was, he had to admit, pretty funny, even if at least ninety per cent of it had to be untrue, and even if it placed some unfortunate images in Peter's head.

On they walked, past wilting plants not designed for the climate. Several half-built structures claimed new spots along the water's edge. The sounds of rough male carpenters' voices carried across to them, the conversation mingled with hammering and occasional swearing.

It became painfully clear just how much Stanford was determined to stall when they kept walking and he kept nattering. Suddenly the tale wasn't just about missing drawers, but a missing corset, too. The man chatted easily, his tone never sounding as suspicious as his behaviour was. He managed to not even sound suspicious when he forgot various details of the tale, changing everything as he went along.

By the time *the* lady in the story had become *three*, they were a good way west, where the town's most affluent residents had chosen to construct their obscenely large homes.

It was there that he came to an abrupt stop.

'The mayor's residence,' he told Peter, nodding in the direction he looked. Laid out beyond the old stone chapel were extensive grounds, greener than any other place in the district—improbably so.

A grand colonial homestead, complete with iron-laced trimmings and a veranda stretching the entire way around sat on an elevated spot back from the river, providing the sort of privacy only afforded to those with more money than sense. It was perfectly positioned to take in the view at the point the Murrumbidgee curved and flowed into the centre of town.

Peter noted, with dark satisfaction, that those gates had failed to keep out the colossal mob of kangaroos that grazed lazily from the top of the slope all the way down to the water.

'And so those ladies will have a hard time showing their faces in church next week.' Stanford continued, becoming ruminative. Peter stood straighter at the change in tone.

'My grandfather knew a man once, years ago. Secretive sort of chap, the way I was told the story. He wasn't much interested in becoming friends with anyone in town—nor out of it, if it came to that.'

Stanford looked across at the residence again and Peter's senses sharpened.

'Back then I was constantly being taken back and forth from Goulburn for school. It was long before the railway, you know. When we used to take the Cobb & Co and imagine bushrangers chasing us down. Excellently timed of you to arrive when you did, by the way. You'll never know how hellish that journey used to be before the tracks were laid and the station here opened.'

'Er, thank you, I suppose.'

He received a swift smile.

'Not all change is helpful, however,' Stanford continued. 'I'm making assumptions, but I'd say you didn't come all the way out here for the work, nor for the brilliant company. Things are changing fast, and I'd recommend you move faster if you're here for answers.'

'Answers?' he asked blandly, feeling stuffy beneath his necktie. Underneath his cheery exterior, the bloody man saw too much.

Stanford wasn't to be deterred.

'This hermit type of fellow my grandfather spoke of. I don't remember much except that the surname started with a T. I'm not sure *which* name it was, though. I'm still not sure. Taylor? Tierney? So many to choose from. I thought you might have a better idea than I do.'

Stanford continued walking, not paying attention to anything or anyone in particular and again Peter was forced to follow.

'*Towner.*' Yes, he'd taken the bait. No, he wasn't happy about it. But—*yes*—he was curious as to where this was going.

'Ah, yes. That's the chap.'

Stanford shouted a greeting to someone across on the opposite bank and then gave Peter his attention again.

'It's been a good few months. For business, for all of us, and yet I'm seeing far too many people around me moping at the moment. *Honestly...*' he scoffed in mock disgust. 'Look at this beautiful weather we're having. Look at how beautifully our work is going. A man would think this was a time for happiness, not gloom.'

'Who are you accusing of being gloomy?'

'*You,* obviously, amongst others. If all these groans and glares you direct at me are about Miss Farrer, I wouldn't worry on that part. She's almost as much my sister as my real sisters are, the poor soul.'

'I don't know what you mean.' It was hard to lie without prior warning, so Peter left it at that.

'Yes, you do, but it's all right. I won't call you on it for now.'

He walked faster; manners dictated that Peter *again* follow suit. The methodical sound of scraping and crunching drifted around in the air.

'I really am here to work, John, not anything more.'

'If you insist,' the other man replied after a pause. 'I might even pretend to believe you.'

Stanford's posture suddenly changed, his step faltered, and then he came to a complete stop. Peter did the same, eyes searching for whatever had given the other man pause.

'This is where I abandon you to your thoughts. All of a sudden it's occurred to me I actually *do* have business to conduct today. In fact, I remember now I had an errand to run over there ... somewhere...' He indicated over his shoulder, back the way they'd come.

And, with a firm handshake, and a pointed look in the direction of the mayor's property, the man was gone as quickly as he'd appeared.

Perplexed, Peter checked his surroundings—and then saw what Stanford had.

A man, at least as wiry as William Adamson, worked a rake across the grass, scooping and crunching up leaves that had dried, deadened and fallen months too soon. Some sense alerted him to the fact he was being observed, and he stopped what he was doing to watch Peter warily.

The odd conversation forgotten, Peter braced himself for a reaction of any sort, and made a beeline for the gardener.

***

'Everyone likes holidays. It's only men who go funny about admittin' it.'

Alice's proclamation was delivered with confidence as she and Elizabeth travelled out across Endmoor land, eyes searching the horizon as they went.

'If you say so, Alice.'

Not quite as convinced, Elizabeth shifted Duncan on her hip. He was getting to be too big to be carried for long, but he wasn't to know that, and she wasn't about to tell him. Hands occupied with the infant, she had to blow away the fly that kept hovering around her face.

Their skirts swished through the grass, the sounds occasionally punctuated by a bang or a clunk from the enormous basket of provisions Alice lugged along with her. The child was content to be carried, even if it was a little hard to hold onto a boy who kept turning this way and that, in awe of his surroundings. They'd been taking turns, swapping baby with basket and back again, but there was only so much energy a person had available at midday in summer.

It was Epiphany, Twelfth Night—or twelfth *day*, as things were—and it was as good an excuse as any to head out to find the men, most of whom had been occupied with fixing fences for the bulk of the morning.

'Grapevines will be easier in the long run,' Robert had commented at breakfast. 'Unlike sheep, they don't see a gap in a fence and feel the need to escape through it.'

However, as grapes took even longer to grow than livestock, Endmoor's income would depend upon those merinos for a while to come, and in the meantime those fences needed mending, holiday or not.

Elizabeth blew at the fly again.

'I reckon the basket's just about heavier than Duncan is,' Alice observed a few minutes later, breaths laboured.

'But significantly less squirmy.'

Elizabeth slowed when Alice did, and watched as her sister-in-law plucked a large prickle from her dress.

'It's all so bloody—I beg your pardon, Duncan—*blasted* dry an' dead out here. At this rate we're goin' to have a fire soon.'

'*Blasted* is hardly a politer word than *bloody*, dear,' Elizabeth said, amused despite her exhaustion. She started off again only to realise the other woman hadn't done the same.

'What's the matter?'

Alice stared at her. 'You swore.'

She laughed at that. 'I do know those words, Alice, even if I think them more often than say them.'

The woman appeared dumbfounded. 'Well I never.'

Alice adjusted her grip on the basket and indicated they should continue. Elizabeth offered the dark grey clouds on the horizon a hopeful look as they set off.

'I feel as though we should have packed something more exciting than the remains of Mrs Beeton's pudding,' Elizabeth said as they set off once more, swishing and catching on twigs and prickles, wondering if any of it would be edible by the time they found the men.

'And jam tarts. We have Epiphany tarts, too, with stars on 'em. That's festive enough, I reckon. Elizabeth, you should've seen how hard it was to get that pastry to stay the right shape when it was cooked.'

'And still, we could be more festive than that. We should be singing something. It's the done thing for the occasion. "Three Kings of Orient",' Elizabeth suggested, 'or "As With Gladness Men of Old", except I hardly remember the words to that one.'

'It's a good thing your memory's bad, then, because I'm not singin' in front of anyone, no matter how jolly I feel.'

Duncan chose that moment to announce something gurgled and unintelligible, fist clinging to a curl of Elizabeth's hair with more strength than someone of his stature should possess.

She summoned a grin to hide her wince of pain as she met his wide eyes. 'Really? That's fascinating.'

She hefted the boy a little higher, and glanced at Alice. 'I think the song talks about a guiding star. And there's definitely a mention of a *rude and bare cradle*.'

'Rude *and* bare? In a Christian song? Lord, I think I ought to be payin' more attention in church.'

'*Where they need no star to guide...*'—there was another line of the song. It made Elizabeth think of a night in September, when she'd caught a certain man sneaking about the property in the darkness.

They passed a dying old tree with a couple of lounging ewes beneath it, the animals' wool coloured perfectly to match their surroundings.

Alice was suspiciously quiet.

'What are you thinking about?' Elizabeth asked reluctantly.

The other woman walked a few more steps before replying, eyes on the horizon. The basket rattled.

'Miss Hall seemed to think you were headin' off somewhere. England.'

It was not as much a question as an accusation.

'Alice, I think I might *have* to go.'

'Why?'

'My art. If I stay here, I'll only be—'

'Wildly successful? I don't know for certain, Elizabeth, but I reckon it's not common for men from Goulburn to come chasin' after a woman in Barracks Flat unless she's special.'

Elizabeth spluttered. 'Mr Evanson is an *art dealer*, Alice, not a *suitor*. And nobody has come chasing me.'

They reached a little bump in the landscape and spent several quiet seconds navigating the rocks scattered across its peak, baby and basket held aloft. When they were clear, Elizabeth was still not finished being appalled.

'Besides anything else, Mr Evanson is *married*. And, and—well, he hardly has the appeal of, of—'

'Mr Rowe?'

Elizabeth took an intense interest in smoothing the baby's little patch of fair hair. Alice snorted and sent her a knowing grin she was determined not to hear or see.

She couldn't go on living her life for a dead man, but other than his ill-advised jaunt to fight in the Mahdist War, Edward had never seen much of the world. And he'd been *desperate* to.

They'd bumped into each other in the street, she and Edward. He'd steadied her with an apologetic laugh, and his cheeky smile had stirred something in her from the outset. For someone as steady, as measured as Elizabeth, it had seemed like madness had taken hold of her.

'*Will you marry me?*' he'd asked one week before he took himself off across the Indian Ocean. '*We can stay here, or I could return to the country and make a go of it with you there. It might take me a week or two to learn how to wrangle a sheep, but it can't be any worse than surviving my officer's endless lectures.*'

He'd made her laugh first, and then she'd said yes without any reservations. And then, so soon after, he was gone.

Beneath the neck of Elizabeth's gown the pendant pushed against her skin. She really needed to stop wearing it.

'You absurd man,' she murmured. Duncan's curious eyes met hers.

Edward's end hadn't come in a blaze of glory. Nothing so dramatic for such an enthusiastic man. No ... her fiancé had died of a short illness while guarding a railway line somewhere between Suakin and Khartoum. He'd never even seen combat.

Now her sister-in-law trudged on beside her, muttering under her breath when she swung the basket a little too enthusiastically and something inside it clattered and clanked. Epiphany didn't feel quite as joyous as it had half an hour earlier.

'Tell the truth, Elizabeth.' Alice huffed with the exertion. 'If you'd known how far away this broken fence was, would you have come out today?'

She was about answer that she wouldn't have when they finally spotted the stockmen some forty yards away. Off to one side, Robert strode towards Mr McCoy, saying something the women were too far away to hear. The women drew to a stop and sighed with relief. The baby reached for his mother, Elizabeth took control of the refreshments, and they started onwards.

'Well,' Alice yelled once her husband noticed them and changed direction. 'About *blasted* time we found you!'

***

Peter didn't know what—if any—sort of welcome he'd receive when he approached the improbably lush lawns of the mayor's residence. The man, the gardener, watched him with detached interest the entire way. Peter got the impression he had no idea what to say or do either.

He came to a stop a short distance from the fellow and felt a lifetime of inadequacies wash over him. More than three decades of pretending he was wholly white. More than three decades of knowing nothing.

The gardener was older than him by a decade or two, he guessed. Here was a man who might have some answers for him, and he'd become a mute.

A good, assessing look at Peter's face was taken, and he allowed it. Moments passed, and the gardener's dark, dark eyes gave the firm indication that if any conversation was to be had, it would be Peter who would have to begin it.

'This is an impressive garden.' He received a nod and more silence for his efforts.

Oh, what a wonderful start.

'I gather it takes a lot of work to maintain it.' *And that was so much better.*

Another nod.

First meetings were hardly ever a lark—he was sure Elizabeth Farrer would have liked an amendment to theirs—but rarely were they this bad.

And then, when the man took a smidgen of pity on Peter and spoke, the words were as foreign to Peter as they would have been if he'd spoken in Persian. It was a language he'd never heard before, but he received the message clearly: he *should* have understood.

Ducks quacked while one man waited for a response that would never come and the other tried to hold his head up despite his shortcomings. The latter couldn't think of anything at all to say. He could have responded in student Latin to sound fancy but knew without being told his companion would be less than impressed.

They watched each other. The sun became too warm for all the layers Peter wore.

'You understand?' The other man eventually asked, switching to English. It was a test, and they both knew it.

A drake, emerald head glistening, waddled past, happily oblivious.

'No.' Peter could only admit failure.

'It's not a surprise.' This wasn't said unkindly.

A vehicle came past, and they both watched it until it was gone. Nothing about their conversation was private; yet it felt like *all* of it was.

'Your people are Walgalu?' The gardener rested his hands on the top of the rake and thought about it a little more. 'Ngambri?'

An invisible vice clenched around Peter at the name. It'd been an expressly forbidden term for so much of his life.

'Ngambri,' he'd confirmed, though his family was at least as English as anything else. 'I have reason to believe that I've family in the region. Or at least, I *had*. My mother...'

He went on to give him the scarce details he had, well aware of the shuttered expression spreading across the man's face as he did. Fearing he'd gone about the whole thing the wrong way, eventually Peter let his words fade away.

The duck came back past, quacking to himself.

'Don't much like talkin' about all of that. The past, you know, not something I think about,' the man said after a lengthy pause. He gripped the rake with both hands and went back to the endless chore of dragging fallen leaves into piles.

Peter looked past the residence's grounds to the crumbling old barracks and the abandoned territory beyond.

He knew so little about what to ask. Furious, helpless with his own ignorance, he chose to wait in silence rather than leave the man to his work. He'd a sense that if he were to walk off now his chances of getting the fellow to talk to him again were slim.

Manners told him to go. Desperation told him otherwise.

Peter had held his ground.

And finally, *finally*, the gardener spoke again.

'Not much likin' what's happenin' now, with this town. Too many people. Too many come 'ere from far away and stay, like they've the right. Those people you're lookin' for? Most are movin' out. If you mean to find your people, I'm no use. But you might try *Weereewaa*.'

And then he swiped the last of the leaves off that obscenely green grass, and stalked away before Peter could ask who—or what—*Weereewaa* was.

Chapter 13

There was more than enough food and drink to go around, even with Alice throwing a substantial amount of shredded ham to the persistent magpies. They served their plain pudding and their jam tarts with the pastry stars, and it was collectively decided the fences were mended enough to last the remainder of the day.

Nobody suggested singing anything, religious or otherwise.

Alice poured more wine and cut a tart into neat triangles to pass around, giving her own berry-topped slice an uneasy glance before taking the tiniest of nibbles. The next moment her face dissolved into a picture of relief.

'Thank the Lord Mrs Adamson wasn't so enthusiastic with the brandy this time. Still not for you, Duncan,' she scolded gently, placing a dull old bread crust in his fist instead.

Robert came and went from where they sat in the shade. Someone was always after his attention.

'They're hungry, too,' Elizabeth felt compelled to point out when he caught the two women throwing more ham the birds' way.

'Yes,' Alice readily agreed. 'And you'll be thankin' me for maintainin' a friendship with them so they won't come and attack your son when they're in a mean mood.'

'You do have a point,' he conceded, and then bent to scoop the child up, leaving Elizabeth on the picnic blanket with Alice. The crust dropped to the ground, snatched immediately by one of the birds. It was then a familiar figure approached from the main road.

Peter hid his agitation well, but Elizabeth still saw it.

No matter how he smiled at the enthusiastic greeting he received from the other men, his shoulders remained squared and set. His laugh, in response to something she was too far away to hear, didn't seem very natural.

He caught her watching him and gave her a funny little bow that teased the corners of her mouth upwards despite her unease. Smiling slightly, he strolled off after Hutton, who had a stick in his mouth and a game in his plans. Elizabeth switched to watching the other men.

There'd be no more grand romances for her, she reminded herself. She preferred to stay silent about her loss nearly three years before, and there was another side to her grief she didn't say a word about to Alice, even then. The side's name was Victoria Abraham, the woman whose betrothal to one Edward Sumner had been announced in the *Herald* three days after the contingent set sail for Africa.

'Was he handsome, your Edward?' Alice was watching her husband and son.

'Handsome?'

'I know I oughtn't to ask that before learnin' if he was smart or a dunce, or funny or serious, but I'm tryin' to get a picture of him in me—*my mind.*'

Elizabeth thought of the day she met him on that Sydney street, of stumbling into him and making her hasty apologies, and of Edward's hand on her arm as he steadied her.

'He was the opposite of Mr Rowe in most ways.'

'Ah, so he was ugly,' Alice said immediately. Elizabeth threw a strawberry and her sister-in-law ducked, giggled, and then got a sparkle in her eye. 'Why're you mentionin' Mr Rowe, hey?'

'It was just an example. He was in my line of sight when you asked.'

'Funny. Because I only asked now, and I see him right over there, playin' with the dog.'

'He ran. The man moves fast.' *Oh, what a believable excuse.*

The other woman scoffed her disagreement, looking too amused.

A shout rang out from across the clearing, and Elizabeth watched as one of the stockmen produced bats and a ball from Lord only knew where. Evidently repairing the fences hadn't been the only thing on their minds when they'd set out that morning.

'These are sweet strawberries, Alice. I don't want to throw any more of them. Edward was fair. His eyes were blue.' What had Martha accused her of that day in town? Of describing a handsome man the way a person described a horse?

She thought harder.

'He had an idea that he needed an adventure before he settled.'

She remembered the way Edward's eyes had shone at the prospect of travelling all the way to another continent. *'You don't understand, Lizzie,'* he'd said to her. *'You've come from the other side of the world, and I've never been past Wollongong.'*

To Elizabeth it didn't sound like the best reason to race off across the sea in the general vicinity of Khartoum, but his enthusiasm had been untameable, and—stupidly, and desperate to please him—she hadn't tried all that hard to stop him.

'Adventure?' Alice scoffed. 'We've enough of that here. More than enough, when it comes to it.'

Elizabeth traced the gold chain around her neck, and then she drew the pendant out from the bodice of her dress. Outside, on such a beautiful day, the sapphires were a rich, deep, luminous blue.

'This is what came for me in that parcel from Sydney. He bought it for me before he left, and it's been waylaid all this time.'

She shouldn't wear it. Even if she wasn't furious with the man—a dead man, at that—it was too fine a piece to be wearing around the station.

'Lord,' Alice gasped, saucer-eyed, and touched the battered silver locket, her late mother's, at her neck. 'That sure is fancier'n mine.'

Yet Alice's spoke of loyalty, and Elizabeth's...

'I thought ... When Mr Rowe handed me the parcel, and when I saw Edward's writing on it? For a mad few hours I'd almost convinced myself there'd been a mistake. That he'd not died in Africa as I'd thought.'

They'd been so focused on their conversation neither of them noticed when Robert, Duncan in tow, drew up beside them, the tips of his boots touching the edge of the blanket.

Robert was much too kind to pry as he moved his attention from one woman to the other. Elizabeth closed her hand around the pendant, again warming the gold against her skin.

Alice looked to the side and was suddenly on her feet.

'You're bored now, Robert? Want some entertainin'? Come, then,' she gathered her little family up with her words. 'I see crowea growin' over there, and I've of a mind to pick some.'

The man was visibly startled by Alice's spontaneity, but when two shadows appeared over her, Elizabeth rolled her eyes. They were Mr Rowe and the heeler, the latter panting, the former perspiring genteelly. Alice was cunning. And determined.

Robert and the baby exchanged glances, and then her brother called after his wife. 'They can't be blooming now. You told me they grow in the autumn and winter!' It had no effect. Alice was already off across the grass, pausing only once to cast Elizabeth a conspiring look over her shoulder.

'She is distinctly lacking in subtlety,' Elizabeth told Peter when the rest of the Farrers were out of earshot. She was half amused and half mortified, and thought he probably felt about the same.

Elizabeth shifted across to one side. 'I promise I won't complain if you sit down.'

He laughed at her from behind a bland façade. 'Thank you.'

While he relaxed onto the blanket, leaving a polite distance between them, Elizabeth broke off a piece of piecrust and tossed it to the adolescent magpie that was toddling around after its parents on lanky, unsteady legs.

'They're not all that different to children, are they?' Peter murmured as Robert, Alice and the baby continued off into the distance, with not a wildflower in sight.

'Not really. However, I don't remember a hungry Duncan ever once resorting to squeaks.'

'Poor bird, he's trying his best. We shouldn't laugh.'

It was a silly conversation, but he relaxed as they spoke, altering his posture so he leaned closer to her.

Elizabeth wondered if he'd noticed.

'I bet you'd drag a husband off with more grace and beauty, if not as much determination,' he said when the others paused to talk in the middle of the paddock. It wasn't long before Alice took off again, her pace even faster than before.

She couldn't help herself; Elizabeth's mind went immediately to the past. She gave Hutton, who'd returned to sniff at the basket, intense attention as she patted him.

Edward had not been from the land. Marriage to him would almost certainly have kept her in Sydney—nearly two-hundred miles from home. She hadn't had time to even imagine the realities of such a change before her grand romance had prematurely ended.

The dog wandered off and Elizabeth sneaked a sideways glance at the man beside her. He sat with his face tipped up to the sun, eyelids half lowered.

The day really was too hot to be lounging about outside. Elizabeth could feel herself becoming *ever so* attractively sweaty beneath her chemise, and felt the increasing trickles of perspiration down her back.

Elizabeth smiled at the antics of the increasingly boisterous stockmen and turned towards Peter a little shyly, only to find herself snagged. She made a sound of dismay to find the hem of her skirt tangled in dry, prickly, overgrown grass and set about extracting herself from it.

'It's too hot for picnics,' she decided, and saw Peter's lips curve as she moved a little closer to him, further onto the blanket.

'That's probably why the English perfected the business. Many British traditions were not made to work in Australia, I think.'

'Perhaps not in summer. The ground is certainly softer in my homeland.'

She surreptitiously mopped a bead of perspiration off her temple and watched her brother and family become smaller and smaller figures in the distance.

It was wholly unintentional, but when she placed her hand back down it came into contact with another, bigger and far more masculine one.

***

Peter's breath caught. His little finger moved against Elizabeth's involuntarily, making the tiniest of strokes.

Was she aware? How could she not be? He did it again, but right then she gasped a laugh and nodded in the direction of her family.

'Soon they'll reach the fence, and then what will they do? Knowing Alice, she'll probably insist they climb over it and continue walking.'

'I think that at some point even Mrs Farrer will tire and march everyone back.'

'Perhaps.' Elizabeth didn't sound convinced. 'What do you think she's expecting us to do?'

He decided there were a number of excellent answers to that question, none of which were appropriate to be discussed with an unmarried lady. No matter how familiar Elizabeth Farrer might be with Lady Audley, the book's authoress hardly went into great detail on such matters.

He stroked her hand again, and again she hardly appeared to notice.

'Judging by the pace she's marching your brother away from us, I'd say she's expecting us to do at least one shocking thing. When she returns, she'll be very disappointed.'

'I can be shocking,' Elizabeth informed him in a tone that might have been fractious if it wasn't so determined. Peter nearly asked her to prove it, and then remembered he wasn't supposed to be seducing her—not even with words.

'You'll have to do it on your own, then. I've no plans to be shocking with anyone.'

She turned curious eyes his way. 'What do you mean?'

'I hadn't planned to marry. Not anyone. Not ever. Shocking behaviour tends to lead to matrimony, so I'd best avoid it altogether.'

Elizabeth nearly sprang off the blanket in surprise. 'What do you mean? All men marry at some point.'

He adjusted his cuff, feeling the loss of her touch against his own, and then patted the space beside him, encouraging her to resume her position.

'Just as I said. Elizabeth, I'm a Ngambri man. No matter how much education and how many manners my parents installed in me—and, believe me, I was driven nearly mad with my extensive education—I can't hide my face. People decide who I am the moment they meet me, and I'd wager few of their thoughts are kind.'

She shook her head slowly. 'Peter ... Do *you* regret your life? Do you regret who you are?'

'No. However, there's anger sometimes. Sometimes a lot of it,' he admitted.

He was a man who wasn't wholly one or the other, brought up in a white world but thought of differently. He searched for a way to explain.

'My mother ... She wasn't a happy person a lot of the time. I don't think she ever truly was. She never admitted it, but I always felt she regretted many things about who she was. She was raised to be ashamed.' He exhaled sharply. 'I'm bouncing about all over the place. It doesn't matter in the end. Ignore me.'

Elizabeth studied the pastry star adorning the top of one of the tarts, frowning. A fly took a chance and landed on a patch of jam. She shooed it away.

'No,' she said softly. 'No, I will not ignore you.'

'Rowe? Will you play?' Harry McCoy called. A couple of stockmen, bats in hands, looked ready for a serious bout of cricket.

'Not today. Sore back,' he called out reflexively, and didn't miss Elizabeth's scoff at the response.

The man turned her way.

'What about you, Miss Farrer?'

'Oh, thank you ever so much. I do enjoy being the afterthought.' She grinned. 'I'll stay where I am, thank you.'

'All right, but don't blame me when you miss all the fun.' The stockman changed the ball from one hand to the other. It looked like a proper cork-and-leather construction this time. The man meant business.

'I thought it was your hamstring,' Elizabeth chided in a whisper as McCoy moved on.

'Ah. I think you misremembered.'

She pressed her lips together and narrowed her eyes him. 'I'm sure I didn't.'

The game began, hampered by a dog determined to catch the ball before the fielders did. They watched for a while, and it was she who broke the quiet.

'You know, just because I'm too overheated and lazy to play doesn't mean *you* can't. Go and join them if you wish.'

'If I'm being honest, I'm not sure what appeals to a man about having a ball pitched directly at him, with only a bat to defend himself.'

It was the perfect time for the *crack* of a hard-hit ball to ring out across the paddock.

'Anyway, that hamstring of mine wouldn't cope with all that exertion.' And, despite his better judgement, he'd not give up the opportunity to sit with her longer.

'Your back,' she reminded him gently. 'It's your back that's troubling you today.'

Whoops. Peter pressed his hand to the small of it and tried to muster a pained expression. Elizabeth did not appear particularly impressed by the dramatics.

'Did you know the first cricket team we sent abroad was Aboriginal?' he asked quietly.

She looked at him sharply. 'Yes, I did.'

They'd been dancing around his heritage for months, and it was some time before she continued. 'Because of your family's history you intend to be a bachelor forever?'

'Hmm,' he said, which wasn't much of an answer. Recently he'd allowed himself to imagine a different future, but those thoughts were so private he rarely even shared them with himself.

An army of ants marched in a trail along the blanket's edge. Soon he'd have to brush them aside, but for the time being he let them be.

'I was thinking of becoming a spinster myself.'

The words lightened his mood but she could not be serious. 'Are you?'

'Spinsters are infinitely more interesting people than wives.'

'They are? How did you come to that conclusion?'

'To begin, there's more time. A spinster can be anything she wishes to be and do anything she wishes to do. She can travel the world, or become a famous eccentric.'

Peter supposed the idea had some merit. 'Or she could become a famous artist?' he suggested.

'Or a famous artist, precisely. If I'm ever to be one it will surely happen because I've not wasted my days entertaining a husband. Ouch! These critters are starting to bite.'

Peter made a great, valiant show of shaking the ants off the edge of the blanket, and when that was done he resumed his position, picking up her hand outright now and tracing an abstract pattern across the back of it.

'Spinsters still take the time for picnics, I'm sure.'

'Occasionally we find a space in our day for one, yes.'

'It's amazing that you've the time to waste sitting out here with me.'

She liked that. He squeezed her hand when she smiled.

'You should feel proud I've carved out a little time for you. It's a great compliment.'

She stilled his caressing fingers and turned her hand so that she held his.

'Mr Rowe, if you're to be an eternal bachelor, and *I* a spinster, then what are we doing?'

He laced his fingers through hers and squeezed again. 'I'd say we're ignoring our better judgement. Elizabeth, if marriage makes a person dull, then what of Mrs Farrer? She seems ... Um, I'm trying to think of a polite way to describe her.'

'Do you not like her?' She sounded personally affronted.

'I like her enormously. Which is why I mentioned her. She seems—er—vastly interesting to me.'

'Yes, well.' She clearly didn't appreciate having her outrage dismantled so swiftly.

He laughed at her and stretched out a leg. 'You've nothing to reply with, do you.'

'You did make it a little difficult,' she grumbled and he angled himself to face her.

'You and Mrs Farrer were deep in conversation when I arrived.'

Her attention immediately switched to the blanket they sat on.

'Lozenge,' she whispered, and traced the diamond pattern. It was a sorry excuse for a distraction.

'I take it by that response that you'll not be telling me.' She didn't owe him her secrets, and he ought to let it go.

Peter was about to release her hand when she squeezed again, gently, a silent request to stay exactly as he was.

'I was telling her about Edward.'

Chapter 14

Something changed as Elizabeth shared her story yet again. Now she'd begun telling it to others she supposed she might as well talk about Edward another time. Secrets caused too much tension, too much hurt.

However it wasn't *she* who changed as the words came out another time. It was Peter.

She'd said something wrong. Very wrong. Even as she prattled on against his silence, Elizabeth knew she'd taken the conversation somewhere that stirred tension in him—anger. Even if he'd not said a thing, the atmosphere had changed.

'From what I understand it was quite the adventure to go to Africa. A person is willing to overlook a lot of discomfort on the journey across if they expect excitement at the end of it, I think.'

What had seemed like such a fine afternoon moments earlier now felt dark and shadowed. Peter smiled slightly; it wasn't his real smile.

Another ant made an attempt to scale Elizabeth's foot. She watched it a little desperately, too tense suddenly to move and brush it away.

Scrambling for a distraction from the dark mood that had so clearly struck him, she did what any floundering person would do then, and gave the sky her attention. Those clouds were moving across the mountains, ominously grey.

'It's such a nice day, but too warm. The last picnic I—we—Alice and Miss Wright and I attempted was interrupted. We went out to that place west, near the estuary. There's an old graveyard there. I'm not sure if you know it. The McCoys have begun to clear their land out that way.'

The story went on and on. She was blabbering again, but she'd seen the unexpected whiteness of the knuckles of his free hand.

'Clearing *their* land,' he repeated when she ran out of words.

A sensible person would have reacted to that tone by shutting up, but Elizabeth was desperate.

'Yes. Well, it's her father's land, but he's an invalid now and doesn't want it. It's not the best soil out that way, and there's nobody else around laying claim to it.'

Again, that tight little smile of his was all *wrong*.

He released her hand and drew back so far he nearly sat in the dirt. Elizabeth nearly warned him that he'd have ants biting his bum, but it registered then that he was angry. He was really, truly angry.

'What's the matter?'

'Your Edward went to the Sudan.' He repeated her earlier words. 'To fight for the Empire's cause.'

'Edward? Yes, he did, but...' The man was jumping about everywhere; the swift change left her dizzy.

Peter's knuckles whitened again.

'And he was part of the New South Wales Contingent you mentioned? Off to do their part for Britain?'

'Yes,' she said finally, voice small, not sure why it felt like an admission of guilt.

He pressed his lips together and watched the horizon for long, terrible seconds as the cicadas carried on their song. When he spoke again he'd visibly regained his control.

'Your family came here some twenty years ago, didn't they?'

'Yes.'

'And the town was founded some thirty years earlier?'

'Yes. This year will be our golden jubilee.' How did he know?

'And, before everyone started celebrating jubilees, who was here?'

It was a rhetorical question, and Elizabeth met his eyes, and found she'd lost her voice. She *knew*. She knew then everything he implied but wouldn't say.

It was astounding how large the blanket had grown in the past few minutes. There had to be a mile between them now, perhaps more.

Peter's jaw was set as he got to his feet and made a show of dusting himself off.

Elizabeth climbed up too, scrambling back when his manners gave in, his hand twitching and then extending to steady her. She did not need his help to *stand*. What she needed was an explanation. She'd said something dreadful and hadn't even realised.

'Where are your mother's people from?' she asked, raising the topic every single person at Endmoor had been avoiding from the first day. Why *had* a company in Sydney been so keen to send a man as qualified as he was so far out into the country at such short notice? Why *had* the original man they'd offered employment to been swapped for Mr Rowe?

He regarded her a long, excruciating moment before he spoke.

'I think you already know.'

***

The rain would not stop. What had been the promise of an afternoon shower at Epiphany quickly became something far more ruthless. Unprepared for the onslaught, the countryside sagged under the intensity of it, as did every structure on Endmoor's grounds.

Elizabeth couldn't remember seeing anything like it before, at least not in Australia. It was merciless enough it dominated every discussion that night and into the next day, no matter what the topic had been when conversation began.

On the second day Mr Rowe was at last convinced to move into a guestroom in the homestead, and on the second night they sat around all but shouting mundane things at each other over the sound of the storm.

'We need to stop this. We must be boring you senseless.' How they'd been talking about the Rhineland one moment and blocked gutters the next was a mystery. Elizabeth had directed the apology at Mr Rowe. It was about the only thing she'd found the courage to say to him since their conversation across the picnic blanket had disintegrated into a quarrel.

He held her eyes long enough to convey something she didn't quite understand, and then relaxed back into his chair.

'I'm not worried. Gutters are a much more interesting topic than grey mould.'

Mending done, newspapers read, everyone wandered off to bed earlier than they usually would. Even the cranky cat who wished to go prowling but disliked wet paws. Elizabeth lingered just a little longer than the others, watching Peter's tall form as he disappeared around the corner, whatever he said to her brother as he left disguised by the endless drumming on the roof.

Nothing had been said between her and Peter about their conversation at the picnic. They'd instead drifted into infuriating politeness. She'd not called him by his Christian name since, not aloud at any rate. It felt too much like they'd become strangers once more, like she knew him no better than she had the day they'd first met.

Worst of all was that she hadn't any idea how to mend the rift between them.

When the shadows of the men in the hall disappeared, she rose and crept to the door, waiting another minute or so just in case before making her way to her own bed. She didn't hear a thing from Peter's room as she passed.

'This rain'll be bringin' out the spiders,' Alice had pointed out after the evening meal, and naturally all Elizabeth thought of as she poked around in her room was arachnids crawling out from every nook and cranny, from the shadows around the fireplace to the curves and crevices of the ceiling rose directly above her, to the tangle of bedsheets brushing at her feet.

It wasn't a thought conducive to a good night's rest, but whenever she turned her mind away from creepy-crawlies all she could think of was grey mould. *Botrytis cinerea*—noble rot, Peter had informed her. He mightn't be the most romantic of men, but surely he was better that way.

She began her valiant attempt at sleep curled on her side, face in the direction of the window. The brute force of the pounding on the rooftop was impressive, if annoying.

When the wind changed, sending hard sheets of water whacking repeatedly against the windowpane, she rolled onto her back, and then her other side, pulling the blankets over her head, trying her best to drown out the sound.

Lightning struck, throwing the room in stark relief, followed only half a moment later by thunder so loud she jumped and the dog began barking. In the next instant something—probably a branch from one of the trees surrounding the house—clattered onto the roof. It was going to be a very long night.

'Hutton, hush,' she ordered, but of course he couldn't hear her. The next flash of light drew her attention to the dark outline of her dresser. Edward's pendant sat there amongst the other clutter, teasing her even though she couldn't tell exactly which of the shadowy lumps it was.

The name *Victoria Abraham* drifted through her thoughts again. Groaning, she rolled back the other way, closing her eyes as the dog finally tired and ceased his commotion.

Naturally, the instant sleep took hold the ceiling began to drip.

Her paintings! The thought got her out of bed faster than any spider could have, hand-sized or otherwise. Hurrying always made a person clumsy and slow and it was no different then. She all but tripped over her shawl in her haste, and then bumped into the bed while she went to the lamp. She ought to have dressed properly, but if her room was capable of dripping, so was any other in the house.

After what felt like an hour to get herself sorted she hurried to the door and flung it open, rushing to the linen closet for something—anything—to cover her work with in case the rest of the house got any funny ideas and began to leak.

Something crashed outside, and Hutton barked once, and then a second time, before giving up. Elizabeth smoothed a sheet over an easel and gave the ceiling a warning glare. Crisis over for the moment, she headed back to her room but changed course when she found a light on in the nursery.

'Dunno how I got him off to sleep in this *blood*—in this racket,' Alice whispered when Elizabeth joined her at the cot. Duncan was sound asleep on his back, one arm up by his face, legs frog-like beneath the blanket.

Elizabeth chose not to point out that if a storm wouldn't wake the baby, there probably wasn't much need to whisper.

'I envy his talent for sleep,' she whispered back. 'This storm is awful.'

Her sister-in-law snorted and moved away from her son, towards the door.

'There's not a word I know good enough for what this storm is. I bet I'll be up the rest of the night. So much for that drought we've moaned about for months.'

'So will I. Alice—did you hear that branch fall on the roof just now?'

'I sure did. I reckoned if anythin' was goin' to wake Duncan up, it would've been that. He's a strange baby.'

They moved out to the hall, Alice pulling the door mostly, but not entirely, to.

Elizabeth paused, struck by a thought. 'I wonder if the roof has any damage. My room's already dripping a bit.' Right on cue something else clattered onto the corrugated iron.

'Well,' Alice said, and changed directions, 'we'd better go and check that out.'

***

Peter supposed he was more used to rain and storms than the Farrers were living out on a dusty station, but halfway through the night even he had to admit the weather had become ridiculous.

He managed to drift off twice, only to be startled awake both times by the clap of thunder. Whomever was up there in the sky was in a bloody bad mood, and determined to make it known to each and every one of them.

The third time he'd managed to fall into a doze the sound of something scraping across the floor outside stirred him out of it. Immediately alert, he cast his senses outward, anticipating the next sound—which came almost immediately.

He winced at a loud bang. It was immediately followed by a hastily cut-off exclamation.

All right, that was it.

He was out of the bed, robed, and edging into the hallway in moments, and just in time to catch a flash of movement at the other end of the corridor. He was quite sure that long, dark braid did not belong to a burglar.

Curious rather than cautious now, he approached with soft steps. Behind him another door opened, and Robert Farrer stepped into the hall, a question on his shadowed face.

Peter shrugged, and both men set off. Inside the room he found a sight he was not expecting.

'I wish you'd let me do it,' Mrs Farrer was saying as he arrived in the doorway. She sounded defeated, but it was not the fairer woman who made him jolt in surprise.

'You're not tall enough, Alice,' Elizabeth said as—*good Christ*—she stretched higher than she already was on the top of a ladder. 'I've almost reached it, and—'

And she broke off without concluding her sentence as she wobbled a little and then continued with ruthless determination. The too-short Alice Farrer gripped the ladder with even more determination. She'd admirable strength for one so small, but any second now this whole debacle was going to turn dangerous.

Both men strode forwards. Peter reached her first.

It wasn't the best idea he'd ever had; once he'd more or less steadied her he realised he'd gripped her by the thighs, and that nobody in the room was dressed in any way respectably. *And,* judging by the way she only wobbled more in reaction, she'd definitely noticed which parts of her he held.

Her brother stirred. 'No, don't move. Don't wobble. Stay just as you are.' Then in a deceptively even tone, he asked, 'Elizabeth, would you mind explaining what you're up to?'

'Ceiling's leakin',' Mrs Farrer answered for her. 'Somethin' fell on it outside a while ago, and then somethin' else just now. We thought we'd better fix it. There's a spot here we thought we might block until we can see better in the mornin'.'

She finally found the sense to give up her post when her husband slid into her place, taking the bottom of the ladder in a steady grip.

'And it didn't occur to you to come and wake me for assistance?'

She shrugged. 'We were both already up.'

With a shake of his head, a barely concealed snicker, and a sigh of long-suffering acceptance, Farrer looked up at his sister.

'Elizabeth, if you wouldn't mind coming down? Giantess that Alice seems to think you are, I'm significantly taller, and more likely to deal with the issue without breaking my neck.'

Farrer afforded his wife an amused glance at her loud scoff and then gave the situation a closer inspection.

'If the roof's leaking, shouldn't you be finding buckets, rather than stuffing scraps of fabric into the hole?'

Lighting gleamed through the curtains, bringing on the predictable thunder seconds later.

'Yes, that'd make sense if...' Mrs Farrer began just as Elizabeth threw all concern for her safety to the winds and stretched up onto the tips of her toes.

Peter's hands flexed.

'This ceiling rose is made in the old style, and irreplaceable. I need to save it.' She wobbled; straightened herself instantaneously.

'The ceiling rose doesn't matter if—oh, never mind. Hurry and finish and then come down,' Farrer said. He lifted a palm in defeat as the woman on the ground handed the one atop the ladder another tattered, torn piece of cloth.

'One moment.' The voice from above them was muffled as Elizabeth reached up higher, fussing with the cloth, but only seconds later she relented. Peter stepped up and held onto her as she summoned the courage to lower her hands from the ceiling, reaching down tentatively, hands stretching blindly in search of something to hold as she descended.

She was not lacking in coordination or courage, and was on the ground in no time, springing off the last step, and then looking up into his face when she'd landed. That she hadn't known he was there—that it had been him holding her—was held in the shock on her face.

That they'd still not discussed what had happened at Epiphany was in the way she immediately looked away, a murmur of *thank you* on her lips.

And then she switched her attention to her brother, stiff with annoyance.

'I'll have you know, Robert Farrer, that the plastering in this room is said to be the same as in Vaucluse House. It's *irreplaceable*,' she repeated, but the man still didn't seem particularly impressed.

Farrer set his eyes to the Heavens but had the sense not to argue the point any further.

The next clap of thunder was loud enough to wake even Duncan, and then Alice and Robert were off to fuss and dote and soothe, and—wordlessly—Elizabeth and Peter drifted to their rooms.

***

Elizabeth stayed in her bedroom only long enough to struggle into a dress and find some slippers. It was a little late to have concern for propriety, but she could hardly go out again as she had the first time. She waited with an ear pressed to the door until Duncan was settled and doors began to close once more, and then she waited longer, counting all the way to one hundred before easing her way back into the hall.

Peter opened his door almost as soon as she scratched on it, and drew her in in a hurry, closing them both inside. His lamp was lit, and it was impossible to ignore the mussed bedcovers. A few personal things were scattered across the dresser.

Oh, this was more inappropriate than she could have imagined it would be. She'd not blush. She would not.

'Your brother'll want to shoot me if he knew you were here,' he whispered, leaning close, his breath stirring the fine hairs at her temple.

It was an even more inappropriate situation than being on that ladder, and—oh—the memory of where his hands had been minutes earlier brought that blush she'd been fighting to the surface.

'Robert's not the shooting sort. I'd say you're safe.' The sentiment was close enough, however.

'Mostly, safe,' Peter amended, and she bit her lip.

'I came to apologise.'

'You don't have to.'

She held up a hand. 'Yes. Yes, I think I do. I daresay you see *the Empire's cause* a little differently, and I spoke without thinking.'

He nearly protested again; Elizabeth lifted a hand again.

My mother ... She wasn't a happy person a lot of the time.

'Your mother's people are from here?'

'Yes. Yes, they were, but it seems there's no one left.' Peter braced an arm against the wall. His sigh was heavy. 'Forget what happened. It was an odd day, and I had something else on my mind. I didn't mean to be an ogre.'

He was so near to her. Elizabeth wondered if her face looked as hot as it felt.

'You weren't so very ogre-like. What *was* on your mind?'

He didn't answer for a long time, and then moved away, giving her air, giving her a chance to breathe.

'I want to show you something. You know the area better than I do.'

He drew her further into the room, closer to the light, then took something from beside his pillow. It was then she saw the letter on the chair beside his bed. *Daisy,* it said at the bottom, in large and clear lettering.

Elizabeth discovered she wasn't brave enough to ask about it, and silently reminded herself she'd not seen a single dishonourable facet of this man yet. He was *not* Edward.

Peter came back, looking more hesitant than she'd ever seen him be before.

'Here. This is what I wanted you to see.' He held an old picture out to her, and pointed to a woman in its centre.

'Who is she?' she asked, though she was sure she knew.

'My mother. Charity Rowe—née Towner. I don't know what her family name was before that.' He ran a hand though his hair and looked apologetic. 'I'm trying to discover where it was taken. I thought you might recognise the background.'

He was so hopeful. So optimistic. And Elizabeth had no idea. She was almost desperate enough to make something up, or take a wild guess, but that would only make things worse.

She gave the woman in the centre a closer inspection, and drew a conclusion based on the ladies' outdated fashions.

'This woman? She looks like you.' It was hard to see well in the lamplight, in an image so small, but she believed it to be true.

Peter was unimpressed. 'The poor woman. Do you know where it is?'

She peered harder, wanted badly to help him, but no matter how hard she tried to form the unfamiliar building, and the odd landscape behind it, into a place so that she might know, nothing came to her.

'I'm sorry, Peter, no.'

He sighed.

'It was a long shot.' She wasn't fooled by the false cheer in his voice.

'Peter ... Perhaps if I—'

'No.' One side of his mouth kicked up as he set the picture aside. 'Don't worry about it.'

She wanted to ask him how she was supposed to *not* worry, but he stepped closer and took her upper arm in his hand. She heard her breath catch as he bent, and couldn't stop herself from resting her hand against his solid, warm chest. Elizabeth closed her eyes as she felt the softest, lightest brush of his lips against the top of her hair.

He smelt faintly of cologne she noticed absently as she became aware of his size, of the fact she'd never expected ... *this*. Not with him. Not ever. And definitely not with her brother and Alice, aspiring chaperone, a couple of dozen steps away.

It was hard to speak but if she didn't, Elizabeth was in danger of being overwhelmed. 'We're being pretty naughty, aren't we, sneaking about in the middle of the night?'

She managed to say it in the most appropriate and amenable of voices. She hadn't been a child for a long time, and nobody—not even Robert—could scold her as one, and still...

Peter murmured something noncommittal, and it would have been a good moment to leave the room with her reputation intact. She'd almost found the motivation to do it when his other hand brushed up from her hip to settle on her waist. Elizabeth gasped quietly and he inched closer.

Their toes bumped and she stammered out an awkward little apology. His hand at her waist tightened in reaction.

'People have been naughtier. I'd say we're fine.'

He lowered his head again, resting his cheek against her hair, and they stayed that way for long, comforting seconds. Elizabeth became acutely aware of his warmth, of her heartbeat.

Being like that, so close, what had happened out in the paddock seemed a long time ago.

'I think I might be a little boring—in need of some corrupting,' she admitted.

'Lizzie, if—'

Her head snapped up fast enough she bumped him on the chin. Such grace, such elegance.

'Ow,' he said softly while she stammered out *another* apology.

'Lizzie?'

He grimaced, and then offered her a rueful smile.

'I thought I'd try it at least once. It doesn't really suit you, does it?'

'I'm painfully immune to pet names,' she admitted apologetically. Only Edward had tried before.

They watched each other. Peter's hand flexed once, and his head dipped infinitesimally. This, she thought, was exactly the right moment to be kissed.

Their breaths mingled, and something within Elizabeth swelled and anticipated, and—Peter released her, fast.

'I beg your pardon.'

Confused, a little bit humiliated, Elizabeth stood there uselessly and watched him potter about the room putting the picture back where he'd got it from, and straightening a chair.

The baby saved her from having to say a thing. The wail, the sort that said he was serious, ricocheted towards them, and bounced off the walls of the room.

'I must go,' she said, and barely heard his grunted agreement before she was out his door and across to her own.

She didn't look back—there wasn't the time—before throwing herself into her room, jumping at how loudly the door clicked into place, and thanking God Duncan had been granted such an impressive set of lungs. And then she pressed her back against the cool wood and didn't hear a thing over the pounding in her ears.

Chapter 15

There was heavy rain, and then there was what struck them mid-morning the next day: a deluge that felt like punishment from a higher power. Never before had Elizabeth felt so trapped in the valley.

The animals and grapevines were checked on and worried over, and the roof watched for more leaks. The footpaths surrounding the house became rivers, and everyone was forced to speak at a shout over the relentless drumming of water on the roof.

Elizabeth returned to the linen closet for more sheets to throw over her canvases, and was in the middle of covering one of her more favoured pieces when through the window she saw a hazy figure moving towards the house. The figure slowly formed into the shape of a man, and by the time he was within twenty feet of her he'd assumed the appearance of John Stanford.

'The town road isn't going to last much longer,' he told them all once he was inside and dripping all over the sitting room floor.

'It's that bad?' Robert asked, and serious looks were exchanged.

'I'd say that this far out we'll be fine. The same can't be said for the centre of town.' He grimaced. 'If it goes on much longer the mills will be in trouble. And my house, when it comes to it, but I won't be thinking about that at the moment.'

Alice gave the grey haze outside the sitting room window a disgusted perusal.

'We should've guessed how bad it was when the house started leakin'.'

John's news was ominous, and within minutes most of Endmoor's men were preparing horses and vehicles. If Barracks Flat was to go be submerged, it wouldn't be without a fight. Elizabeth watched Peter stride out to the drive with her brother and John, and she followed Alice outside. They stopped a few paces back from the steps, but still rain misted the fronts of their gowns.

'We should come with you,' she called, and she didn't know which of the men protested first. Perhaps it was all three at the same time.

'You'd better stay here. There ought to be someone at Endmoor just in case.' Peter attempted to sound diplomatic, but she noticed he didn't look at either her or Alice as he said it.

It was then that something clattered to the ground out by the stables. Nobody bothered to look and see what it was; things had been dropping and collapsing for a full day now and they were accustomed to it. The sound reverberated around the clearing and Elizabeth relented.

'Go,' she told the men. 'There isn't time to quarrel about it.'

Mr Adamson and Mr McCoy emerged from the stables, horses ready to go. When Elizabeth turned her attention back to the others she found Peter watching her, and all she could think was of a strong hand at her waist—and that accidental whack on the chin.

'Be careful.' It was not loudly said. She didn't know if he heard her or not.

And, less than a minute later, the men were gone.

***

Stanford hadn't exaggerated. The state the town was in when they dismounted near the park was appalling.

'Damn,' Farrer muttered as they made their way through the surging crowd, down a street that had changed into mud overnight. The Murrumbidgee had already broken its banks. Water seeped up towards them, covering pavements at the southern end.

Peter hopped over a pond-sized puddle. 'I take it you've never seen something quite like it.'

'No. I've not.'

Stanford was called off somewhere and Peter and Robert stopped side by side, taking in the developing crisis. The southern side of town was bearing the brunt of it. Water welled up and over the bank, rising to touch the base of the bridge, and threatening to rise beyond it. The first few streets had already been struck; Peter hoped the houses' foundations were solid or else they'd soon be swimming.

The rest of the residents were lucky nature had provided them with a reasonably steep hill to live on. He saw people across the other side, climbing the slope and congregating at the top, watching hopelessly.

In a display of his infuriating efficiency Stanford was already wading into the fray, up to his knees in water as he lunged to grip the end of a poorly made boat that had somehow crossed the river with its passengers, surviving the powerful pull of the current.

Peter stepped up to help. The family had piled in, and they were bloody lucky they hadn't sunk. Two adults, three children, a dog, and a—*good Christ*, they'd even brought a budgerigar in a small cage.

He hoisted one of the children, a frizzy-haired girl clutching a toy soldier, over to dry land, suppressing a curse when a spiky piece of broken bush got him around the ankle as it swirled past. The adults grabbed their possessions, and Robert saved the cage, and then, freed, the family marched away up the street in a flurry of gratitude, the budgerigar chattering the whole way.

When Peter stepped back the world around him had altered again. He could have sworn the water had been a good yard further off minutes earlier.

A man he'd never before seen appeared beside him and flashed Peter a grin. There was no humour in it.

'And it's only getting goin'. This'll be fun.'

***

At Endmoor buckets were placed anywhere they thought them necessary. When they ran out of buckets, Mrs Adamson allowed them access to the less lovely pieces of china and pottery from the scullery. Elizabeth's mind had been elsewhere the entire time. It was impossible to feel safe in the homestead when Heaven only knew what was happening to the others in town.

And then, once everything had been prepared and checked, and then checked again, the women found themselves standing in the corridor, at a complete loss as to what to do next.

'I suppose we still must eat,' the housekeeper said, and was off to the kitchen.

Alice turned her attention to Elizabeth. 'What d'you think we should do?'

'I wish I knew,' she answered honestly. Some things, she'd begun to discover, were well beyond her control. It wasn't a nice lesson to learn.

'I'm goin' to go mad if the best we can do is stand in the house starin' at the ceilin' and waitin' for another leak to come through.'

But standing and staring was about all they had left to do. There were farmhands to care for the land, and there were servants who'd already—silently—been appalled at the sight of Miss and Mrs Farrer crawling about the house, plugging leaks here and catching drips there.

Alice became ruminative. 'I wonder how high the water will get this time.'

It was always this way: an appalling drought broken so thoroughly nobody was able to cope. Thunder rattled the windows.

'At this rate it will probably turn the park into a lake.' Elizabeth didn't think she was exaggerating.

'And then there's Miss Wright's house right on the river road,' Alice added. 'It's a very nice-lookin' house from the front. It'd be a pity to see it drown.'

'It's a very nice house from the inside, too,' Elizabeth said softly.

They drifted into thoughtful silence. The rain pelted down around them and plates clattered in the kitchen. The men would be in Barracks Flat by now. The last time conditions had been so bad, back when Elizabeth wasn't much more than a girl, the river had come halfway up Monaro Street.

'We can't just sit here while the town drowns.'

'It'd be pretty rude to do so, I reckon.'

Elizabeth plucked a pin from her hair and used it to fasten a stray curl back into place, and then she removed the borrowed apron she wore, folding it and laying it over the back of a chair, wondering how well her boots would stand up to the elements.

Alice followed suit, laying her apron beside Elizabeth's, and then by silent mutual agreement they turned for the hall.

The wind was so bad the front door almost slammed back in their faces when they opened it, but they wrestled it back again. It slammed closed behind them hard enough to make Endmoor's foundations rattle, and it was enough to give Elizabeth a moment's pause.

'Coward,' she whispered.

'Well then,' Alice said. 'Let's go.'

'Can you swim?' Elizabeth asked belatedly as they prepared the old wagon by the stables. She twisted her hair into a more practical style, catching it on something in her haste, and tugging hard in frustration.

'Yes, I can swim. It's the only good thing my no-good brother ever taught me to do.' As they settled into place in the vehicle, she glanced sideways. 'Can you?'

Elizabeth squared her shoulders. 'I think I can float.'

Chapter 16

'Bloody hell,' Alice said once they'd pulled up near the park, climbed down from the wagon, and rounded the corner onto Monaro Street. 'This is worse'n ever before.'

Elizabeth drew up beside her and surveyed the area with cold dread bundling inside her. They'd both lived in the region a long time, and had both seen the Murrumbidgee misbehave, hopeless against the freakish downpours that hit every five or ten years. What they'd never seen before was the town's main street—wide, long, and lined with sturdy buildings—looking like it wouldn't survive the afternoon.

Water edged its way up, heading towards the two of them in murky shades, picking up the foundations of the town as it rose. Already it had come further along the road than Elizabeth could ever remember seeing before.

'It *is* worse,' she said, and then they set off towards the rising water, cloaks pulled tightly around them against the conditions—two small figures going unnoticed in the chaos that unfolded around them.

'I hope Robert and John aren't doin' stupid things today. They'd better be savin' their own lives before anyone else's.' Alice said fiercely.

Their footsteps on the unpaved road sloshed instead of scuffed.

And what about Peter, Elizabeth thought. 'Robert doesn't do stupid things. And he manages John well enough when he must.'

'You reckon they can save those mills?'

'I hope so.' Barracks Flat's livelihood depended on wheat.

They passed the post office to their left, and the Hobsons' shop to their right. Though the flooding hadn't reached them yet, workers from both places were already piling stuffed hessian sacks and anything else they could find to form barricades.

'And what about the fancy houses?'

Martha's family lived near the river's edge, as did anybody in town with the money to build there. All the same, Elizabeth had thought the Wrights would be safe. Their house was up on an obnoxious rise, set back in those grand gardens. But now she'd seen the situation for herself nothing seemed certain.

'Are we just gonna be in the way?' Alice's question echoed Elizabeth's thoughts.

'Perhaps ... But now I've seen how bad it is I think we should try and do something to help.' *Anything* was better than nothing.

They came to a stop beside each other in the middle of the street, in a place that on a normal day would be a gauntlet of carriages and carts and horses.

Alice looked from side to side, her gaze falling—and stopping—on the Hobsons' shop, a place she'd worked years ago, before she'd become a Farrer. They paused to let two burly men pass.

'They're makin' more sandbags.'

Which probably meant they were in danger of running out.

'I think we can help them with that.'

Elizabeth nearly stumbled over her own feet as she took off again; her boots were much more appropriate for respectable outings than for trudging about in the middle of a disaster.

'Do you think we could heft those bags around?' Short of lifting the buildings off their bases and moving them half a mile to the north, there was little else anybody could do to stop the impending disaster.

Alice rubbed her hands together. 'I think we ought to try.'

***

There was only so much a man—or a town of men, women, and half-grown children—could do, but everyone continued working against the inevitable. It ceased to matter who was whom when they formed a chain of sorts to pass sandbags down to battle the worst of the flood. When all the sandbags were used, they passed anything else that might stop the rising waters and not be too terribly missed in the process.

Peter became separated from both Farrer and Stanford early on, and found himself plonked beside a woman more than twice his age and around half his height who stood engulfed up to her knees, with her skirts hitched and knotted in a way that displayed more than he'd warrant she'd ever shown the town before.

A man he didn't recognise unceremoniously passed Peter a sack of potatoes, struggling under the weight of it, with the clear indication he was to pass it on down the haphazard and growing line of people.

Despite the circumstances he hesitated before handing it on to the woman. It was heavy, and she was small, and he didn't want to be responsible for incapacitating one of Barracks Flat's upstanding elderly citizens. Had she not been one of the ladies fawning all over Robert in the churchyard that afternoon weeks earlier?

Where Peter hesitated, the woman did not. With a scoff squarely directed his way, she grabbed the thing out of his hands and passed it on.

'I beg your pardon,' he murmured, and then passed her the next one without question.

And so it went on. Anyone who'd had the idea of sheltering themselves from the elements soon gave up. The endless wind gusts came from the side, flipping umbrellas inside-out, rendering them useless. Even those hiding beneath awnings were blasted with unavoidable sheets of water.

After a solid few minutes of hauling and passing there was a lull as a gap in the chain opened up.

'Hurry up!' A man yelled as he scurried past.

Peter hadn't any idea who the order was directed at. The sense of urgency had infected people to the point they were scurrying around like a group of hyperactive chickens.

'Get a bloody move on!'

And, he decided as common sense began to fray, if they weren't careful soon the lot of them would achieve no more than a flock of poultry could manage in the same conditions. It was only then, as people scrambled and swore and the sense of community harmony began to frazzle into disharmony tinged with desperation, that the old woman beside him spoke.

'Have you ever been out to Bungendore?'

He looked down into her shrewd brown eyes.

'I beg your pardon?'

She tutted at the rising water and hitched her skirts an inch higher. Peter averted his eyes.

'Bungendore,' she repeated, saying it more slowly. Peter bent at the waist to listen more closely, straining to make the foreign name sound familiar in his mind. It was no use.

'I don't think so, no.'

She gave him the sort of frank perusal people in cities usually avoided.

'You might want to visit there sometime soon. I'm Miss Hall,' she continued before he could ask her why in the world he'd *want* to do that.

She held out a hand for him and he shook it before he could think to do otherwise. Her grip was firmer than he'd expected, but then he'd not shaken hands with a woman ever before in his life.

After tutting again, this time at his reticence, she inspected him closely for a second time, grey hair plastered across her forehead and down the sides of her cheeks, and then swatted at the hand of a man of middle years who'd come over, intent on removing her from the chain of workers.

'I'm doing a better job than most of this lot. Leave me be.'

With the man successfully disposed of she looked back at Peter and beamed. It was mildly disturbing.

'Bungendore,' she said for a third time. 'Ask me about it another day, when I'm not up to my knees in this mess.'

Bungendore. Bungendore. Whatever she was trying to tell him, it was another new name to commit to memory.

They both turned at the impatient sound of a sturdy-looking woman who'd appeared beside them, a woman who practically threw a bag their way before running off, head shaking at their slow reaction.

'Don't know what their rush is, honestly. The houses on the other side are already a lost cause, and the Magee mill here's as good as gone. We could stop and chat much longer and it wouldn't make much more difference than the praying those ladies are doing up at St John's right now.'

To illustrate her point, cries rang out then as part of the river walk dropped into the water. It was a shocking sight.

'I've been here since the days of the Clarke brothers and Hall. Villainy everywhere back then. Sometimes it was a bother to share my name with a criminal, but it's a good name. One I'm proud of. He was a relation of mine, you know.'

The woman was jumping all over the place. It was hard to decide if she was dotty or earnest, or a combination of both.

'Who was your relation?'

'Ben Hall, I mean. Have you heard of him?'

'I don't think so, no.'

She handed him another bag that had appeared from the opposite direction. It was only half-filled, and poorly tied in the hurry, and Peter used too much force to haul it down the line, its lightness taking him by surprise.

'Hm. That's a pity.' It was a statement made matter-of-factly, but—as she adjusted her stance, her footing no longer all that steady—it wasn't possible to ignore the fact she'd started to droop with all the exertion.

Peter was about to suggest she go and dry herself and try her hand at prayer with the other ladies, and had opened his mouth to say just that, when he saw Elizabeth.

It couldn't be. He'd left her installed in a mostly dry homestead. Hadn't there been a silent understanding that she'd try to keep herself safe and sensible for the remainder of the day? It was the least she could do after that performance with the ladder the night before.

He squinted. He tried his best to focus on turning the delicate, refined features of the face of the woman halfway up Monaro Street into those of a stranger.

It didn't work.

'Damn...' he breathed. Incredulous, not wanting to believe it, he took a few steps in her direction. The longer he watched her, the more familiar she looked.

It *was* Elizabeth Farrer, of that much he was certain, even though her form kept disappearing behind the rising mist. She stumbled along without paying much attention to her surrounds, attention fixed determinedly on the growing barricade behind him. The bag she dragged was surely too heavy for her, but she didn't once slow her pace.

'Damn,' he said again, and then he was off jogging, wondering how and when she'd got herself out from the estate.

For the love of God, could she at least *once* in her life live up to his expectations of a proper English lady and sit around the house being dainty and appropriate? He reached her at the same time she passed the bag on to the first man in the chain, and then he followed her when she spun around and hurried back up off the street.

'Miss Farrer?' he called, but she was too focused on her self-imposed task to hear.

Peter increased his pace and raised his voice.

'Elizabeth! What in God's name are you doing?'

***

Elizabeth started at the roar of a too-familiar man's voice behind her.

'Oh dear.'

She continued onwards, wishing she might have been able to help a little longer before being caught. She'd done nothing wrong, she reminded herself. The town needed as much help as it could get.

However, when she turned to face the incredulous man bellowing from behind her she found a Peter Rowe unlike she'd ever seen before. Stormy and stern and—for once—not entirely put together. His jacket was long gone and his sleeves were pushed up, the fabric sticking to his skin. The colours of his waistcoat had deepened in the rain.

'What are you doing here?' he asked in a slightly more reasonable voice, like she'd not heard him the first time, and she struggled to form an appropriate explanation.

It wasn't an especially good time for an argument. It took a lot of courage to bend to one of the remaining hessian sacks and begin shovelling again—having a grumbly ogre hovering over her, glowering with disapproval was a bit distracting.

After arriving in Barracks Flat she'd almost immediately become separated from Alice, and she hadn't seen Robert nor John since she arrived. It didn't matter; speed, not camaraderie, was the only thing they needed right then, because—as Alice had said—the flooding was worse than they'd ever seen before.

Nearby several men attacked the dirt with shovels, creating a ditch and guaranteeing the street would be rendered useless to traffic once the storm passed. It was a scene that would have caused outrage all around town on any other day, but there were so few hessian bags left, and they were desperate. A road could be fixed faster than a town rebuilt.

'I'm helping,' she told Peter. 'Short of watching the buckets fill at Endmoor, there wasn't anything useful left to do there.' How could she *not* help? This was her home as surely as it was anybody else's.

'You're helping,' Peter echoed, but instead of scolding her he bent to take hold of the edges of the bag, holding it open for her to scoop the earth into. There'd been a trowel around somewhere a few minutes ago, but it had disappeared somewhere, and so she continued with her bare hands.

'Here,' he said, sounding unhappy but resigned. '*You* hold it, and I'll scoop.'

'No. My hands are filthy already.' And there really wasn't time for a debate.

And so he watched her work, radiating a frustration that was oddly comforting. Elizabeth paused once to give him a companionable nudge with her elbow—it was the cleanest part of her right then.

'It's all right, Mr Rowe. If it wasn't raining quite so much I could almost say I was enjoying myself.'

He grunted. 'I don't suppose you'd be amenable to going inside one of the shops and supervising from there?'

'Ask me again in half an hour, when I'm sodden all the way through.' She suspected her petticoat was still dry enough. 'For the time being the answer is definitely no.'

Not much more was said for the long, precious minutes it took to fill first one bag and then another, and then a third. Peter made a few more grumbling sounds about her hands being ruined, but she continued with her work, scooping and packing until there were no more available bags.

'Carry those two down, and I'll drag the last one.'

He was gone before she finished fumbling with the string to tie the tops.

Inspired by his efficiency, and hopelessly optimistic, she took off, realised she hadn't half his strength, and then instead grabbed her own makeshift sandbag—*earthbag*, she supposed—by the top and dragged it beside her, only crashing into two people on her way.

By the time she reached the other end and handed her sack over to a gentleman she knew by sight but not name, she found Peter off to one side of the street, engaged in a debate with a boy of nine or ten years old.

Chapter 17

'Me dad's got a bundle of money in there.'

The boy, with more carrot-coloured hair than any person could surely require in a lifetime, pointed exactly where Peter dreaded he would: to the slowly collapsing gristmill directly ahead.

There were now two things Peter hadn't expected to come across in town that day. The first had been Elizabeth. And the second, after he hefted the two bags onto the growing makeshift fortress, was a financial crisis.

He searched hopelessly for the father in question, and then—resigned—studied the mill. The current was steadily eating away at everything in its path.

'Is there anybody in there?' Elizabeth asked as she drew up beside them. She released her grasp on the earth-filled sack as a couple of men came to relieve her of it, her eyes fixed on the collapsing building.

The boy shrugged. 'Don't think so. Maybe I oughta climb back in there and see if—'

'No,' she said at the same time Peter did. He reached out and caught the boy's arm before he could trot off to do as he'd suggested. The kid twisted, freeing himself.

'Are you absolutely certain about the money?' It would be just his luck the kid was sending him to a watery end for nothing more than an overactive imagination.

'Of course I am.'

Peter briefly wished he'd chosen to spend the day watching buckets fill at Endmoor.

'All right. Then wait here. Please.'

'But I could—'

'No,' Peter said another time, cutting off the boy's protest, and then closed his eyes for a moment. 'Stay here, and stay back from the water. Please. You too, Miss Farrer. *Please.*'

He started off, but stopped when she called after him.

'Is it safe?' A ridiculous but understandable question. They both knew it wasn't.

He did her the honour of not lying, and instead stepped back close for another moment, eyes focused on hers.

'The structure looks sturdy enough at the moment. I'll be as speedy as I can.'

He might have brushed his hand against hers then, or perhaps he only imagined the contact.

'For the love of God, Elizabeth, whatever you do, don't come climbing in after me.'

'I'll try my best. Don't drown.' It seemed an important caveat, even if it had Peter rolling his eyes.

***

With her boots toeing the edge of the water alongside the boy's, Elizabeth curled her hands into fists as Peter's large form disappeared into the mill. Irritable with worry, she noticed not a single other soul offered their assistance.

The crowd had to keep retreating as the river seeped out in every direction, but Elizabeth held fast as long as she could, until the water bumped against the tips of her boots, and then even after, when her toes were covered by the encroaching sludge. A few people hovered, watching. They'd done about as much as they could—all that was left to do now was hope the sun made an appearance soon.

The boy fidgeted, and she distractedly recalled he was one of the Magee children. The hair was a giveaway. His father's business was—quite literally—going under. Elizabeth tried not to imagine what was happening inside that listing structure.

What was taking so long?

'It's got worse,' the child announced, but even when Elizabeth gave in and edged back a few feet she watched the damaged mill the entire time. Was it only her imagination or was it tilting to the left more than it had a minute earlier? She worried over each creak and groan around her, her head filled with visions of the entire building sinking away.

The boy, still fidgeting, drifted off to share his story with people who'd only then stumbled across the unfolding drama. Elizabeth looked around for Alice but there were too many people about, some still helping, some simply waiting to watch the destruction progress. Her sister-in-law wasn't always the easiest person to find in a crowd.

Wrapping her arms around herself, she watched the building Peter had disappeared into. She was almost silly enough to believe something dreadful would happen if she looked away. It was why she nearly jumped up in the air when a voice spoke from somewhere in the vicinity of her shoulder.

'I'd say someone up there in the sky is pretty cranky with us today.'

'Miss Hall.' She'd not noticed the woman's approach. Elizabeth tore her attention from the mill just long enough to acknowledge the other woman, and strove for a rational tone. 'Wouldn't you be happier out of the rain?'

"Course I would. But nothing much'll get done if we're all cowering in the church like that lot of Auxiliary ladies.' She nodded at the gristmill. 'Looks like the Magees are in a spot of trouble there.'

Elizabeth hugged herself tighter. 'That's one way to describe the situation.'

Something within the building snapped, and her imagination threw up a hundred different possibilities of what was happening inside, each one far worse than the one before.

She dug her fingers into her arms hard enough to hurt.

'The floods've been bad in the past, but at this rate I doubt my family's graves will survive this time. They were already halfway into the river, and that was when the ground was hard, not mud. I hear it's even worse out west than here in town.'

'Who told you that?' The worry that had niggled at her all day began to blossom into something worse.

Miss Hall shrugged. 'People. Glad I was out there to pay respects at Christmas. My Ben and the others buried out there'll be floating halfway down the Murrumbidgee by the end of the day.'

'What makes you think that?'

The older woman gestured at a small horde of people moving in from the opposite end of the settlement.

'If they're coming in from the south, it means the road up the other way is all but gone.'

Elizabeth pressed a hand to her stomach. Miss Hall was right. Scanning the swelling crowd, she searched anxious faces, lingering on the children, looking, looking...

Mrs McCoy was nowhere to be seen. Nor were her children.

'Have you seen Mr McCoy?'

'Who?'

'Harry McCoy? My brother's stockman?'

The woman peered up at Elizabeth through spiky eyelashes. A droplet landed—and stayed—on the tip of her nose.

'Who?' she asked again.

Of all the times for the woman to go dotty...

A shout came from the direction of the collapsing gristmill, and Elizabeth started towards it without thinking. In her distraction she hadn't noticed the appalling new lean the nearest wall had taken on. Good God, that was the part of the building Peter had to climb back out of.

Where was *he?*

'I think I should—' she took another step, and Miss Hall's strong fingers grabbed her in a tight grip.

'I'm thinking you really shouldn't.'

She would have argued the point, but it was that moment a very irate man began blustering in the direction of anyone who would listen.

***

It was impossible.

It didn't take long to ascertain that all the crucial parts of the mill were already inundated, and that the unimportant parts would soon follow. If there had been a small fortune stashed in the building—on that point, Peter was still doubtful—it wasn't retrievable anymore.

There was decent, gentlemanly behaviour, and then there was suicidal behaviour. Peter could have dived into that murky water and tried his best, but there was a woman and a child waiting for him outside, and he'd prefer that the next time they saw him he was alive and relatively intact.

He stepped over an upended chair and then tripped over a sack of flour. A bowler hat floated past in a vision that might have been comical if the hoist hadn't chosen that moment to veer sideways, missing Peter by a fraction of an inch.

Papers drifted past, absolutely ruined. If there was a packet of money amongst them it was too dark and shadowy inside to see it.

There were few benefits to ending one's day squashed beneath heavy equipment. Uttering a couple of choice things better left unheard by others, Peter decided self-preservation was more important than a wild-goose chase.

Navigating his way out wasn't as easy as it should have been, not with the force of the flood rearranging the layout of the mill faster than he could find his bearings.

For one precarious, ridiculous moment he started wading the wrong way, a mistake he only caught when a floorboard underneath his foot sank lower under his weight. The last thing he needed then was to take a jaunt downstream. The mill might be on its way to the ocean, but it would be without him in it.

Backing out of the structure while it was still strong enough to hold his weight, he emerged on the street to the sounds and sights of what could only be described as an argument. Tension was turning people cantankerous.

'It's hopeless,' he called when he found Elizabeth in the crowd, and was on the verge of explaining there were better ways to help than being crushed under a freed pit wheel when movement off to his side grabbed his attention.

'There!' a man shouted, and pointed. 'He's been in there robbin' me. Can't count on everyone in this world to be trustworthy.'

It was the disagreeable man from the bank, the one who hadn't the faintest understanding of interest rates, and as he advanced on Peter then he named a laughable sum of money he claimed to be missing.

'Dad...' the boy—clearly his son—tried to interrupt but was not heard.

Over the years, Peter had learnt restraint. He had had to, in order to preserve his sanity. His father's good reputation helped, as did Peter's solidly British education. And still he had no control over the assumptions of others. The flash of rage at the man's audacity took him by surprise, and he had to fight hard to convert it to something numbing, to hold himself in check before he reacted in a way they'd see as justification for their accusations.

They would *not* have that satisfaction.

From a distance he felt the light pressure of Elizabeth's touch on his arm, gone as soon as it came, and Peter raised his eyes beyond the man in front of him, searching the crowd. Most were making excellent work of pretending they weren't listening.

It was then, in amongst the others, he saw the gardener from the mayor's residence.

Weereewaa...

The other fellow's gaze was steady and meaningful, and then he dipped his head, bent to heft a hessian sack, and was gone.

And the rest of the world came back to him. The growing assembly of onlookers. The drone of accusations.

'*How* many pounds, you claimed? Please,' Peter said, injecting all of the politeness Sydney society had taught him to use into his words, 'that might be a fortune to you, sir, but it's nothing to me. I can't see why I'd bother.'

'Why'd I take a stranger's word?' the man asked. Peter saw, though, that he'd begun reconsidering his accusation in the face of very little support.

'Imagine,' Elizabeth interrupted, 'being foolish enough to accuse the only person who tried to help you.'

'Why're you always causing trouble where there is none, Mr Magee?' That odd little Miss Hall had waded into the fray.

'*No trouble?* Look at my bloody mill!'

'Still not a cause to swear at an old lady. And I'd say that mill's sinking into the river because of shoddy foundations. God's not too pleased with you, sir. I wonder why.'

The man said something vile under his breath and then dismissed the woman with a turn of his shoulder, sending his rage back Peter's way.

Peter stepped closer and lowered his voice. 'Would you have made the same accusation if it had been another man?' The way the fellow's eyes shifted to the side was answer enough.

A few people who'd not been there to see the worst of the argument continued to rush past. The barricade continued to grow. The commotion unfolded around Peter as if he was merely a spectator to someone else's drama.

This was not a first for him, nor—he was sure—would it be a last. However, never before had it been played out so spectacularly, and so melodramatically. The insanity of the accusation was lost in the heat of the anger.

Something cracked and splintered, and an almighty crash came from inside the building.

'Dad, the mill's sunk.' The boy's early concern had transitioned into awe.

Another crack came soon after the first, drawing the curious closer and sending the sensible several steps back. A few men dashed past, shouting orders, doing their best to save the rest of the building.

Peter folded his arms.

'I'd say you might want to help them.'

'Dad,' the eternally ignored boy tried again, 'You'd better do somethin'.'

The man was so far gone in his outrage he was blind to sense, but his son grabbed him then and tugged with more strength than was imaginable in such a bony pair of arms, and it was the thing that snapped his mind back to reality.

'I guess I'd better,' he murmured, eyes on Peter's. 'Excuse me.'

It wasn't an apology, but then Peter didn't expect he'd ever receive one. For the time being, it would have to be enough. It would never be the time for fisticuffs. Much as he might like to, he wouldn't be punching anyone that day.

Realising someone was missing, Peter turned this way and that, searching for Elizabeth and finally finding her off to one side, talking to a woman he recognised from the shop on the main street, and looking mightily alarmed.

***

A new fear gripped Elizabeth as Mrs Hobson passed on the news she'd heard. The road to the McCoy house was impassable, and the family had not been seen all day. She had to go. Immediately. There were enough people in the town's centre to do what needed doing, but none outside it.

Peter caught her arm as she spun, desperate to be off, and released her the moment he had her attention.

'What's happened?'

'I must—I must go. Now.'

'Go where?'

Her mind was already on the task ahead. If the river had risen so much on the outskirts of the township then her chances of following the usual road west were slimming fast. If she didn't go immediately she would have to take the longer way around, and then it might be too late.

The McCoys were not stupid people, and they'd know the land as well as she did—better, even. The problem was the way the river curved. From the viewpoint of their house they'd likely not even know they were in trouble until they were trapped and it was too late.

She had to—

'*Elizabeth*. Tell me what the matter is.'

It was the use of her Christian name that caught her attention and broke her from her frantic thoughts.

She took a deep breath, released it, and then focused.

'Harry McCoy. He's one of the men I saw climbing into that collapsing mill just now. His family lives beyond our estate, and if what we were just told about the newly broken banks is true, then his wife and children are in trouble. Someone has to go and help them, and all those men are occupied.' She could no longer see Mr McCoy at all.

She whirled, searching the heaving mass of townspeople, and then started off through the horde of men hauling bags, old boxes, and anything and everything they could think of to use to build barriers. Peter called her name, but she didn't stop as she continued towards the river, sensing rather than seeing him on her heels.

She scanned the crowd again. Barracks Flat wasn't a big town. Why did it suddenly seem to house the population of London?

'We'll never get to him in this. There's not time to find him. By now—' she broke off when a magnificent shudder took hold of her—her petticoat was soaked now, too—and then she spoke again.

'I could ask Robert, but I haven't seen him since I arrived.'

'So nobody knows anything about the McCoys' predicament?'

'Nobody who'd know the way out to find them. Peter, will you come with me?'

'Why do you even ask?'

He took her arm and set off up the street with enough purpose that Elizabeth didn't even think to waste time questioning what he planned. Instead she went with him, trotting ahead faster and faster as she pictured the landscape between town and the McCoy house, speeding up to the point Peter was forced to lengthen his stride.

'We can take the wagon I came here with Alice in.' Elizabeth didn't need to ask what he was thinking, nor what he was doing. He was aware of the urgency, and he was going to help her, just as she'd known he would. Why *had* she even asked?

'We'll take it as far as we can,' he agreed, and she pointed, directing him to the place they had pulled up not very long ago, near the magistrate's house.

He moved faster then, and she had to double her steps to keep up with him, but the urgency was reassuring. She jogged the last few yards, and accepted his help up.

They were away in moments. As soon as they'd passed Monaro Street the town's roads were completely deserted. The park was abandoned, the small ponds as flooded as everything else, and the church's doors were pulled firmly shut against a miniature waterfall running the length of the stone path.

'What a disaster,' she declared. And Peter urged the horse on with a shake of the reins.

Chapter 18

They'd known that at some point the road out west would become impossible to navigate in the wagon, but discovering it was true, and seeing it with her own eyes, was another matter.

Already, the wheels sloshed rather than rolled.

'I'm sorry,' Peter said, voice a little raised. He drew them to a reluctant but necessary stop and Elizabeth gripped the edge of the vehicle and climbed down. Her boots skidded a little when she landed.

'Half the track has dropped into the river. We'll have to continue on foot.'

'I daresay you're right. Elizabeth ... You don't have to come with me.'

He checked their surroundings as though a magical, cleared pathway might appear, and she extended a hand and tugged when he slipped his into it, pulling him from the seat to his feet.

'I'm not sure standing about here will be any better than walking about down there.'

He was visibly reluctant. 'You could sit under the wagon.'

She didn't immediately realise he was serious, but then he ducked to take a look under its bed, and she had to fight to stop her jaw from dropping. Thunder cracked and the horse stamped. The vehicle swayed half a foot—and sitting beneath it definitely didn't seem like the safest option. Elizabeth decided against honouring the suggestion with a response.

She set off instead. 'We should hurry. The McCoy children are quite young.'

They plodded on, occasionally holding onto each other, and then walking single file when it became too narrow to go on that way. Occasionally one reached back or forwards to touch the other for balance, or in warning of a pesky tree root or poorly placed rock. Elizabeth took an odd step as one of her boot's laces came loose, and wished she'd made a more sensible choice of footwear instead of rushing *quite* so fast out of Endmoor with Alice.

After a while the conditions forced them off the track entirely. Peter stepped to one side, holding back a branch for her to pass.

She dug up a smile from somewhere. 'Thank you. That was very chivalrous.'

'Every now and again I do try my best.'

Moments later a branch further above gave into the weight of the water and dumped the whole lot of it directly onto Peter's head. Elizabeth pressed her lips together—firmly.

'Don't laugh at me.' Peter's voice was a rumble over his shoulder.

'I'm sure that I didn't. I am glad, though, you chose that instant to step in front of me. You probably wish you still had your hat...'

Despite her teasing he was kind enough to hold another branch back for her, and Elizabeth murmured her gratitude.

'I don't suppose you expected any of this when my brother wired your firm back in August. I'm sure this nonsense wasn't in your employment agreement.'

'Not precisely, no.'

'It bothered you, didn't it? The way that mill owner spoke to you.'

'Yes.'

She took his hand when he reached back for hers and then moved up beside him when the path widened enough to allow it.

'Does it happen often?'

His fingers flexed. 'It happens sometimes. I suppose everyone's definition of *often* is different.'

They reached the clearing sooner than Elizabeth expected; the world had changed so swiftly overnight she hardly recognised the place anymore. Everything had altered. Had she not seen the oddly shaped and now overflowing pond, with the antiquated graves beyond it, she'd have struggled to believe she'd ever been to this part of the valley. Soon—very soon—the pond would join up with the Murrumbidgee, and then they'd be swimming.

One of the headstones hung precariously at the edge of the grass, the angle defying gravity. It'd not be there much longer.

'Miss Hall was right.' Elizabeth wished it wasn't the case. Silly stories about ghosts rising from the river's edge, the tales she, Robert and their friends had spooked themselves with when they were younger, looked likely to come true.

'I beg your pardon?' Peter came to a stop and put his hands on his hips, orienting himself.

'Nothing—it doesn't matter. I didn't know it was possible for this to happen so fast,' Elizabeth whispered, the wind stealing her words before they could reach her own ears. Peter hadn't a hope of hearing her.

They kept going. There was no sign of the McCoy family; there was hardly a sign of the track they needed to take to reach their property.

'We should find higher ground,' she said more loudly, and thought he made a sound of agreement. She might have said more, but Peter stopped then, so fast she whacked into his tense body. It did not take long to understand what he'd seen.

Mrs McCoy and her two children came into view, and Elizabeth gasped as the reality of the situation struck her.

'Oh no,' Peter said.

The people they'd come to find weren't trapped on the wrong side of the flood. They were trapped *in* it.

The little boat Moira McCoy and her two children travelled in would have been perfectly serviceable on a normal day. Now, though, it connected with something hidden beneath the surface and tipped dangerously.

***

If her sound of dismay was anything to go by, Elizabeth saw the McCoys right after Peter did. They were in a lot more trouble than he'd prepared himself to deal with on the trip out, and that was saying something after what he'd seen in town.

The family was impossible to miss, a trio in a boat that would have survived a regular journey, but now rocked and tipped and spun in a swell, bouncing off the bank and spinning halfway around again.

A dropped paddle bobbed just out of reach. Grabbing the side of the boat, Mrs McCoy stretched an arm out for it. Everyone tipped wildly and the children shrieked as they struggled to steady themselves again.

'Come on,' Peter said to Elizabeth, grim. He didn't have a plan, but if they didn't get there soon and try something, the boat would capsize and probably take the two children with it.

They rushed to the ridge. Elizabeth drew up beside him and gasped again as the boy made a grab for a low tree branch, nearly launching himself into the water in the process.

'What can we do?'

An excellent question. If the family drifted closer Peter might be able to reach out and grab them, but the incline was so steep he wasn't confident about it.

'Stay back.' He threw himself down onto his belly, gripping at the vegetation for support, and reached as the boat completed a full pirouette, spinning them closer to the bank another time.

'Moira!' Elizabeth yelled, and the woman whipped around, hair in her eyes, hands gripping either side of the boat as it wobbled this way and that. She was astonished to see them.

The children, a half-grown boy and a younger girl, gripped the one remaining paddle, waving the thing uselessly between them, risking clobbering their mother over the head with it in their panic.

A wooden plank, freed from some unseen structure upstream, sailed past then, clipping the side of the boat at a convenient angle, slowly knocking it in Peter's direction with its strength.

'Perfect,' he muttered, and braced himself as they neared.

The woman reached. Peter reached. The current finally decided to behave.

It nearly worked.

And then one of the children moved too suddenly in their desperation, unbalancing the lot of them. Just as Mrs McCoy's fingers brushed Peter's, gravity took over and she toppled directly into the river.

***

Various people screamed. Elizabeth might have been one of them.

She lurched further down the track, anticipating the boat's progress. She had to do something—she didn't yet know what—but the sight of those children caught in the swirl, alone now and still waving that paddle about...

Despite some atrocious judgement trying to cross the Murrumbidgee that day, Mrs McCoy was not stupid, and with grim determination on her face she kicked out and lurched in Peter's direction. She grabbed his hand and fought her way up, shouting instructions to her panicked children along the way.

The stray paddle that had been circling in the swell came up against her side of the slope, was immediately drawn back out, and then was drawn back her way again.

Elizabeth had half a second—less—to choose the sturdiest hanging tree branch, and hoped against hope she'd more strength than she thought as she braced her bare feet on the slope and swung outwards, stretching an arm in either direction until they hurt. The lace of her boot chose that moment to snap completely, and she nearly fell with the surprise of it.

The ends of her fingers made contact with the paddle, but then the blasted thing slipped away.

'Good God.' She stretched further, feeling that any moment something important would pop out of a socket.

God must have been listening then because a miracle struck and she grabbed the paddle on the second try. Praying for extra strength, she angled it towards the boat until the boy clutched it in both hands.

Little David's knuckles whitened with the effort as his sister wrapped one arm around his waist and grabbed the side of the boat in the other.

Somehow, and Elizabeth would never remember exactly, it worked. The connection anchored them enough that when the boat came up against the bank a second time they were able to scramble out of it, sloshing through the shallower water at the river's edge.

Fiona, the little girl, dragged Elizabeth into an embrace tight enough to cause a serious injury. 'Thank you.'

In the next instant Moira McCoy was there, face grim, hair limp, most of it now hanging down her back. She took Elizabeth's hands in a fierce, determined grip.

'My da,' the other woman said, gasping, as she struggled out of her panic. As she spoke she simultaneously gripped her children in a hold strong enough to raise matching complaints, and twisted enough to look up at what remained of the trail to her father's house. There was little time left for them to reach the place before the entire clearing would be immersed.

'Go,' Elizabeth said and, with a final whisper of gratitude, Moira shoved the children in front of her, son and daughter alternating between tears and hysterical, excited conversation as they disappeared into the trees.

They'd done it. Relieved, she took a step back, rocked sideways on her ankle, and—tutting—knelt in the muck. Her dress was as good as ruined anyway. Her troublesome boot was tossed aside, and after less than a moment's thought—and because it seemed she ought to have some dignity and symmetry—she quickly discarded its partner.

Freed, she looped the laces around her hand and stood, the boots thumping against the side of her leg.

Mud and twigs and sodden grass felt disgusting beneath her toes, but it was hardly the most pressing concern right then. The trip back to the wagon would be an ordeal but she'd not ask Peter to carry her; the man was so honourable he'd probably do it, and likely expire from the effort in the process.

Only then did Elizabeth become aware of the stranger up ahead, making steady progress along the higher, drier, part of the track. He led a pony and gig slowly towards them as if the drama he had to have seen was nothing more than a humdrum pantomime.

She hadn't the chance to make out his features before, at a snap of a splintering tree, she swivelled. The now-empty boat tangled with the fast-moving debris was pulled along by the river's increasing speed, and then vanished beneath the straining branches of a crooked tree some twenty yards downstream.

'Good afternoon.'

Startled by the nearness of the voice, Elizabeth swung her gaze around to the strange man with the gig, narrowing her eyes until she realised he wasn't quite so strange after all. Mr Towner had neither died nor disappeared from the valley as she'd suspected, and had chosen to grace them with his presence several minutes too late to be of use.

'Good afternoon,' she echoed, nonplussed. What an inappropriate sentiment it was to apply to the day. Something revolting squished between her toes where she stood.

'Elizabeth!' She whirled at Peter's shout, and with her attention captured, he raised a hand in a gesture that was clearly meant to be an order.

He probably thought she was in danger, but she didn't think she was. Not from a crotchety old fellow who'd never made the effort to pose a danger before.

Smiling her reassurance, she took a couple of steps towards him, about to explain that there was no danger in having Mr Towner about—well, not much, anyway—and there was no warning of the trouble she was in, no sign whatsoever.

It was then the ground under her shifted, a whole chunk of the land collapsing, and taking her with it.

Chapter 19

Peter was some ten yards from Elizabeth when the inevitable happened and her footing was lost to the power of the flood.

'Christ.'

He broke into a run, but it was far too late. By the time he reached the spot she'd been standing on she was long gone into the water. His hand, extended to grab at any part of her before the bank gave way completely, grasped only air. And then he was clinging to the branch of a weeping willow, digging his heels into the mud in order to stop himself tumbling in after her.

'Elizabeth!' he called uselessly, and stumbled back another step when more of the land beneath him shifted. He was a decent swimmer, but if they both got trapped in the pandemonium...

He could only watch as, mostly submerged, she kicked and reached for an exposed tree root—for a fraction of a second it seemed like she'd latched onto it. But the water's force threw her back against the dirt, her swirling skirts fanning out across the surface.

And then her bare hand emerged as she flailed again, and then she was off with the current. He lost sight of her for a moment and swore viciously.

'Damn,' he said, and took off along the overgrown path, tearing through the tangle of long grasses, low bushes, and sagging, rain-laden branches, his clothes catching here and there, his bare hands and forearms scraping against wayward twigs and prickles.

Again, she emerged, and was swept up against the compacted dirt. Again, she stretched a hand out for a grip on one of the trees. And again she was dragged back before she could manage it. Her head was still above the water, the momentum of its pull so fast that it'd not yet dragged her down.

Peter edged alongside her, struggling to move as fast as she was when the ground sagged and slipped under each step he took.

He caught sight of her every so often as he raced to outrun the Murrumbidgee's speed, every effort hampered by yet another obstacle nature threw in his way. For a few heart-stopping seconds Elizabeth, her dress billowing around her, finally managed to grip a branch that drooped into the water but the current took her away again—and part of the branch with her.

The scrub in front of Peter disappeared and at last he could run ahead to the river's curve where she'd next appear. *He hoped.* He was so focused on Elizabeth that it took several seconds to realise someone else was shouting his name.

'Here.' Vernon Towner shoved a coil of rope in Peter's face. Its other end was secured around the trunk of a solid gum tree up ahead. 'Me aim's not the best anymore. You'd better bloody do it on the first try.'

The next instant Elizabeth came around the bend and he shouted her name as loudly as he could—twice. She was paddling, completely helpless to stop the river's pull, but still with enough strength and sense to keep herself upright and to turn partway around once his second shout registered.

Knowing he'd only have that one chance, Peter tossed the rope so it uncoiled in an arc, praying he'd judged the timing and the conditions properly.

Elizabeth came past and he was sure he saw her take hold of it. And yet she continued to drift downstream.

As she continued along, away from him, Peter's mind filled with images too horrific to contemplate. He was about to jump in after her when there was sudden tension on the rope and Elizabeth jerked to a stop midstream.

'Hold it!' Peter shouted, digging his feet in and struggling for traction on the slippery ground. 'Wrap it around your arms and don't let go!'

She tried to do as he ordered but was hampered by dangerously large pieces of debris coming at her—leafy branches, sharp sticks. An entire bloody log.

'Help me,' he ordered the old man, not knowing what more could be done. He couldn't drag her in if she was only to lose her grip the moment he started pulling, but her strength wouldn't last forever.

Elizabeth struggled, and kicked upwards to avoid gulping down the muddy, murky water as she called to him.

'Just do it!' The wind and the constant drum of the downpour nearly carried her shouted words away. He had no choice but to trust her, and so he did.

Peter was vaguely aware of Towner swinging himself partway down the bank, gripping at branches that'd looked like they'd break any moment.

Nature decided to behave at last. Nothing gave way, and the other man somehow didn't fall in, defying every assumption Peter made. The man managed to keep his grip and his balance while extending a hand to Elizabeth, hauling her a couple of feet up the slope when she was free enough of the current to find her footing.

'Keep holding the rope!' Peter shouted, and then dropped to the ground, scrambling along and downwards until he lay on his belly in the carpet of fallen needles and leaves, reaching for her as she dragged herself upwards.

She was a foot from him when he stretched out further, finally—*finally*—managing to clasp his hand. The angle was awkward, and it was a struggle, but he hoisted her upwards while she dug her feet into the bank.

And then she was up and over the rise, falling half across him as she landed on safe ground, both of them panting with the effort and the shock.

She shivered as Peter wrapped his arms around her and squeezed too hard. He couldn't stop himself. She pressed her face into the crook of his neck and gasped a few times, staying there with her hair in disarray across his face, and his chest, until the worst of her trembling faded.

And then she was pressing upwards, forcing him to loosen his hold on her as she sat back and tried her best to put herself to rights with unsteady hands. Peter reached across and took a clump of her skirt in his fist.

'Bit of an adventure, hey?' Vernon Towner had used the rope to manoeuvre himself back over the ledge, and now held it in both hands, giving it a good inspection.

'Nice to see it's robust. How're you, Miss Farrer?' He went to the tree and began undoing the knot.

'I'm all right.' She wasn't, but nobody called her out on it.

'Good to know. At least the weather's easin'.'

It was a spectacularly optimistic take on the situation, but it surprised Elizabeth into laughter as she gathered a section of her skirt and wrung it out.

'I'm not being hysterical, if you're worried.' She sounded matter-of-fact and very much herself, but when Peter sat up, bringing himself closer to her, he saw the tremors still running through her hands.

'Maybe I'm just a little hysterical,' she admitted in a whisper.

'It'll be a nice day for travellin' tomorrow. You wait and see.' Towner coiled the rope again, watching it with the sort of affection normal people reserved for their children.

Enough fear had left Peter and enough sense returned for him to take in the particulars of the situation that he'd not before. He eyed the gum tree by the ridge, thinking it was owed a plaque for its help.

'What was the rope for?'

Towner shrugged. 'I was plannin' on crossing by boat—the thing's long gone in the flood, just like the nearest bridge—but didn't fancy attemptin' it without the extra security. Of course, that was before it got as bad as this. It came racin' across the valley faster than I've ever seen before.'

Peter got to his feet and leaned down to tug Elizabeth up too. Despite her best efforts to stand on her own—namely, tugging away from the grip he had on her arm and uttering something about how *fine* she was—those waterlogged skirts looked heavy. He found he wasn't ready to trust her word just yet.

There was no hope of a return to town, not the way they'd come. Though he could just make out a church spire through the mist and the rain—Barracks Flat was very close, just on the other side of the trees—the danger was too great to even attempt it.

They'd have to take the long way around and return to Endmoor instead. It would be a long, uncomfortable journey, but by far the safest option.

'Do you know whose gig that is?' he asked her in an undertone. In their present state a walk all the way to the wagon was out of the equation.

She shook her head, and he raised his voice to ask the same question of the other man, the one who was presently averting his eyes and looking not at all like an innocent man.

Towner man appeared bewildered by the question.

'I've no idea. The animal's mine. Well, as good as mine, seein' the way her owner neglects her. The gig ... well, I think I'd better not tell you about that. I'll be needin' them both in the mornin', but I'll loan them to you overnight.'

He studied them with too-shrewd eyes. 'Unless Miss Farrer 'ere needs a ride the long way round into town.'

Peter nearly answered for her, but Elizabeth straightened and proved she was stronger than he'd have given her credit for.

'Thank you, but no. I think I'd like to go home. If you meant it, we'll borrow that borrowed gig. And thank you for the use of your rope.'

He liked that response, old Towner. Respect glinted in his eyes.

They started towards the vehicle, Peter with a hand at the back of her saturated dress. Elizabeth had just climbed up when the rough rumble of the man's voice reached them again. Peter heard his name and turned back.

'Where'll I find me horse in the mornin'?'

Peter pointed to the sorry little road up ahead. 'We're going that way. Towards your old cottage.'

That caught his interest. 'Still standin', is it?'

'It is. I've been there a time or two.'

'Hm. I haven't bothered with the place in years. Don't like the memories. Too many people gone from there, but they always leave the bloody memories behind.'

The rain eased just a little bit more, and Peter considered how much of this man's loneliness was self-imposed. He supposed he'd never know.

'And now you're going, too.'

'It's well past time for me to be off from this valley. *Well* past.'

'Thank you for everything.' It had to be said at least once before he left, and Peter thought the fellow seemed amenable enough to the gratitude. He'd just set off towards Elizabeth when his name was called again.

'The house is yours if you like. Way it's going, you'll be the only one left who'd want it.'

***

'I think I can float.'

Thinking back, Elizabeth decided—as she rocked and shook along with the gig, shivering each time her sodden hair deposited another droplet down the neck of her equally sodden dress—she might have overestimated her talents.

She thought Peter was worried about her, which in turn made her think she should be worried about herself. Why she was reacting to her near-death as though she hadn't done anything more exciting than taken a stroll around Alice's rose garden was beyond her.

Perhaps later the surprise of it would strike her. For the time being, she was happy enough to be numb. Now, if only Peter would stop worrying so much.

'I'm really fine.'

'Yes, you said so.'

It wasn't the first time she'd told him, and it wasn't the first time he hadn't believed her. She needed to distract him, but was having trouble keeping her thoughts in order.

'Who is old Mr Towner to you?' she finally asked, and judging by the change in his posture it did the trick.

'He's my grandfather.' The answer was given flatly, but Elizabeth was not fooled.

She spun back towards him. 'Your grandfather? Why have you not mentioned him before?'

He pressed his lips together as he thought. Elizabeth watched a raindrop track a path down his cheek, catching briefly in the stubble of his tense jaw before continuing on.

'I only met him in recent weeks. And I've hardly exchanged more words with him than we had this afternoon.'

'Oh.' How strange that she'd seen the man in question coming and going from Endmoor most of her life. What a pity Peter had never come to the tablelands sooner.

Peter chuckled. 'If only Daisy could see me now, building barriers and tossing ropes in rivers. I wonder if she'd congratulate me or laugh hysterically.'

He loosened the reins when it became clear the pony would go wherever she wanted at whatever pace she chose, and Elizabeth tried to ignore the icy sensation washing over her.

Apparently oblivious to the change in her mood, he chuckled again quietly. 'She'd probably do both.'

'Who's Daisy?' She had to ask. Either way, she had to know.

'My sister. With the people closest to her she prefers it to her first name.'

He looked at her and his inattention had not even the slightest effect on the pony's direction.

'My mother named her after an aunt Edith Daisy'd rather not be associated with.'

'Ah.' Elizabeth leaned her head against his arm. Considering the conditions, it was not comfortable, but she had to touch him somehow. When they went over an unexpectedly large bump, causing her forehead to connect with the pointiest part of his shoulder, she drew back.

'You'd like her. She'd like you,' he finally added, eyes on the nodding head of the animal.

Elizabeth gave his arm a squeeze and then released him to take in the valley from this new aspect. The shakes came in earnest then, and she decided she'd been a little premature in declaring herself well.

'It's really cold today, isn't it?' It felt like winter, not midsummer. Shivers she hadn't a hope of hiding from him coursed through her, and the harder she tried to stop them, the more ferociously they fought their way out.

Peter took her condition in with a swift glance. When the road smoothed enough to allow it, he reached across to grip her hand, each squeeze of reassurance bringing her back from a precipice she hardly understood.

Eventually, as they rocked and rolled along, the worst of it receded.

'I'm really all right now,' she decided, though she'd like to be indoors somewhere sooner rather than later. They were crawling along at the laziest pace imaginable. Had she any shoes available, Elizabeth would have suggested they walk the rest of the way to wherever it was they were going.

The trail forked and Peter didn't hesitate as he took her left along a road she knew of but had never travelled down, navigating the route with the expertise of a man who'd been there a time or two before. The entire landscape was covered with a scattering of fallen foliage, the ruts in the dirt brimming with water.

'We spend so long wishing for rain, and then this happens and I can't remember why that was,' Elizabeth said, giving their surroundings an offended look. She was on the verge of showing *exactly* how miserable and cross she was, but it would be disingenuous to do so with the man who'd slid halfway down a muddy incline in order to retrieve her from the brink of certain death.

He adjusted his hold on the reins and then pressed against her with his arm. The pony snorted in what Elizabeth chose to believe was agreement, and plodded on in its slightly jerky gait.

'It will be good for the drought. We were running a little low on water,' Peter said when he straightened again.

'The land needed to be watered, not *drowned.* The next time anyone in church thinks to ask for rain, I'm going to have someone in the legal profession look at the wording of their prayers first. We'll all have to be more specific.'

She looked up to the Heavens and earned one big droplet directly in her eye for her efforts.

And then, just as everything seemed to be working out better than expected, they reached the top of a knoll and found the road flooded badly enough it wouldn't be safe or sane to attempt to pass. Peter drew the vehicle to a stop.

'Oh,' she said, soaked and miserable, but she tried to rally. 'Perhaps we should try and return to town.'

Town was a long journey back the way they'd come, and now they were so close to home it was the last thing she wanted to attempt. Yes, the worst of the storm had blown off in the direction of the mountains, and the clouds above them were definitely lighter than they'd been an hour ago, but *honestly...*

'Don't worry yet,' he told her. 'See that mark there, running along the embankment? It's already begun to recede.'

He was right. A line of debris formed a stripe across the top of the bank, higher up than the level of the water. Having done its damage, the Murrumbidgee had finally decided to behave.

'I suppose that's something to be thankful for.'

'Oh, good,' Peter said then, perking up and looking happier than he ought to. She glanced askew to see what precisely was *good* about any aspect of their situation. Raindrops dripped off the ends of his dark hair as he pointed to a place off to the side, and it was only then that she saw the hut nestled in a small clearing amongst the eucalyptus trees.

He turned them down the old, overgrown road that led to the place, drawing them to a stop right at the door.

'Go inside while I take care of the animal. The place shouldn't be locked, and I shan't be long.'

'Are you certain?' she asked, and the question earned her a knowing smile—Elizabeth felt justified in her suspicion.

'Trust me.'

She supposed she'd have to. As soon as she'd hopped down from the gig, one of his hands steadying her descent, he was gone off to do as he said.

Elizabeth stepped up to the door, wondered if she should knock, and felt distinctly like an intruder. With one glance back over her shoulder to see Peter leading the pony and vehicle towards a crooked old shed, she rapped once on the door in warning and then let herself in. There was, after all, only so much time a woman could spend out in the rain.

She knew immediately the place was unoccupied but hadn't been left to rot, unloved, as so many others in the region had been since bushrangers were driven out. More prosperous residents chose larger, newer, and more comfortable residences close to town. In this empty place there was really only one room, though someone had constructed half a wall between the bed and the door to provide a modicum of privacy.

Elizabeth relaxed with relief to see the place wasn't the dangerously rundown hovel she'd suspected it would be. *Trust me...*

She hadn't brought gloves with her when she'd set out, she had no hat, and by then her boots had spent so long marinating in the mud she assumed they were beyond saving. It all left her feeling exposed in a way she'd never been before, but they were well past the point of decorum—she and Peter, surely. There'd not been much time to worry about manners or humiliation when they'd been fighting against the river's currents, skirts swirling and arms and legs akimbo.

Now, though, in the loud silence of an empty hut and surrounded by a downpour to raise the dead, things felt different.

She rushed to remove her stockings, and then looked at them bunched in her hands for a moment, horrendously self-conscious. What should she do with them? Hide them? Burn them? She bunched them more tightly and stuffed them under the table, sending an apology out to whomever would discover the things in the future.

When Peter returned a few minutes later, arms loaded, he took note of her studying the sparse decorations on the wall as he struggled through the doorway, bumping against the musty collection of papers and books. Elizabeth turned her attention his way. Her eyes fixed on the pile of firewood he'd produced from Heaven only knew where, and he grinned at the disbelief on her face.

'It's dry,' he assured her. 'Mostly. I'll get the fire going and then you can show your profound gratitude for my ability to plan ahead.'

He again asked if she was all right; she again said she was. It still wasn't quite true, but she felt a lot better now there was a roof above them. Peter brushed vigorously at the debris clinging to his waistcoat and it suddenly seemed uproariously funny he still wore it. Elizabeth pressed her hand to her mouth—hard.

He glanced back at her and then knelt on the ground, going about the business of starting the fire.

'Whose house is this?' She'd never even known it was there.

'Now? Nobody's. Well ... that's not quite true. It's quite likely it's mine. It was just given to me, more or less. My grandparents lived here once, and possibly my mother, too, for a time.'

Gradually, the details of the place began to seep into her consciousness. The nicks in the wood of the walls. The scent of timber, stronger than usual that day, she was sure. The careless stitching of the sampler on the wall.

'I'd hoped...' Peter turned rueful. 'I suppose I hoped I'd come here one day and find all the answers to questions I've had for years. It was a bit silly of me.'

Elizabeth tried to sound positive.

'You have your grandfather now.'

Ruefulness turned to exasperation. The kindling was already half gone and Peter added a log to the fire.

'Such as he is.'

'Such as he is,' she agreed faintly. The walls seemed to be closing in around them, pulling them nearer to each other in increments.

A tiny part of her anxiety melted away. She blamed it on the casual way he went about his work. He appeared so relaxed there, crouched on the earthy floor, more handsome in his dishevelment than she was, and had she not felt like a drowned rat right then she might have enjoyed the situation.

Against all odds he built a snapping, sparking fire and then rose, eyes drifting to a place somewhere behind her. Elizabeth returned her attention to the sampler, reaching out cautiously, using a gentle touch to shift it into alignment. It would not stay as she put it.

'It's no use. Nothing in this little house will behave as it should. Believe me, I've tried to straighten the thing in the past, but the whole building is on such a lean. Believe me,' he assured her a second time as she gave it another try for good measure.

She didn't dare touch the sampler again; the thing was likely to drop right off its nail. Instead, she leaned closer, making out the initials sewn into the corner, jagged and lopsided as they were.

'C.T.?' she asked, but didn't immediately receive a response. The firelight danced around them.

'My mother's name was Charity. Such a good *Christian* name.'

'It stands for Charity Towner?'

'It's only a guess. I doubt I'll ever know for certain.'

'I'm sorry.'

'You've nothing to apologise for.' He hands went to the fastenings of his waistcoat, his movements precise.

He continued to undress, apparently too distracted to realise how inappropriate it was. Elizabeth wondered if she should remind him where he was and whom he was with, but that naughty side of herself she had only just discovered kept her quiet. *Soon*—soon she'd stop him.

Maybe...

Elizabeth forced herself to stop watching, eyes drifting to the table, to the fire, and then back to the embroidered lettering. And then, somehow and despite her better judgement, her eyes drifted back to Peter.

'It seems the person who stitched it didn't seem especially pleased about the task.'

'And if there's one clue that piece is my mother's, I remember she always did hate to sew.'

He was out of the garment now, and she watched him move a chair closer to the hearth and spread the waistcoat out over the back of it. His hands had reached the hem of his shirt when he finally caught himself and froze. Wide eyes snapped to her and he stammered, clearly mortified.

'I apologise. I wasn't thinking. I'll just—' he reached for the waistcoat again, and she stepped up and reached out a hand to stop him.

His eyes were very, very dark as they met hers. Luminous, too, somehow.

Even though she trembled, Elizabeth forced lightness into her tone.

'You might as well leave it off. If it's woollen it'll be hopelessly waterlogged now.'

He watched her in a way she didn't know if she trusted. Elizabeth fiddled with the mess of her hair, and noticed his attention shift. More self-conscious than before, she scrambled for a more suitable topic, thoughts drifting back across their extraordinary afternoon and settling back in the town.

'In a way it's a good thing we're so isolated. There are a few people in town who'd be more than mortified to find us like this.'

It was true. If they were to have the respect of the sticklers of Barracks Flat society they'd be expected to tackle that flooded road back to Endmoor—fully dressed—and die trying.

'Not all of them, though. Miss Hall, for example. That little woman,' Elizabeth demonstrated with her hands. 'She'd congratulate us for our common sense.'

'I take it she isn't really a relation of *the* Ben Hall, the bushranger.'

'It's a story she loves to tease people with, but no. Everyone humours her but we all know it's just a fantasy on her part.'

Peter took up the rusted poker from the side of the hearth and gave the fire a few unnecessary stabs.

'She mentioned a place to me. *Bungendore,*' he offered, sounding the word out carefully. 'Why would she do that?'

'People—your people—have moved further and further out over the years. Perhaps some of them are out that way,' Elizabeth replied quietly, mesmerised by the collection of colours in the embers. He murmured something unintelligible in response.

'I wonder why she does it. Talks of bushrangers, I mean.'

Oh, he had to ask *that*. Elizabeth took a breath and made herself face him directly.

'I'm told that decades ago she took a fancy to a Ngunnawal man from around here. He'd been given the name *Hall* by the missionaries; I've no idea what it was before that.'

'A Ngunnawal man?' Peter reacted to that as though the words were a physical force.

Elizabeth took the poker from him and gave the log a good prod. The metal wobbled in her hand, the handle was loosened from years of use and neglect. The fire did not react well to her abuse; sparks flew up as the log rolled over, glowing.

'Yes, that's what I've been told. I've heard nobody was especially happy about it.' It was something she didn't want to share. Not then, and not with *him*.

'And what became of that fancy of hers?' he asked evenly, after a significant pause.

'By the time the infamous, other Ben Hall was bailing up hotels and raiding towns, Ada's—Miss Hall's—Ben had succumbed to smallpox. He died before he could leave for the north with the rest of his people.'

'Why does she use his name?'

Elizabeth took her time returning the poker to its spot. She didn't want to share the rest of it.

'I suppose it was the closest she could come to being his wife.'

Above them the sky dumped such a huge load of water on the roof it nearly rattled the walls. They both looked up at the ceiling, anticipating the inevitable, but it never came.

'I can't believe nothing has leaked yet.'

Peter made a sound of agreement. 'I'm pretty surprised about that myself.'

A remnant of a shiver struck her then. Peter noticed and knelt to add another log, momentarily breaking whatever odd sensation was passing between them.

'Here, come closer.' He grunted his approval as she did. 'There's nothing dry here for you to dress in, but at least stand over here by the fire.'

She stepped in a puddle as soon as she moved.

'My clothes are dripping everywhere.'

The flames cast shadows across his face as he studied her. 'So they are.'

Something about it all felt inevitable. The timing was dreadful, but a lot of things were dreadful right then. She couldn't control the weather, but there was one thing she could decide for herself.

'Peter.' She bit her lip. He'd either say yes or no.

'Yes?'

She couldn't believe her boldness, and she rehearsed the line twice in her head before she managed to voice it.

'Will you help me out of this gown?'

Chapter 20

'I'm not sure you want me to do that.'

It had been over Christmastime that Peter admitted to himself whatever had been growing between the two of them was more than friendship. And it had been upon his return to the countryside that he'd decided it was best ignored.

Ignorance was easier, however, when the other person involved wasn't standing there asking him to strip her. It might have been a good time to ask if she'd hit her head in the past hour, if she was in her right mind, but there wasn't a way to do so without causing enormous offence.

There she stood, looking hopeful—and *sane*—wide eyes fixed on him, as if her request was normal. *Good God.*

Hadn't she *any* idea what images she'd just put in his head?

Did she have *any* recollection of what she'd already been through that day?

He took too long to respond.

'Shocking of me to ask, wasn't it?' Her bravery faltered and then collapsed entirely; she focused determinedly back on the fire. Whatever mad bout of bravery had driven her to ask in the first place dissipated, and Peter hated himself for being the cause of her humiliation.

He felt pained. 'What if you spend a few minutes drying out the front of your gown and then turn and dry the back?'

As plans went, it was a pretty stupid one, but what in the world did she think was going to happen if that dress came off? He thought she'd spent the summer months reading scandalous books. Had she no idea?

Elizabeth shook her head and dripped more of the Murrumbidgee onto the floor.

'I'm not a rotisserie. And I'm quite serious that I'd rather not spend the next few hours wearing this.' She looked so earnest, and so oblivious. It was dark in the little house, and when she found the courage to look at him again, her eyes were a deeper shade of brown.

Peter silently admitted he'd known how the two of them would end up from the moment they saw the road home was still unpassable. He could—and should—have let his grandfather return her to town instead, no matter how long it took. Vernon Towner might have a passion for shifty behaviour when it came to things of the four-legged or two-wheeled variety, but an instinct told Peter he could trust the man with Elizabeth.

The fire snapped and sizzled as stray raindrops worked their way into the crooked chimney. Its poor construction meant the cottage filled with more smoke than it should, and that the two of them would probably return to the homestead sporting an unfortunate reek.

He knew they could sit and wait for the storm to lose its power in companionable, well-behaved silence. He also knew he was lying to himself.

'Think about what you're asking. Please.'

She made a sound that matched the frustration on her face.

'I feel so ignorant sometimes, about things other women my age know. Other times I feel like a child. I don't want to be that woman anymore, Mr Rowe, and I think that if you weren't so determined to be chivalrous you'd admit *you* don't want me to be, either.'

Noticing details others might overlook was a characteristic of an artist, he supposed, but for once he wished she was less observant.

She smiled a little. 'Don't suggest I'm not in my right mind. I'm cold and a little grimy, which I'm quite sure is to be expected under the circumstances, but that near disaster back at the river made things clearer for me.'

Near disaster wasn't what Peter would have called it.

'Elizabeth ... are you sure?' he asked and she nodded, not looking away this time.

'I *am* sure.'

She didn't move as he approached, only doing so when he took her shoulders in his hands and turned her so he had her back. Peter found *he* was the one trembling then, but she stood straight and obedient and much like a soldier on parade, and it was so very, very *Elizabeth* of her that some of his guilt ebbed.

She tensed very slightly when he began on the fastenings of her dress, but didn't pull away.

'This is where you've been coming, those times you ventured out and—' she stopped abruptly.

'And?'

'I saw you, that first night you were here, when you went wandering in the dark, and I wondered. I hadn't any clue how to ask what you were up to without sounding like I was accusing you of something shady.'

The fire sizzled again, and when she looked across at it her long hair, now completely free of its pins, brushed against him, dripping on his hands. Peter watched a droplet trickle along his skin and then well in the space between his forefinger and his thumb.

His hand slipped and he nearly ripped a button right off its stitches.

'Sorry. It's a little hard to undo these when they're wet.' It was a convenient excuse.

She grabbed a hunk of her hair and pulled it over her shoulder. 'Better?'

'Yes. Thank you very much.'

He wasn't the slightest bit surprised when she giggled. He sounded ludicrously formal.

'I saw you, too, that first time I went searching,' he told her, voice lowering, and she rounded on him, astonished and guilty all at once.

'You did?'

'How could I not? I couldn't approach you, of course, when you were ... not dressed to be greeted. And I didn't want to embarrass you by mentioning it. I didn't want to embarrass *myself*, for that matter. It's a little ironic, considering where we are now.'

Elizabeth thought about that as she turned back to let him finish unfastening her gown. 'Evidently I would make a terrible spy.'

The last of the buttons came loose and she pressed a hand against her chest a moment, holding the garment where it was before she found the courage to wriggle free.

'There.' It felt very much like they'd crossed a hurdle so high they could never scramble back.

***

Her pendant was gone. Where Elizabeth should have felt a chain at her throat, there was nothing.

Edward!

She'd not noticed earlier. In amongst everything else that had happened, she hadn't even thought to notice. It could be anywhere by now. If she'd lost it in the river it was surely gone forever.

'Thank you,' she told Peter as evenly as she could manage, and reminded herself she'd not wanted the blasted jewellery in the first place. It didn't matter anymore, it truly didn't...

'You're welcome.'

Now that he'd committed to the situation Peter was awfully helpful, leaving her standing in layers unmarried men were not supposed to see as he shifted his waistcoat aside and went about draping the gown across the back of the chair. There was something reassuring about his sudden ease with the situation.

If he could be sensible about it, so could she.

While she watched him add another log to the fire she touched her throat again. There was no chance of finding Edward's final gift. Not any chance whatsoever. Tamping down the gnawing ache, she focused on the man she was with now, the one who was alive and close and twisting to study her in a way she'd been unaware a man ever would.

'Do you think that now we are going to ... do ... this?' She'd no words for what *this* was.

He rose and came to her, taking a lock of her hair between his thumb and his forefinger, straightening it over her shoulder, and down her front. The touch was light, something she could barely feel, and it caused her to arch forwards, hungry for more.

'If you're certain.'

'And afterwards?'

What would happen? Would he be honourable, or would they both pretend it had never occurred? There were always consequences for actions, and just being together as they were then would be enough to start rumours.

Would he back away for her to find someone more *appropriate*? She didn't want the guilt without the fun of committing the crime.

'And afterwards, God help you, we'll be—'

Naturally, that was when the stack of old books and papers by the door crashed to the ground, and he broke off, twisting to find whatever new danger planned on striking them that day.

'Blasted hoarders,' she heard him mumble, and even though she could have suggested he leave them where they were, she was grateful for the minute's reprieve it gave her as he set about returning everything to order.

Elizabeth thought she should have offered to help, but this was all very new to her, and even though she was determined she was also acutely aware of how she was—or wasn't—dressed. And so she stood there, feeling rude and terrified and exhilarated and more than mildly embarrassed as Peter hefted a hunk of papers in his hands and used the surface of the table to tap them into alignment before adding them back to the pile.

'That's very fastidious of you,' she told him, mightily surprised how steady she sounded. Lady Audley, she knew for certain, never found herself caught in such preposterous situations. Not even the time she was committed to an institution in Belgium.

Peter was done then, and prowling back in her direction. He looked like a man still wrestling with his conscience, and she felt an urge to shake him for it.

'Elizabeth...' He again fussed with her hair as he looked beyond her, and then directly into her eyes before his own drifted away again.

'Just tell me.' She wasn't sure she wanted to hear it, but it had to be voiced all the same.

He let go and met her gaze. 'Elizabeth, in a town where everyone is so closely aligned, I'm a huge oddity.'

Not so huge, she wanted to tell him, but there were some things a man had to come to terms with on his own. She knew he was reaching for any excuse, but also knew he hadn't moved away from her. She looked at the pounding pulse at his throat, and then at the way his free hand clenched at his side.

'You want me to reject you.'

'Think of what you told me of Miss Hall just now. You know I do.'

'Well, then,' she eyed the clothing draped across the chair pointedly, 'perhaps you ought not to have removed me from my clothes. It's a little too late for propriety now.'

He didn't want to be amused by her, but she didn't miss that barely concealed gleam in his eyes. She'd crossed her arms, and—*goodness.* Now he was looking at her chest, and for far too long beyond any casual glance.

'And,' she continued needing to distract him, 'you should probably have left me back at the river. Your grandfather was willing to take me with him.'

He grimaced at the mention of the man, and she didn't blame him. Mr Towner was one of the last men alive she wished to think of while barely dressed.

'You'd have contracted some sort of chill or fever travelling all that way to get home,' he protested weakly. 'And I don't trust you around rivers. Not at the moment, at any rate.'

'Nonsense. I wouldn't dare do something so pitiful as catch a fever because of a bit of water.'

'I think,' he told her, swiftly earnest, 'that I might need a few more months before I'm able to joke about that.'

'It honestly wasn't that bad. I'm here now, and I'm sure my skirts kept me afloat. I was never in *that* much danger.'

He spluttered a bit and seemed ready for another quarrel, and Elizabeth thought it a good time to deftly change the direction of their conversation.

'Mr Rowe ... Do you think that sometime soon you might kiss me?'

'I shouldn't,' he muttered, and then scooped an arm around her back, raising her to the tips of her toes, and did just that.

Chapter 21

Kissing wasn't new to Elizabeth, but she was hardly accustomed to it, either. And never, ever before had it come close to being such an overwhelming experience.

Peter's bristly cheek brushed lightly against her own, raising bumps on her arms. He made her shiver when he ducked his face to her neck, kissing her there and then pausing to inhale deeply against her skin.

'I'm sure I stink,' she told him matter-of-factly. There was no point denying it.

His kiss became a smile, and he clasped her to him tightly for a long moment.

'Elizabeth,' he murmured when he pulled back a fraction, searching her eyes for something that she knew he wouldn't find. She didn't want or need him to be honourable anymore.

She was resolute now. Determined. And she didn't know if it terrified or comforted her that she'd never been more aware of his height and his strength than right then. If he wanted her to change her mind he should have tried being a little less handsome.

'Peter,' she countered, and clasped at his damp shirt, tugging a little, knowing what she wished for even while the infuriating man insisted on a last attempt at chivalry. He relented and tugged his shirt over his head, and she was treated to the sight of his bare, broad shoulders, shoulders she'd noticed that first day on the carriage drive and many times since.

She tried not to laugh as he rushed over to the fire and made a great show of laying his shirt neatly alongside the waistcoat, but her chest hurt with the effort. When he'd finished that silly little task and returned his attention to her, the laughter disappeared as suddenly as it had come.

Edward's pendant was best gone, she decided, and then cast all thoughts of her first love far away, well past the wobbly old walls of the cottage.

She was aware—so very, very aware—of each touch, each press of the lips and movement of the tongue, and of each sigh and sound. There was precious little between them, and minutes later even less, and she'd not ever been so close to a man before.

Peter walked her backwards to that alcove, to that bed, and again showed infuriating consideration, breaking their kiss to check the mattress, mumbling various frustrated things about insects and mould that were hardly conducive to romance.

And then he was there again, encouraging her to lay across the bed, and then checking the infernal fire again, and then denting the mattress as he *finally* came down beside her. She felt him against her, from their intertwined legs to their chests pressed tightly together, and to the places in between that she was still too shy to acknowledge, even as she felt him—*all* of him.

And then, despite her best intentions since that afternoon in September, she broke out in romantical shivers after all.

She hadn't known ... She simply hadn't known.

He placed a hand on her thigh, and it felt like a brand. She startled a little as his fingers curled around it and tugged it up around his own.

It wasn't fear she felt, not as she'd felt in the swirling torrent of the Murrumbidgee, but the anticipation. The implication of what they were about to do had her turn shaky and trembly as she snaked one of them up under the last of his clothing, feeling the muscle of his belly and the comforting warmth of his skin.

When he moved a hand to the hem of her chemise, she let him. And when he reached her drawers and paused, a question in his eyes, she nodded her permission and he drew them from her body.

She was nearly bare to him then, and somewhere a distant knowledge warned her she ought to be ashamed, or embarrassed, but there was no room for that. She was too full of the moment, of *him*.

He rose then, fingers trailing down her leg and eliciting shivers as he moved away just enough to remove the rest of his own clothes. She watched in fascination, in interest, and—*yes*, she had to admit—in a little bit of fear as the reality of what was happening settled around her.

He returned to her, drawing her close again, and kissed her breast over the fabric of her chemise.

She could not stop sneaking glances down ... there. Because—*goodness*. What on earth was supposed to happen with *that*—that ... oh she hadn't the words for any of it.

'How much do you know about this?' The words sounded forced from him, and—strangely—she liked that he seemed to be struggling. It meant she was not alone in her predicament.

'This?' It was difficult to focus on the question when there were so many other distractions.

The hot flush in her face was as much unease now as need. He toyed with the damp, crumpled fabric of her chemise. She was vaguely aware it hid next to nothing from his sight, but then she was doing plenty looking of her own.

He was rather large down there—not that she had any comparisons, but surely he was.

'About this, what we're about to do.'

'Well, it's not generally something included in a girl's education. I've learnt drawing and embroidery and a little bit of French—I'm terrible at it, so please don't ever ask for a translation.'

She took a breath. He was looking at her oddly, and she could hardly blame him, but she kept going.

'And thanks to you I now know a thing or two about noble rot, which isn't typical for a woman, I'm sure, but it's only a recent—'

She broke off again, knowing she was chattering like a parrot, and then took a bigger breath.

'Don't worry, I'll muddle through it.'

Even though the strain on his face was plain to see, his teeth flashed at her, and just for a second he drew her very close, holding her hard.

'That's awfully brave of you, if not particularly romantic.'

'Oh, I'm not sure I *am* romantic.' It seemed an important thing to share with him, all things considered.

He rolled onto his back and encouraged her to sit up beside him. She came to him awkwardly, unsure of how such things were done, misjudged the movement in her uncertainty, and found herself falling half across him before regaining her balance. She did not miss his wince.

Grace and beauty, indeed.

'I beg your pardon,' she said quickly, feeling that primness hovering around her, seeking a chance to reclaim her. 'I hope I didn't injure your ... your...' she waved a hand when she couldn't bring herself to say the words.

'My bollocks?' he asked softly. An involuntary giggle escaped her, and suddenly everything was all right.

Peter's hand began searching all over her; there wasn't a place he'd not claim now she'd ordered to be claimed, it seemed.

'Come here,' he said, a demand in his voice she was loath to deny.

He touched her in places that ached badly, providing one sort of relief at the same time as making her much more desperate. The last rational part of her was almost shocked—and very surprised—that anybody had ever thought to touch a woman where he did, between her legs, in a place that was *definitely* too private to be mentioned in conversation, but once she overcame her shyness she was very glad they had.

She clung to his head as he kissed her, curling her fingers into his thick hair. The beating of the rain on the rooftop hypnotised her. And then, long minutes later, he drew her over him, and—oh, apparently there were many ways to do such things—he compelled her to lower herself onto him in. Surprising her, astonishing her.

Later on she'd decide whether or not to be embarrassed—there was so much more intimacy to the entire thing than she could ever have prepared herself for.

'This really is all quite unusual, isn't it?' she commented after several minutes. It felt like a time that *something* ought to be said.

He huffed out a laugh and tightened his grip on her thigh, and then he turned them around again and she learnt another lesson in those secrets that had been kept from her for twenty-six years.

***

Peter came back to himself with the knowledge things had changed in ways that could not be undone.

'*Merde*,' he said, and the pattern Elizabeth had been tracing along his upper arm came to an abrupt stop. She sat up quickly, the chaos of her hair falling across her shoulders and down the front of her chemise. The fabric clung to her and hid so little from him it was essentially useless, but it was the expression on her face that gave Peter a fission of unease. He had the sudden—belated—good sense to assume he was in a bit of trouble.

'What did you say?'

'Never mind, it was nothing.'

'*Merde*,' she repeated. 'I hope that wasn't an assessment of what we've just done. I might not be an expert on such things, but it's not the nicest description.'

Oh dear. 'You weren't supposed to understand me.'

'Remember I told you I learnt French?'

'Well, yes, but I thought you probably weren't taught *all* the words.'

She was *definitely* laughing at him.

'Of course not. I'm too delicate for that. Mr Stanford, on the other hand ... Boys like to be shocking. And John shocked me as often as he liked, as a brother would. *More* than a brother would, in my case.'

As much as Peter loathed hearing Stanford's name under the circumstances, he chose then to believe him about Elizabeth. *She's almost as much my sister as my real sisters are.*

He ran a firm hand down her arm and brought it to rest on top of her own, stroking her skin.

'I'll keep my French polite from now on.'

She nodded like they were having a perfectly normal conversation.

'Swear in Spanish next time, if you like. I don't know a word of it. Or Walgalu, perhaps ... Do you speak it?'

He touched a fingertip to her lips.

'No. No, I don't.'

He encouraged her to relax back down against him, and warmed inside when she did immediately, without resistance.

There's nothing wrong with unconventional matches. He, of all people, should believe that.

Again he tangled and then untangled his fingers from her drying hair, and then sifted them through it, combing, stroking. Her hand tightened where it rested around his side, but she said nothing. The rain still fell, he realised then. It had eased a little, though there was a constant dripping sound somewhere nearby. He hoped it was from the awning on the *outside* of the hut, because he was in no state of mind to fix yet another leaking roof.

Shifting slightly, he angled his head to look down at Elizabeth's face. Her cheeks were flushed and her eyes half closed.

'By the way, you weren't supposed to mention that ever again.' Her voice, when she eventually spoke, had regained a great deal of

England in its tone, and even more primness. And he hadn't a clue what she was talking about.

'Not mention what?'

'You know. What I said back when we first met.'

Ah.

'The bollocks or the book? Because I've only mentioned the bollocks so far, and—Miss Farrer—I'm sorry to tell you this, but I never promised to forget about it.'

She gripped his side tightly enough to tell him she was unimpressed.

'I wish you hadn't such a good memory.'

He kissed the top of her head and smiled against her hair. 'No, you don't. Things wouldn't be half as fun otherwise. Speaking of shocking things you've done in recent months, I have a question about Lady Audley.'

'What about her?' Her voice was resigned and entertained all at once.

'How did I compare to Sir Michael?'

She pulled away with an outraged gasp; Peter tugged her back.

'I cannot believe you'd ask that. How do you know I even finished reading it?'

'Oh, I'm sure you did. It's the sort of story that must be read the whole way through.'

A groan. A shake of the head.

'Well, yes, all right. I did finish it. However, I *know* you've read it. And therefore *you* know that they don't discuss anything like ... this in the text. There's certainly no mention of—of...'

'Bollocks?' he suggested, and she nearly choked.

'Would you *please* stop saying that word?'

He gave the request a lengthy consideration. A burst of lightning struck somewhere in the distance, lighting the tiny window, and thunder cracked over the mountains before rolling away across the sky.

'At least admit you read it.'

'Ah, well, even *I* become tired of numbers every now and again, and a man must do something to pass the time. In any case, it's a convenient excuse to read such things. Sometimes even bollo—'

'Mr Rowe!'

More lightning. More thunder. Whomever was up there in the Heavens was still mightily angry with their little part of the world.

'For now,' Peter said when they could hear again, and stroked her hair—again. 'I will stop just for now, but I can't make any promises about the future. There's a sequel of sorts, did you know? Maybe Mrs Farrer has the second book stashed away somewhere for you to borrow. Or to hand over to unsuspecting guests.'

Elizabeth sighed. 'It is only with you that I make such a fool of myself. And so often.'

'Fools are much more entertaining. Please, don't ever change.'

'I'm almost resigned to my fate.'

He held her a little tighter. 'That's the spirit.'

As they lay there he told her his odd little story about that seagull in Sydney and its oversized lump of bread, and then about the political rants and raves he'd heard on every corner of the city.

'I can't tell you how relieved I am the election is finally over. If I hear one more debate about voting rights, I'll—excuse me. This isn't an especially romantic conversation,' he admitted, lifting his head to catch a glimpse of her face.

'No, it isn't, but it's better that way. We wouldn't want to become sentimental.'

He relaxed back against the saggy mattress and Elizabeth tucked her arm back around his waist.

'Miss Farrer, I'm not wholly averse to a bit of sentimentality from time to time.'

Elizabeth turned her face more fully against his chest. 'Peter...'

His fingers caught in a knot in her hair and he gently worked it free, worried about the change in her voice.

'Yes?'

'Can you ... Could you live here, do you think? Even when people are utterly awful to you? Or is it *too* awful? I think anonymity might have been easier for you in the city. I think people take so long to change...'

A gust of wind rattled the hut to its foundations but Peter barely noticed.

'I'll admit, there's not a lot I can do about who I am or how I look.'

'Hmm. I feel like this is the moment in the conversation I ought to tell you how devastatingly handsome you are.'

He gave her a squeeze. 'Please, don't. I'd have to reciprocate by waxing poetic about your spectacular beauty, and then you'd become embarrassed.'

'No. I'd just accuse you of lying, and then we'd probably quarrel. I'm too exhausted to quarrel today.' She sobered. 'You came back. At Christmas, you came back. I didn't think you would.'

He ducked and pressed his forehead to hers. The wind changed and the hut shook again.

Reluctantly, Elizabeth drew back. 'What do we do now?'

Peter groaned, knowing he sounded like a man three times his age, and stretched his legs out so far his feet stuck off the end of the bed to touch the wall.

'We should probably try to return before sunset,' he conceded. Such as sunset was; the day hadn't once risen out of its grey haze, but if they didn't leave soon it would be dangerous to even attempt the journey.

She rested a hand back on his chest. 'We could stay here...'

'I doubt that would work well. Your brother will worry, and then feel obliged to come searching for you, and then some new disaster will surely strike. I've had enough excitement to last the year.'

'The year has barely begun.'

'I know. My point precisely.'

Elizabeth sighed and began to move off the bed.

'Mr Rowe, I've had enough of it, too.'

Chapter 22

Peter knew they'd make it back to Endmoor eventually, but some higher power kept throwing obstacles in their way. He didn't doubt Robert Farrer was aware he was missing a sister by now, and if they waited much longer they'd all be on a merry chase across the valley in search of each other.

By the time they'd dressed, both of them a little shy with each other now the moment had passed, he pulled the cottage's door open to discover the rain faded away to little more than a drizzle. Remarkably, when she came up beside him a few seconds later, Elizabeth was able to point out a few blue patches of sky off to the east, the clouds drifting away from the town as a calmness gradually returned to the land.

Still, though, the drizzle was just heavy enough to be a pest.

'It seems a pointless exercise to dry our clothes only for them to be ruined again,' Elizabeth said on a sigh but trudged dutifully out the door and off in the direction of home, those old shoes he'd found weeks earlier on her feet—a replacement for her own mud-splattered pair with the torn laces—before he could suggest they wait a little longer.

Peter closed the door just as she stumbled, steadying herself before he could help, and then laughed. She kept her head down, focusing on the uneven trail home, plodding along at a steady pace.

'These shoes are a little big.'

'I'll go back for the gig and pony.' He was already slowing and looking back the way they'd come.

'No! No, we'll keep walking. It's almost fun trying to get around in these. I'm fast developing sympathy for circus clowns.' She kept going, lifting her feet higher than she normally would, holding her skirts higher too, to accommodate her odd new gait.

'I think I should feel more preposterous. I'll wager you'd never see one of your city girls looking like this.'

Peter was about to tell her there hadn't been as many *city girls* as she assumed when she tripped over the boots again and he steadied her with a hand at her waist. It gave her a chance to give him a long perusal.

'It's actually really rude of you to look so clean and handsome at the moment. Why isn't your hair frizzing like mine?'

'It wouldn't dare.'

Elizabeth pulled a face at him.

'I actually don't know how to get home from here. The landscape's changed since I was out this way. Please tell me you've been this way before.'

'I've been this way before. Don't worry, I'm not walking you to the ocean. We're heading in the right direction.' He checked their surroundings. 'More or less.'

And so they continued, clinging to each other now and again when the muck left by the slowly receding water threatened to upend them on their backsides, laughing when they weren't moaning about how uncomfortable a journey it was.

It was when they were most of the way back that he saw the bogged wagon on one of the side trails, and the young man trying hopelessly to dig it back out. Elizabeth came to a stop when Peter did, assessed the situation, and sighed.

'We have a talent for finding people in predicaments.'

They truly did.

'I feel like I have to play the hero for one final time today. The lad looks miserable.'

Elizabeth lifted her chin. 'All right. I'll help you.'

'No. Please,' he added, 'go somewhere dry and take your clown shoes with you. If you keep walking this way, you'll find your way back easily enough.'

She watched the boy another few seconds, undecided, and then lifted a foot for inspection.

'All right. Knowing my luck, if I try and help I'll probably just trip into the ditch.'

Peter snorted in agreement.

***

Elizabeth swatted at Peter as they parted ways, prompting a chuckle out of him before she set off down a path that looked more familiar the further along it she went. She was glad there was nobody there to see her the next time she tripped—nor the half-dozen times after that. Thanks to her lack of stockings she'd begun sprouting blisters as soon as she left the hut, but it was unfair to moan about it until she was alone. Peter had done his best with very little.

On she walked, looking back occasionally until she could no longer see him or the boy, occasionally spotting a mob of sheep huddled under a tree. The drizzle eased even more.

She was so busy rescuing herself from a close call with a shrub that had decided to grow in the middle of the track that she missed the man approaching from behind.

'There you are,' a familiar, incredulous voice said, surprising her from her thoughts.

Her brother, it seemed, had also commandeered a gig from somewhere. She was enormously relieved to see him, but her feet were even happier about the vehicle. He stopped several feet from her.

'Robert! You've no idea how glad I am to see you.'

'And *you* have no idea how relieved I am to find you so quickly. You've saved me the need of forming a search party.' He studied her.

'Are you all right?'

'Oh, yes. I'm just out taking a spot of exercise. There's nothing to worry about.'

They both glared at the sky when it attempted one errant lightning flash, and then he approached slowly, wobbling along on shaky old wheels.

'Mind the bush. You don't want to get bogged like the other fellow.'

Robert drew to a stop and scanned their surroundings. 'Which other fellow?'

'The one over near the—oh, I have absolutely no idea. He's somewhere around. Peter was helping him get free of a ditch, and sent me on home.'

She was sure she didn't trust the way her brother sat up straighter and looked intensely interested at the mention of Peter's name. Robert saw too much for his own good.

'So far Alice has kept your secret, the little rascal. However, I'd wager she wasn't the only one sneaking out to Barracks Flat today to save the world the moment I was gone.'

The thunder hit, far away now.

'Alice is a good sister-in-law.' She wasn't admitting to anything yet.

'Hop up with me and I'll take you home. It's been a very interesting day.'

Elizabeth rested a hand on the horse's neck. 'I'll bet your day was only half as interesting as mine.'

'I hope to God that it wasn't. We've a lot of stories to share tonight, I think.'

She accepted his assistance up, slamming against his side by accident, and then laughing along with him as they disentangled themselves and settled into their spots on the hard, unforgiving bench, comfortable in the way of siblings, in a way—Elizabeth had to admit—she'd missed. Greatly. Dearly.

'Mind that bush,' she reminded him, and he had the grace to not scold her for her fussing.

'You seem...' he began.

Elizabeth braced herself for anything. 'Do I want to hear this?'

'Well, to be honest, I'm trying to think of a tactful way to tell you that you look a mess.'

She might have been offended, had her body not still been singing, and if she hadn't recently taken an involuntary swim in the Murrumbidgee ... and for the fact she knew it to be true.

'I'll be honest with you, I've had easier days than this one.'

His smile was gentle.

'Where's Alice?' she asked.

'Home—*now*. I found her wading into The Dog and Stile to help—wading! And I knew if I'd said anything to stop her she'd simply stay in there longer.'

'So what *did* you do?'

He cast his gaze upwards for a moment and shook his head.

'I waded in with her. What other option did I have?'

It warmed something in her to be there with Robert, despite the circumstances. They'd been through more together than either of them ever had apart. She'd felt excluded for a couple of years, even though not a single person on Endmoor could be blamed for it. Life changed for most, but until recently hers had very much stayed the same.

Things *would* change now. She'd miss her brother. She missed him already.

'It really has been quite the day.'

He grunted.

'Don't expect a rest yet, Elizabeth. I've the impression we'll have quite the scene waiting for us at home.'

'Oh, I'm *so* looking forward to it. Robert?'

They lurched hard enough for Elizabeth to grip the vehicle, *hard*. Even the horse snorted at the impact.

'Hmm?'

'Before we get there, I want to tell you about Edward.'

***

Endmoor's grounds looked more or less like they'd exploded. Nothing was where it was meant to be, and as people started trickling back from wherever they'd seen out the storm they began to congregate, standing around and shaking their heads. Alice stood there amongst them.

'Lord, where'd *you* get off to?' she asked when Elizabeth moved over near the stables to join her.

'The McCoys were in a little trouble. We went to check on them.'

'We, huh? I suppose you mean you and Martha? Or maybe you and Mrs Hobson? I know it wasn't you and Robert because he was too busy followin' me around and complainin' under his breath.'

Elizabeth might not have been able to look at Alice right then, but she *could* put an elbow to good use.

'You know who I mean.'

'I do. Saw the two of you in a tussle over sandbags. Would've been funny to stop and watch, but I was a little busy at the time.' She elbowed Elizabeth back. 'I'm ticklish there, by the way.'

'That's a good thing to remember.'

Around them bedraggled, exhausted folk laughed and shouted greetings. Now the worst of it was over everyone seemed determined to remember the entire disaster as a bit of a lark.

Hutton trotted past, looking thrilled. He was wet from head to toe and stank with it.

'The McCoys are all right?'

Elizabeth thought back to Moira and her children scrambling away from the torrent and into the bush. It felt an age ago.

'They were all right the last time I saw them.'

'And how about Mr Rowe?'

While her brother's suspicion had been subtle, Alice's was delivered with a grin.

'Alice...'

'I suppose we'll see him soon. Now I've gotta go and check on Duncan. I'd say he's about the only person here who doesn't mind the rain.

Give my regards to your man, whenever he returns.'

Off she went, smug as she could possibly be, and probably assuming her matchmaking at the picnic had played a part in what had happened since. She was probably right.

Elizabeth was on the verge of returning to the house, desperate to be out of her soaked clothes and to finally have the chance to brush the wild tangles out of her hair, when Peter walked through the gate at the town road, cutting a tall, imposing, familiar figure with a wealth of hair that still hadn't frizzled.

He watched her intently as he approached, and it was one of those times she wished he didn't see her so clearly. The sunnier it became, the scummier she surely looked.

'Rowe!'

Mr Adamson bustled over from the stables and claimed his attention, and—for the time being—the connection was broken.

There were many, many people who wanted to speak to Peter when he reached the top of the carriage loop. Elizabeth used the toe of her too-large boot to move some debris off the gravel while he was asked his opinion of the situation in town, of the time he thought it would take for the water to recede, and of every other thing he couldn't possibly answer with any expertise or certainty. Something had shifted in their opinions, and suddenly the suspicious stranger from Sydney was an oracle.

Sneaking off while his attention was occupied elsewhere, Elizabeth bent to pat Gertrude as she passed. The cat was alternately fascinated, by the new sights and smells nature had delivered her, and horrified, that she had to get her paws damp to enjoy them. When the tabby moved on, Elizabeth was about to follow but a dull gleam caught her eye.

Breath hitched, she crouched and sifted her hands through the mess of gravel and leaves, and across the grooves made by wagons that had rolled over earlier in the day. She pinched the filthy gold links of the chain and drew it up slowly, her breath catching for a second time as the chain snagged once before coming free of a twig.

The pendant was a little dirty. The little rows of pearls, however, alongside the sapphires, were all in their fittings, including the largest stone at the bottom. The chain, as well as the rest of necklace, could be saved with a thorough cleaning.

'Thank God,' she whispered. No matter what had happened in the past with Edward, losing the piece would *not* have been for the best.

She climbed back to her feet, tucking the jewellery away into a fold of her dress, and looked around. Robert crossed the drive to greet stockmen returning from the outskirts of the property. Bertie and Bessie bustled down the path bearing various implements to clear away the worst of the damage. If there were any spitfires crawling about the garden that day, they'd been well and truly extinguished.

Everything was back to normal—or at least it would be soon.

'Miss Farrer? D'you know what became of that ladder?' the maid, Bessie, called from across the courtyard. The woman had a broom in her hands and a smudge of something grimy across her forehead.

'It's up in the—no. Don't worry. I'll get it myself.' Elizabeth was already in a state; she might as well ruin her gown completely clearing out the eaves. And this time Peter was too distracted to disapprove of her climbing it.

Bessie's eyes narrowed as she considered a protest, but then her name was called and she was off before she could admonish the landlord's sister for doing something as helpful as sweep.

If you were to return home, we wouldn't be surprised, and you'd be very welcome here.

Yes, Elizabeth knew her parents would welcome her back in England, but that evening she was needed in Barracks Flat.

And only when she realised this truth did she breathe freely.

Chapter 23

The next morning Elizabeth slept in longer than she should have. When she woke, astonished at the angle of the sun, she jumped out of her bed in confusion. She devoted a good few minutes to standing in the middle of her room, bare and lightly blistered toes curling against the floorboards as her heartbeat steadied. Her life had changed irrevocably, but she didn't know what she was supposed to do about it.

Forgoing breakfast—there was no chance she could do something as mundane as sit about gnawing on toast—she wandered the rooms of the homestead, catching a glimpse of some rich riesling vines from one window and of several of Endmoor's workers laughing as they set off across the property, Mr McCoy amongst them. Plants and people in the tablelands, it seemed, were both doggedly resilient.

She was halfway to the homestead's front door when a familiar smiling face attached to a familiar tall man appeared in front of her. John Stanford was in good spirits, characteristically indestructible in the face of the past few days' events.

'Good morning,' he said when he spotted her. 'I thought I'd swim my way up the town road to deliver some news. Your Martha's house survived yesterday.'

He grimaced before continuing. 'That father of hers is smug about it ... Naturally the town's least affable man won't suffer any damage while the rest of us marinate in river water over the coming weeks.'

Elizabeth gave him a solid inspection. He was impeccably dressed, as always, and the sunlight tinged his hair golden. As it always did.

'You're nowhere near soggy enough to have been in the water today. John, how is it that you never manage to look ruffled?' She was genuinely curious.

'It's a talent a person is born with.' He grinned at her. 'You look more or less untarnished. I heard you took a dip in the Murrumbidgee. Might I recommend you choose a finer day the next time you decide to go for a swim?'

He came nearer and gave her a nudge with his elbow, and then reached past her to retrieve something from the table near the door.

'I thought I might as well relieve the post office—which, by the way, survived thanks to your little sandbag escapade—of some of their correspondence while it was still salvable.'

He sifted through the various papers and then handed her three letters.

'The post, it seems, won't even stop for a minor disaster.'

'Thank you,' she said absently, noting the familiar handwriting on the first two envelopes.

'Well, then. Postman's duties complete, I think I'm superfluous here. I'll be off, inspecting grapevines and such, should anybody like to offer me their thanks for my thoughtfulness.'

'John?'

He stopped and looked back at her, waiting.

'If yesterday was a *minor* disaster, what's your definition of a catastrophe?'

He smiled at her once more. 'A *catastrophe* would have been if I'd been up to my ankles in the Murrumbidgee when I got out of bed this morning. My new oak floors ruined straight after they were laid? Utterly unthinkable.' He shook his head and was gone.

Soft footsteps sounded in the hallway behind Elizabeth as she watched him step back outside, and Alice arrived at her elbow, peered at the letters, and then scoffed.

'We've almost no decent fruit left thanks to that bloody downpour, and the stockmen are claiming the road'll be a mess for the next few weeks, and yet that man brings us the mail? Somethin' about this is more than a little ridiculous.' She tied the strings of her apron around herself as she spoke. 'I'll be in the drawing room inspecting another soggy spot on the ceiling.'

She was halfway to the door when she realised Elizabeth hadn't moved. 'Aren't you going to open them?'

'Yes, I suppose I have to,' she responded, her voice sounding like it came from another woman entirely as she read the messily scrawled address of the third letter's origin.

Cascade Street

She braced one hand on the table and watched until Alice was gone.

She couldn't open it; she *had* to open it.

'Not here,' she murmured, and returned to her room for her hat, oldest boots and her sketchbook. Drawing might, just might, provide the comfort she'd need after reading her news.

But probably not.

***

What now, Peter wondered when he woke the morning after the flood, again in the cottage on Endmoor's grounds, which had somehow managed not to leak in its old age. Despite its slightly dilapidated exterior, the place had solid foundations.

The world, or at least their little part of it, slowly put itself back to rights. Nature moved on to cause problems for some other unfortunate souls, leaving the remnants of chaos behind for the people of the tablelands to fix. The birds were louder than ever, in ecstasy with the conditions where everybody else was knee-deep in mud.

I was thinking of becoming a spinster, she'd said.

Had it really happened? Had he really spent an afternoon with Elizabeth Farrer in another, less robust building, doing every single thing he wasn't meant to?

There's nothing wrong with unconventional matches.

'Bloody hell,' he told the wallpaper, and immediately felt bad about it. It wasn't the right thing to say about what had happened between them.

His father had an excellent old copy of *Roget's Thesaurus* that sat in his office with other important, impressive and rarely read books. Peter searched his memory for a word to describe how his life had changed in a matter of hours. Amazing? Enlightening? Astonishing? None of them were quite right.

'I need to read that book,' he announced to the room at large, and then threw back the covers.

Sunshine sneaked through gaps in the curtains. People were already bustling about on the property with so much to do now that nature had taken pity on them and carried its misery away somewhere else. It would take some time before Barracks Flat was restored to how it had been before, and Peter was just mean enough to hope the damaged gristmill beside the Monaro Street bridge wasn't the first place in town anyone rushed to repair.

He lingered in the cottage longer than any respectable man capable of lending a hand should, reflecting on all the things he hadn't dared to think of the night before.

That he would marry Elizabeth now was a given. That was if she'd not already come to her senses and gone running for the foothills, or rowed herself halfway down the Murrumbidgee to escape him. If he was allowed a say in such things, she wouldn't be going anywhere near water of any kind in the future. Whether she accepted him or not, he was still banning any and all activities involving rivers, sandbags and small boats for the foreseeable future.

She'd probably wallop him for it.

Peter shaved and dressed and allowed himself a few thoughts about his future. He'd have to dip his feet into the sea a little longer the next time he was Sydney, to make up for the fact he'd not be doing it much in the future. There wasn't a beach anywhere near the *usually* dusty Barracks Flat.

***

After stopping to help clear a couple of fallen branches from the roofs of the stables and the shed, and reliving the previous day's events with the abnormally talkative Endmoor staff, Peter didn't see his employer until the middle of the morning. They'd found themselves at the homestead's front doorstep at the same time, Peter on his way into the office, and Farrer on his way out.

The other man changed his course, a dip of his head inviting—ordering, perhaps—Peter to join him there.

They set their hats side by side on the railing and together watched as the estate's various workers scurried around the muddy grounds. Sunshine gleamed and rippled in puddles; the carriage drive would not be easy to mend. Peter would wager it had been a long time since Endmoor had been in such a state.

Mrs Farrer marched past with a broom, barely sparing her husband a glance as she muttered something about chaos in the rose garden. Despite whatever was hanging in the air between the woman's husband and himself, Peter smiled at the sight of her. Apparently the estate wasn't averse to oddities.

'There's something to be said for a storm that can clear off so fast,' he remarked when the man beside him remained silent.

Farrer looked over at him.

'Yes, and there's also something to be said for a downpour that dumps so much misery and then leaves us to deal with the aftermath, while it blows off somewhere else without a care in the world.'

The sounds of brutally vigorous sweeping reached them and both men stopped to listen for a while. There was nothing soothing about how Alice Farrer attacked a misbehaving garden.

'I've been out to check the vines,' her husband said. 'The damage is nowhere near what I worried it would be. I'd say we're still all right to proceed as planned.'

'That's good news.'

'It means I'm going to be busier than ever from now on.'

There was something *not* being said that had Peter perking up. He wanted to ask; he waited for Farrer to tell him instead.

'I was thinking of a new arrangement. Something along the lines of a partnership. Me, John, and you, if you're willing. God knows, you've taken on a lot more than we expected since you arrived. And you've no idea how happy I am to have that extra time out on the land.'

The sweeping stopped.

'A partnership?' Peter found he'd lost his words. Already he was picturing a new future, a different one than he could ever have hoped for or allowed himself to want until the day before.

'You're from Sydney, and I understand completely if you'd prefer to return. I daresay we could come to an agreement that had you in the city, working with us out here. *However...*'

There was a wealth of meaning in that one last word, and Peter straightened his spine and waited for it. This *was* Elizabeth's brother, and he had to at least suspect something had happened between them.

'I thought you might like to stay on in Barracks Flat. In town, if not in that cottage, which really is too small as a permanent residence. Or maybe you'd like to build something bigger on your land.'

Your land ... Peter searched the man's words for any alternate meaning but found none.

'Elizabeth said something.' He hoped to God it wasn't about anything that happened in that hut on the Yealambidgie trail.

'She's been fairly coy, but I'd already surmised a lot of it. I'm sorry.' Farrer shook his head. 'This isn't an offer of employment; it's an attempt to right a wrong. Partially, at least.'

Peter looked off towards Namadgi country. 'I might never understand exactly what that wrong was.'

'There are still some Ngambri and Ngunnawal people around. In fact, for a while we had a few working as stockmen here at the station. Have you considered ... I assume you came all the way to this outpost because you once had people here.'

'I did. And I have. And I intend to be here long enough to investigate it.' He glanced to the side. 'I don't suppose you need any more explanation as to why my father sent me in his place last September. Not that he told even me of his intentions, but I've no doubt he expected me to conduct a little investigation.'

'You don't know who your people are?'

'I've an idea or two, but it would have been so much easier if I'd not been brought up to deny it.'

Farrer's posture had sharpened with interest, so he continued.

'I don't know much about that part of me at all, but now I've a few clues I intend to follow. My mother was taught to be ashamed of her heritage, and my grandfather—a white man—he seems even less inclined to share.

Vernon Towner,' Peter added, and saw the recognition on the other man's face.

'Ah.'

It seemed the old man's infamy was in direct contrast with his determination to stay isolated from anyone and everyone.

'More infamously known as The Duffer.'

'Ah.'

Too late, Peter remembered admitting to having a livestock thief as a relation wasn't the way to endear himself to Elizabeth's brother.

'I know no long-term plans were discussed, but would you be willing to stay on? Help us make something more of this business?'

Farrer touched the braided leather brim of his hat and then turned brown, unwavering eyes, so similar and yet so different to his sister's, on Peter.

'I mean stay and work the land? *This* stretch of land?'

'I will.'

Farrer nodded. 'I want to tell you it isn't enough.'

'It's more than I came here expecting.' *It could never be enough.*

'There are always going to be people who'll judge the situation. Judge me.'

Mrs Farrer walked past then, hands full of leaves and bark and twigs, and added it all to a growing pile. A moment later she was headed back to complete her task.

Robert watched his wife until she'd gone. 'There will be people who judge unfairly. Even so, I—'

He broke off abruptly and stared incredulously at the family that had silently appeared, hopping up the steps one at a time until they stood in a neat line at the edge of the veranda. The smallest and greyest of them wobbled to a stop, peeping little hungry noises.

'Alice,' Farrer bellowed in a tone louder than Peter had ever heard from him before.

The sweeping stopped again.

'What?' The response was equally as loud, if more feminine.

'Will you *please* stop feeding the magpies.'

The adult birds regarded them with steady amber gazes as Mrs Farrer considered a response to the request. It came a couple of seconds later.

'*Never!*'

Sighing and shaking his head, Robert went to the bucket in the corner and retrieved what looked to Peter like remnants of the past several days' meals mixed together, and threw a couple of handfuls out onto the pockmarked carriage loop.

The birds were off in an instant.

Peter caught the other man's quickly concealed smile.

'As for my sister...' he continued, and Peter wondered if this was the point in the conversation they discussed pistols at dawn. When he found it in him to look across at the other man, Peter saw deep awareness in his eyes.

'If you want to ask for my permission, I think I'd better grant it, seeing as our father's several thousand miles away and not easy to reach. Though Elizabeth would likely lock me in the housekeeper's cupboard if I stood in the way of her wishes.'

He changed his focus back to the sodden landscape. A respite.

'Have you asked her yet?'

'Not yet.' Not officially, at least.

'Well, you'd better go and do that.'

Chapter 24

Deciding to propose marriage was one thing. Finding the woman Peter intended to propose *to* was another.

After searching the entire homestead, and then the garden, and then—because he was getting a little desperate—each and every outbuilding within reasonable walking distance of the house, Peter had to concede she was nowhere to be found. Everyone claimed to have seen her at some point that morning, but it was no help when the woman refused to stay put.

When a stockman he passed near the town road claimed Elizabeth had walked away into the distance a little while ago, and directed him off cross-country, Peter changed his course and hoped the fellow wasn't joking.

He walked. And then he trudged when he hit a muddy spot. And then he skated when things became a little slippery.

There was a sense of inevitability that it wasn't Elizabeth he found first, but the man who'd avoided him for over three decades. After being nowhere for so long, Vernon Towner was suddenly *everywhere*.

'I'll be away soon.' The man spoke before Peter reached him. 'If you've somethin' to say, now'd be the best time.'

The pony had been retrieved, as had the gig, as well as most of the rubbish that'd been scattered around the crooked cottage the afternoon before. His grandfather had secured it to the back of the little vehicle with rope in a way that didn't look like it could hold for more than a mile or two. However, the rope—as Peter had learnt the day before—was capable of magical things.

'Thank you for what you did for Elizabeth yesterday.'

The older man paused at that. His bushy grey eyebrows rose.

'*Elizabeth*, is it? Not Miss Farrer?'

'Elizabeth to me, yes.'

'Interestin'. Anyway,' he said after a short pause. 'I didn't do much to help, far as I remember it.'

Peter shook his head. 'Yes. You did.'

For the first time that day his grandfather gave him his full attention.

'The pony might not be mine, but the books and papers are, if you're wonderin'.'

Peter didn't care about the papers, but he noticed the sampler was not amongst the junk.

The man was washing his hands of his daughter, as he'd washed them of everyone else.

The animal snorted and stamped, and Towner shifted his attention to the track leading south as he stepped away to take the reins. Peter's heart jumped as the situation took on a new urgency.

'You're really off now?'

'As I said, I got somewhere to be.'

Peter took hold of the reins, stopping him.

'Just a moment. Tell me, do you—' he broke off and tried to gather his thoughts. There were a million questions he'd still have liked to ask, even knowing he'd not get satisfactory answers.

This was probably the only chance he'd ever have. He knew that partly because of instinct—Towner seemed on the verge of disappearing into those blue-grey mountains and never returning—and partly because this old man was fading. It was as though each time he saw him he'd withered a little more.

'What are the chances that any of my mother's family are still alive?'

He could not bring himself to say *your daughter's people*, not to this man who so clearly wished for all of his past to disappear. Peter would be going back for the sampler that afternoon.

'Still livin'?' He tapped his chin slowly, thoughtfully, as though he'd forgotten his urge to be gone. 'Might be one or two who made it through that smallpox outbreak. Anybody who could moved on right after that.'

He'd not express his anger at the other man's casual tone, Peter promised himself. He'd not show his anger that the lives of so many were so easily dismissed. It would achieve nothing, raise the man's hackles, and he'd leave without the information he wanted—*needed*.

A dreadful pause ensued, where Peter convinced himself he'd overstepped, that he'd never receive a response, but then the man shrugged. And spoke.

'Ngambri people. Always' coverin' a big area, they are, but they've been movin' northeast for a while now. You heard of Lake George? Big stretch of water on the way to Goulburn? *Weereewaa*, they call it.' The man's pronunciation sounded perfect to Peter's ears.

Towner inspected his battered old hat and then pressed it firmly onto his head, low enough that Peter could hardly see his eyes anymore.

'If you're determined, that's where I'd go for answers. They built a mission somewhere between there and Bungendore an age ago. As for me? I've enough of this place. Thinkin' of headin' south. Got an old friend livin' down along the Murray River, near Albury. Reckon me luck's not so bad that I'll get two floods in a year.'

'I found this.' Peter removed the daguerreotype from his pocket and held it out reluctantly.

His grandfather, *The Duffer*, the so-called *Irish Convict*, the man who'd hidden in the bush to escape punishment for his life of crime, peered apathetically at the old image of his daughter. How a person became so removed from all that was theirs, Peter would never know. Working in the country, tramping through the bush day after day, he'd come to understand a man's attachment to the land. It seeped into a person before he was even aware of it.

'She was beautiful, wasn't she?' Towner sounded almost surprised.

'She was.'

'Good thing, then, that she got herself out of here and off somewhere she'd be better appreciated.'

'Do you know where the picture was taken?' he asked, trying to hide his urgency. His grandfather was already beginning to drift; his mind was off somewhere far beyond the town.

'Lake George, as I remember it. Could be wrong, on the other hand, but that's me best guess. Wish *Elizabeth* luck. She's gonna need it, marrying one of me grandsons.' Towner relieved him of the reins.

There was no shake of the hands, nor were there any heartfelt words, not that Peter had expected them. The old man set off without a backwards glance, all the things that mattered to him in the world in that gig, leaving the daguerreotype in Peter's hand. The scrub and the trees quickly swallowed him up.

Peter's feet squelched as he set back off the way he'd come.

Surely it wasn't too much to ask for a little more fanfare the moment one of his only relatives drove out of his life.

***

Elizabeth's boots were muddy. Not even the summer sun could dry out the land fast enough to make her walk out to her favourite paddock enjoyable. Thankfully her special perch under the scraggly old gum tree had survived the storm intact, and the countryside was fast returning to its usual life. The mud would dry soon, but not soon enough to save her clothes. She was once again in her old burnt umber dress, and was glad of it, because her hemline hadn't survived the journey across the estate unscathed, either.

As the morning became afternoon she found that, for the first time in a long time, on her own and going over some *very* private memories, she felt inspired. The work poured out of her, and instead of wanting to punish nature for the ordeals it had put them through, she wanted to capture it.

She wiped a bead of perspiration from her temple with the back of her wrist, and then set her sketchbook aside for a while. After a solid couple of hours of work, it was time to simply appreciate the view.

The Slade School welcomes women...

It may well include women now, as her mother said, but no woman painting in the centre of London could capture what Elizabeth could where she sat there and then. Those women would learn from the greats, and it was an enviable situation, but she knew now it wasn't for her.

The first of her letters sat opened beside her. Mr Evanson in Goulburn had several clients up north in New South Wales, in places along the coast, people who were interested in depictions of stockmen in the dry centre of the colony.

'Dry!' Right then that was laughable. She shielded her eyes against the sun sparkling on the surface of a puddle and listened to the cicadas sing.

Women several oceans away would have opportunities Elizabeth would only ever dream of. They wouldn't ever know though, that even after a flood, grass could be so tough it poked a woman through her stockings, or that the smell of eucalyptus so soon after a storm could envelop a person completely, changing their perspective of the entire countryside. They'd have to travel far to see birds in such brilliant shades of green and blue.

Her thoughts brought her back to the pendant, which she hadn't worn since retrieving it from near the stables. It sat beside her now. The big sapphire, freshly cleaned, caught her eye.

Since she'd last been out to the far paddock the old buildings across the fence had disappeared even further behind the encroaching nature. A person would need a machete to cut their way through now. Or perhaps a cannon. There was no need to check them this time to know they'd not been lived in since the last time. And now she knew for certain that Mr Towner, *Peter's grandfather*, was very much alive.

Resting a hand on her sketchbook—she'd done a decent job of capturing the last of the rain clouds as they swirled over the highest, furthest peaks of the Brindabellas—she put her feet on a freshly fallen branch, one she'd splintered her hands trying unsuccessfully to shift, and watched the pointed ears of a kangaroo off by the creek.

She knew Endmoor was getting on fine without her, just as it had for a couple of years, since Alice took over as its mistress, learning one new thing after another at a dizzying pace. Elizabeth had been feeling redundant for a good long while, but now there was no depression in it, nor the bitterness she'd had to fend off in private moments.

It was time for her to move along with her life and think of the future. She had her suspicions about what that future might be, but there was a certain Ngambri man she needed to talk to—*alone*—before she'd allow her daydreams to take her in that direction.

She was not surprised when Peter walked over the rise some ten minutes later. They both knew there were things that must be said. She was more surprised by the timing; she still had a letter to read and hadn't yet found the courage to do so.

He stopped when he saw her, and even though he was still too far away for her to make out his features, she knew that he smiled. Elizabeth stood, arranged her skirts, and as he approached she tried very hard to not look as thrilled to see him as she felt.

'Good afternoon,' he said after studying her long enough, eyes roaming over her features, she nearly squirmed. There was almost a question in his tone, she realised, and felt comforted by the knowledge he wasn't quite as steady, as confident, as he first appeared. That made two of them.

She stepped closer.

'Is it afternoon already? I suspected but wasn't sure.'

'I've no real idea, but it took so long to walk all this way to reach you it must be close to midnight by now. Why come so far out? You could just as easily have hidden somewhere nearer to the house and saved me some time in finding you. My poor legs are aching with the exertion.'

She gave his chest a little poke. 'Good Lord, you can exaggerate. I *like* it out here.'

'It's a beautiful view,' he told her, eyes still on her face.

'Oh, nicely done. If that was your attempt at flattery, I'll have you know it was awfully saccharine.'

He winced, and gave the nearest bleating sheep a funny look.

'I apologise. It *was* dreadful, wasn't it?'

She touched his jaw. 'You're forgiven.'

With a flash of a grin he gave their surroundings a better inspection, taking in the creek and the animals and the particular view of the mountains that she loved the best before settling his attention on her little collection of things she'd brought with her.

He nodded at the sketchbook. 'Capturing the countryside in a state of disarray?'

'I had to, before the world righted itself and I forgot the details.'

He glanced down and then bent to move the branch at her feet as though it was nothing more than a twig. Elizabeth didn't think he managed even a single splinter. If her heart hadn't been too full of him then his casual strength would have been infuriating.

'I might again remind you the mountains can be drawn from one of a thousand places closer to the house.'

She grimaced and pointed. 'Letters came for me, and I wanted privacy to read them.'

'Ah. You want me to go.'

'No!' She tugged at his arm until she had them both sitting on the log. It was quite the squeeze—Peter's *poor legs* required rather a lot of space—but she'd not complain about the closeness.

'My mother wrote, though her advice is no longer needed. I'll not be returning to England. Not now. Not after—' She hadn't the words to say aloud what they'd done together the day before. It was still too new, too special. And still a little bit embarrassing.

He remained quiet, listening as he leaned down and took a gumnut between two fingers. It was a comforting sort of quiet.

'The other letter...' She trailed off and picked it up, turning it over, and then over again, reading the Sydney address yet another time, and then finally found the courage to open it.

Miss Farrer,

Now, thanks to your success, I know where to find you, I thought you might like this.

V. Abraham

Victoria Abraham. Elizabeth's heart sank.

There was a photograph inside, and she studied it a long time as realisation set in, and then handed it over with a grin. Suddenly, and wholly unexpectedly, her whole world was lighter. Evidently, poor letter writing skills ran in the Sumner family blood. Elizabeth decided it was a good thing she was sitting, and wedged so tightly against the man beside her, because the relief would surely have knocked her to the ground otherwise.

As correspondence went it wasn't much, but it was enough—*more than enough.*

'Edward?' Peter asked after a long pause to inspect the youthful face looking back at him.

'Yes.' She smiled and reached across to touch a fingernail gently to the face of the man in the image just once, just for a second.

Peter turned the photograph over to read the writing on the back.

'Edward Sumner and Mrs Abraham.'

'His aunt,' she explained, pointing to the barely legible end of the description. She then accepted the picture back, tucking it away and not minding one bit when Peter's hand came to rest on her leg. She'd confront the renewed pang of sadness later, on a day where her heart wasn't quite so overwhelmed by so much else.

Victoria Abraham *wasn't* a rival after all; she was an elderly aunt. A *married* elderly aunt. That people made mistakes wasn't a new revelation. What she hadn't known until then was that newspapers were capable of putting the wrong name in a betrothal announcement.

A final puzzle piece slid neatly into place. The disaster in the Sudan had caused chaos, and illness, and loss. She supposed that at the time people were too busy succumbing to typhoid to properly address their correspondence and condolences.

Edward hadn't betrayed her. She laughed, as everything finally, finally came still, clarity removing a haze she'd lived with for so long.

Peter appeared confused and entertained in equal parts.

Her empty stomach rumbled loudly and Peter looked at her, amusement written all over him.

'I didn't want to hate him. Edward, I mean. All this time, I didn't want to hate him.'

It occurred to her that she'd never explained the whole sorry drama to Peter, but that wasn't for today either.

'I should go to Sydney one day soon. I need to know where his memorial is. I owe him an apology.'

'I suppose all of this will make sense to me eventually.'

'It will.'

She caught his glance at the pendant.

'Edward bought it for me. I shall return it, perhaps to his parents.' People she had never met. 'It isn't right for me to hold onto it, considering...' Considering she now had another gentleman in her life.

Peter tucked the gumnut into a pocket and tensed as his tone changed.

'Elizabeth, don't.'

She looked at his hand, darker than hers, except where her fingers were once again stained with her charcoal. And then she looked up into his eyes, his expression shadowed a little, silhouetted by the sunshine.

'Don't what?'

'Don't return it. It's *your* necklace. And it was purchased for *you*, not for anybody else. Keep it.'

'Are you certain?'

'Of course I am.'

She considered it a moment longer before pressing closer to him, this man who was the opposite of Edward in so many ways, and who was generous enough to allow her room in her life for both of them.

'I know that Edward will always be a memory for you, but—I'm sorry—you can't escape me now, God help you. You've worn me down, or perhaps I've done that to you.'

His fingers linked through hers, and he used the stronger connection to tug her closer still. Those creatures bouncing around inside her belly began to jump and dance faster.

'Elizabeth ... I didn't hike all the way out here just to ruin my legs. I've been sent here to make my formal proposal of marriage. I was going to ask you anyway, you have to know that.'

'You've *what?* Sent by whom?' She was suddenly too suspicious to be nervous.

'Your brother, of course. And yes, I can see your face turning pink, and don't for a moment try and tell me it's because of the sun. I wasn't told to *propose*, specifically, but your brother's meaning was plain enough.'

Elizabeth was sure she was closer to crimson than pink then, but Peter was kind enough not to mention it. If Robert was sending this man off across the station to make his intentions clear, then he had to know that ... Lord, she didn't—*couldn't*—think about it or she'd never be able to look at her brother again.

'Oh my goodness, what does he know about—'

'If he knows anything, it's all just guesses. Don't worry about that. It was awfully convenient of you to fall in the Murrumbidgee yesterday. Apparently it made the seduction that followed mandatory, and now you've gone and forced my hand. How clever you are.' He paused. 'You really do have to believe I was going to offer marriage regardless.'

She nodded. She did know that.

'I know being married to me will be a hardship.'

'Peter—'

'No, I'm not being maudlin. I'm thinking of your reputation. You told me that spinsters are more entertaining than wives. If we marry you're going to have to work hard to rise above the tedium.'

He lowered his voice. 'Do you think you could manage it?'

'Oh, I think so.'

Peter pressed his foot against hers and kept it there.

'Should I make a grand declaration of love? I rehearsed a few possibilities on my way over.'

'Good God, no. I'd die of embarrassment, and then feel obliged to make one in return.'

'And have you?' he asked, voice lowering. 'Have you rehearsed any of your own, Elizabeth?'

She felt hot and flustered and oh-so-excited all at once. It was too much for a person to experience at once. 'Of course I have, you dolt. You're the one who was fighting this from the outset.'

He released her hand to clasp her to him then, and she was happy to be caught.

'Well, then. That's good to know. Do you plan to sketch much longer? I can wait while you finish.'

'Peter Rowe, if you think that I'll be able to draw a single line after what you just said, you're mad.'

He beamed, and then he kissed her, and she kissed him back.

'Shall we return and share our news? It's a little muddy, as I see you've already discovered, but I could carry you over the worst of it.'

She baulked at the suggestion and jumped to her feet, backing away a step when he followed because he looked serious about it. When he continued looking serious she raised one hand in defence.

'And have you slip and drop me in it? No, thank you. I've good boots on.'

He took a look at them.

'I suppose I won't see you in clown shoes again. I think I should probably be offended by your lack of faith in my manly skills.'

'Don't be. The day is too nice to be cranky.' Her stomach had other ideas, however, sending out a protest so loud it almost drowned out the warble of a magpie in the tree above.

He kissed her one more time.

'I think we need to find you some food.'

'I know.' But instead she returned to her perch on the log and patted the space he'd warmed beside her. 'First, though, let's just sit together for a while. The others can wait.'

Epilogue

March

'I'll leave you to finish your work,' Daisy (*if you'd met my aunt Edith you wouldn't want the name either*) Rowe told Elizabeth one sunny afternoon the next month.

Dressed in a stylishly bustled, fashionable purple dress from Sydney that both complemented her dark colouring and turned heads in town, Peter's sister had come to Barracks Flat the previous week to join her brother and Elizabeth on their newest adventure.

On her way out of the room she paused for the briefest of moments, to look again at *Namadgi Sunrise*. After being driven some two-hundred miles along the rails from Maurice Rowe's Sydney terrace, the painting now hung in its new home above the mantle. It was a wedding present, Daisy had explained when, wrapped tightly and causing all kinds of trouble for the porters, the painting arrived at Barracks Flat Station the same time she had.

'*Though, not a great one,*' she'd told Elizabeth, laughing, '*as Peter already owns it.*'

Elizabeth returned to her canvas with the sort of determination she only needed on days nothing went right, when—with a little sound of surprise—Daisy stopped again.

'I should warn you, I heard a horse outside just now, and saw a very familiar fellow walking towards the house. I doubt you've much time left to yourself.' She smiled. 'Be prepared for another interruption.'

Elizabeth smiled back at her and then fixed as much of her attention as she could manage on her work, tingling with anticipation. That familiar fellow would have to wait; she was soon to be a famous artist, and such an achievement required hours of effort.

Off to one side, and currently covered to protect them from the damaging sun, were two completed works. Ready to be sent off to Goulburn, and then to the cities beyond. She was still adamant she was no McCubbin, and yet she found a great deal of joy in her painting.

It was an unusual thing to be in a new home, but it wasn't an unpleasant feeling. It was an adjustment, mostly, becoming accustomed to the idea that Endmoor was no longer hers. The homestead would always be there, waiting for her whenever she needed it. And anyway, she needed those paddocks and those vines for inspiration to keep her customers happy.

Another letter from England sat opened, read and reread on the small table beside her. Her mother's heartfelt advice was very much appreciated but no longer necessary. Elizabeth had made her decision. When the news she'd sent off a few weeks earlier reached Endmoor—the Endmoor of Cumberland, not of New South Wales—Mary Farrer was going to be very surprised.

She and Peter had been married when the town recovered from the disaster, and as soon as—Elizabeth had made sure to mention then—the church was no longer soggy. Their house was not as large as her old home, but it had the advantage of being directly in town, on Church Lane, a pretty little street close to the river that afforded them a view of the expansive grounds of the mayor's residence on the other side.

Not *too* near the river though, Peter had pointed out with a wry smile the day of their wedding, while they'd watched as some of his possessions from Sydney and her own from the homestead were moved in a flurry of activity and excitement.

Thanks to its slightly elevated position, Martha's house had come away from the flood unscathed, bar damage to the English garden at its front. The same could not be said for some of the gristmills nearby, but Barracks Flat had rallied as it always did and was steadily putting things back as they were meant to be.

Best of all, in this new home Elizabeth had an entire parlour on the ground floor to herself. The room faced in such a way the light was good most days, even if that particular afternoon was a little overcast. A gift of sorts, her new husband had called it. Once she'd finished laughingly explaining that parlours were not standard gifts for new wives, she had been forced to admit he could not have thought of anything better.

A flutter of colour at the window caught her attention, and she glanced up to see a pair of lorikeets working their way steadily around a nearby bush, nibbling at Heaven only knew what on its yellowing autumn leaves. Setting her palette aside, she took a moment just to enjoy the view.

'What time is it?' she asked.

'Near to five,' her husband replied.

She'd known he was there, watching her and yet still giving her space, waiting for her to be finished before he interrupted.

Peter came closer and gave her work a frank assessment.

'The colours are ... interesting...' he eventually decided. The too-kind assessment made her laugh.

'What's so funny about that?'

'*Interesting* is a generous way of implying you're not impressed but don't want to hurt my feelings. *Interesting* happens to be the kindest word I have for it, too. The whole work is disastrous and ought to be abandoned, but I can't seem to do it.'

'You don't like it?'

'Goodness, no. I've badly missed my mark. At this rate I might as well make the birds pink and the trees orange; it couldn't possibly make the scene any less accurate.'

He snatched one of her hands in his with a sudden movement, as though she would make good on her promise and ruin the piece there and then.

'Don't you dare.'

Squeezing her fingers lightly, he kept possession of her hand as he walked around the chair to face her, and then he tugged her up so they stood face to face.

'Lizzie?' he began and she groaned.

'I thought we'd agreed against doing that.'

He stroked a finger across her palm. 'I apologise. I thought it might be worth a second try.'

'And it's still not acceptable. Unless...' They were close enough for her to see the flash of alarm in his eyes, and—smiling—she stopped to think, taking in the strong angle of his jaw and the hint of a shadow running across it. It was a sensible exterior that hid so much strength beneath.

'I don't like the tone of your voice, nor the look on your face. It's dangerous.'

A breeze beyond the windows sent the garden rustling. Dappled light bounced around the room in the shape of a hundred-thousand petals and leaves.

'Perhaps if I'm *Lizzie* you might be *Petey.*'

That strong jaw clenched. 'Don't you dare.'

'It's sweet, and it suits you.'

Her husband's alarm grew. 'I truly hope it doesn't.'

He thought she was serious. Pleased with her newfound power, she bit her lip until she had control of herself.

'You hate it, don't you? Now I know how to best punish you. This is the sort of thing a wife should learn as soon as possible.'

The word *wife* was still new enough to startle a reaction out of him; it startled her, too. Feeling too happy even to tease, she patted his chest.

'What were you going to say?'

His relief palpable, he indicated the painting. 'I was going to tell you it's an impressive piece.'

'I think you are an unreliable art critic,' she told him earnestly.

'Truly? I thought I was getting rather good at it.'

She grinned at him. 'Liar.'

The firmness of his hand at her waist was in stark contrast to the softness of his lips when he brushed them against the nape of her neck.

He turned again, holding her lightly from behind and they simply stood a while, enjoying each other's company, and the silence of the room contrasting with all the squawks and chirps of nature outside. The sun came back again, lightening the room at such speed it felt like a different day and a different season.

Elizabeth ran her fingers back and forth over his hands where they rested, folded at her waist.

She felt his contented sigh, and then a moment later his sudden shift in attention.

'What *are* your plans for the painting?'

'Peter, *please* stop looking at it. When I create a masterpiece you may appreciate it all day, but this really ought to be condemned to the fire.'

His arms tightened. 'You wouldn't.'

'No. It's not terrible, just not my best. Perhaps I'll add those pink birds and orange trees and call it a new genre. I'll rename myself something exotic and pass myself off as a master.'

He thought about that. 'Maybe Angélique Rowe. Or Benedetta Rowe? Juliette Rowe?'

She looked at him over her shoulder. 'I notice all of the names you suggest come with *your* name attached to them.'

'Well, yes. I've only just given it to you; you're not to dispose of it yet.'

She dropped her head back against his shoulder. 'I should be packing.'

Peter paused. 'When you speak of packing, what exactly will that entail...?'

'No,' Elizabeth told him hastily, knowing what he assumed. 'I wasn't planning taking *all* of this with me.'

They were off out of town the following morning. On Miss Hall's advice they'd stop in Bungendore first, where, allegedly, they might find a stray relation or two to share what they knew of the tablelands' past. Then it was off to the north, where Lake George stretched some sixteen miles in the direction of Sydney.

It wouldn't be the usual sort of honeymoon, but there were much more important and interesting things that needed doing first. Peter's quest for a connection to the country hadn't ended simply because one old man with a penchant for horse theft had a disinterest in his family.

'*Weereewaa.*' She tried out the word, still so new to her.

'*Weereewaa,*' Peter echoed, saying it better.

Thanks for reading *The Artist's Secret.* I hope you enjoyed it. If you liked this book, you might enjoy my other title in the Brindabella Secrets series, **The Landowner's Secret.**

Reviews can help readers find books, and I am grateful for all honest reviews. Thank you for taking the time to let others know what you've read, and what you thought.

Sign up to our newsletter romance.com.au/newsletter/and find out about new releases, must-read series and **ebook deals** at romance.com.au.

Share your reading experience on:
Facebook
Instagram
romance.com.au

ROMANCE .COM.AU ESCAPE publishing A novel approach

Bestselling Titles by Escape Publishing...

Discover another great read from Escape Publishing...

The Landowner's Secret
Sonya Heaney

New South Wales, 1885

When Alice Ryan wakes to find thugs surrounding her cottage, on the hunt for her no-good brother, she escapes into the surrounding bush.

It is wealthy landowner Robert Farrer who finds her the next morning, dishevelled, injured, and utterly unwilling to share what she knows. With criminals on the loose and rumours that reckless bushrangers have returned to the area, Robert is determined to keep Alice out of danger, and insists on taking her into his home-despite the scandal it may cause. Convincing her to stay on with him for her own safety, however, is going to take some work.

What Robert doesn't expect is his growing attraction to the forthright, unruly woman staying in his home. Before either of them can settle into their odd new situation, their home and wellbeing come under threat and they will need to trust each other to survive. But they are both keeping secrets, secrets that have the potential to ruin their burgeoning love, their livelihood ... and their lives.

Find it *here*.

www.ingramcontent.com/pod-product-compliance
Lightning Source LLC
Chambersburg PA
CBHW011556010726
47495CB00010B/2804